D1255206

PRAISE FOR LEE GOLDBERG

PRAISE FOR *MALIBU BURNING*

"The author of the Eve Ronin mysteries returns with a fast-paced, over-the-top caper that entertains while keeping readers guessing."

—*Library Journal* (starred review)

"Goldberg returns to the wildfire he memorably chronicled in *Lost Hills* (2020) from a strikingly new angle . . . A businesslike thriller that shows how rewarding it can be to revisit the same story from a new point of view."

—*Kirkus Reviews*

"Goldberg's well-drawn characters will keep readers rooting for both crooks and cops, and he hangs everyone's fates on a clever, complicated con. The result is as explosive as a wildfire."

—*Publishers Weekly*

"*Malibu Burning* is a blistering thrill ride full of Southern California thieves, cops, and firefighters, all facing high stakes and imminent danger. Superbly researched and told, fast-paced, and downright fun, this is Lee Goldberg at his best!"

—Mark Greaney, #1 *New York Times* bestselling author of the Gray Man series

"By turns tense and rambunctious, wildly entertaining, and breakneck-paced, Lee Goldberg's splendid *Malibu Burning* is pure storytelling pleasure from beginning to end."

—Megan Abbott, Edgar Award–, Anthony Award–, Thriller Award–, and *Los Angeles Times* Book Prize–winning author of *The Turnout*

"*Malibu Burning* is classic Lee Goldberg at the top of his game: a fast-paced, funny, and deeply satisfying page-turner."

—Jess Lourey, Amazon Charts bestselling author of *The Quarry Girls*

"An inventive, twisty, and funny caper from one of crime writing's true pros. Elmore Leonard and Donald Westlake would've loved this wild heist."

—Ace Atkins, *New York Times* bestselling author of *Robert B. Parker's Bye Bye Baby*

PRAISE FOR *MOVIELAND*

"Goldberg's compelling follow-up to *Gated Prey* is a fast-paced, riveting police procedural influenced by actual events in California. A character-driven series entry that skillfully depicts Hollywood corruption."

—*Library Journal* (starred review)

"The fourth book in Lee Goldberg's series is his most ambitious and best realized yet . . . *Movieland* is crime writing of the highest order. Goldberg's style touches on both Michael Connelly and Robert Crais, in whose company he now squarely belongs."

—*The Providence Journal*

"*Movieland*, Lee Goldberg's fourth novel featuring Ronin, is every bit as good as the first three. The characters, including victims, suspects, and an assortment of lazy, hardworking, honest, and corrupt cops, are quirky and well developed. The depiction of police procedures feels authentic. The writing is vivid and precise. And with startling twists around every corner, the suspenseful tale unfolds at a furious pace."

—Associated Press

"Lee is fantastic at combining clever plotting, humor, and thrills in his stories."

—Boyd Morrison, #1 *New York Times* bestselling author

"LA noir is real; so is Malibu noir, and no one does it better than Lee Goldberg."

—Luanne Rice, *New York Times* bestselling author

"Finished this on the plane home. Typically classy police procedural from Lee Goldberg—giving Michael Connelly a run for his money."

—Ian Rankin

PRAISE FOR *GATED PREY*

"The seamy side of California dreaming . . . Goldberg not only ties up . . . but links some of Eve's investigations in ways as disturbing as they are surprising."

—*Kirkus Reviews*

"Lively descriptive prose enhances the tight plot of this episodic crime novel, which reads like a TV show in narrative form. Columbo fans will have fun."

—*Publishers Weekly*

"A great series . . . Eve Ronin continues to dazzle and show her gritty side as she progresses in the Los Angeles Sheriff's Department."
—*Mystery and Suspense Magazine*

"Another suspenseful, fast-paced yarn with engaging characters."
—Associated Press

"I whipped my head back and forth reading *Gated Prey*. So twisty, so funny, and so LA—a few of my favorite things. After zooming through these pages, I'll ride shotgun with Lee any day!"
—Rachel Howzell Hall, bestselling author of *And Now She's Gone*

PRAISE FOR *BONE CANYON*

A *Mystery and Suspense Magazine* 2021 Best Book of the Year Selection

"Goldberg follows *Lost Hills* with a riveting, intense story. Readers of Karin Slaughter or Michael Connelly will want to try this."
—*Library Journal* (starred review)

"Goldberg knows how to keep the pages turning."
—*Publishers Weekly*

"Lee Goldberg puts the *pro* in *police procedural*. *Bone Canyon* is fresh, sharp, and absorbing. Give me more Eve Ronin, ASAP."
—Meg Gardiner, international bestselling author

"Wow—what a novel! It is wonderful in so many ways. I could not put it down. *Bone Canyon* is wrenching and harrowing, full of wicked twists. Lee Goldberg captures the magic and danger of the Santa Monica Mountains and the predators who prowl them. Detective Eve Ronin takes on forgotten victims, fights for them, and nearly loses everything in the process. She's a riveting character, and I can't wait for her next case."

—Luanne Rice, *New York Times* bestselling author

"*Bone Canyon* is a propulsive procedural that provides high thrills in difficult terrain, grappling thoughtfully with sexual violence and police corruption, as well as the minefield of politics and media in Hollywood and suburban Los Angeles. Eve Ronin is a fantastic series lead—stubborn and driven, working twice as hard as her colleagues both to prove her worth and to deliver justice for the dead."

—Steph Cha, author of *Your House Will Pay*

PRAISE FOR *LOST HILLS*

"A cop novel so good it makes much of the old guard read like they're going through the motions until they can retire . . . The real appeal here is Goldberg's lean prose, which imbues just-the-facts procedure with remarkable tension and cranks up to a stunning description of a fire that was like 'Christmas in hell.'"

—*Booklist*

"An energetic, resourceful procedural starring a heroine who deserves a series of her own."

—*Kirkus Reviews*

"This nimble, sure-footed series launch from bestseller Goldberg . . . builds to a thrilling, visually striking climax. Readers will cheer Ronin every step of the way."

—*Publishers Weekly*

"The first book in what promises to be a superb series—it's also that rare novel in which the formulaic elements of mainstream police procedurals share narrative space with a unique female protagonist. All that, and it's also a love letter to the chaos and diversity of California. There are a lot of series out there, but Eve Ronin and Goldberg's fast-paced prose should put this one on the radar of every crime-fiction fan."

—National Public Radio

"This sterling thriller is carved straight out of the world of Harlan Coben and Lisa Gardner . . . *Lost Hills* is a book to be found and savored."

—BookTrib

"*Lost Hills* is Lee Goldberg at his best. Inspired by the real-world grit and glitz of LA County crime, this book takes no prisoners. And neither does Eve Ronin. Take a ride with her and you'll find yourself with a heroine for the ages. And you'll be left hoping for more."

—Michael Connelly, #1 *New York Times* bestselling author

"*Lost Hills* is what you get when you polish the police procedural to a shine: a gripping premise, a great twist, fresh spins and knowing winks to the genre conventions, and all the smart, snappy ease of an expert at work."

—Tana French, *New York Times* bestselling author

"Thrills and chills! *Lost Hills* is the perfect combination of action and suspense, not to mention Eve Ronin is one of the best new female characters in ages. You will race through the pages!"
—Lisa Gardner, #1 *New York Times* bestselling author

"Twenty-four-karat Goldberg—a top-notch procedural that shines like a true gem."
—Craig Johnson, *New York Times* bestselling author of the Longmire series

"A winner. Packed with procedure, forensics, vivid descriptions, and the right amount of humor. Fervent fans of Connelly and Crais, this is your next read."
—Kendra Elliot, *Wall Street Journal* and Amazon Charts bestselling author

"Brilliant! Eve Ronin rocks! With a baffling and brutal case, tight plotting, and a fascinating look at police procedure, *Lost Hills* is a stunning start to a new detective series. A must-read for crime-fiction fans."
—Melinda Leigh, *Wall Street Journal* and #1 Amazon Charts bestselling author

DREAM
TOWN

OTHER TITLES BY LEE GOLDBERG

King City
The Walk
Watch Me Die
McGrave
Three Ways to Die
Fast Track
Calico

The Sharpe & Walker Series

Malibu Burning

The Eve Ronin Series

Lost Hills
Bone Canyon
Gated Prey
Movieland

The Ian Ludlow Thrillers

True Fiction
Killer Thriller
Fake Truth

The Fox & O'Hare Series
(coauthored with Janet Evanovich)

Pros & Cons (novella)
The Shell Game (novella)
The Heist
The Chase
The Job
The Scam
The Pursuit

The Diagnosis Murder Series

The Silent Partner
The Death Merchant
The Shooting Script
The Waking Nightmare
The Past Tense
The Dead Letter
The Double Life
The Last Word

The Monk Series

Mr. Monk Goes to the Firehouse
Mr. Monk Goes to Hawaii
Mr. Monk and the Blue Flu
Mr. Monk and the Two Assistants
Mr. Monk in Outer Space
Mr. Monk Goes to Germany
Mr. Monk Is Miserable

Mr. Monk and the Dirty Cop
Mr. Monk in Trouble
Mr. Monk Is Cleaned Out
Mr. Monk on the Road
Mr. Monk on the Couch
Mr. Monk on Patrol
Mr. Monk Is a Mess
Mr. Monk Gets Even

The Charlie Willis Series

My Gun Has Bullets
Dead Space

The Dead Man Series
(coauthored with William Rabkin)

Face of Evil
Ring of Knives (with James Daniels)
Hell in Heaven
The Dead Woman (with David McAfee)
The Blood Mesa (with James Reasoner)
Kill Them All (with Harry Shannon)
The Beast Within (with James Daniels)
Fire & Ice (with Jude Hardin)
Carnival of Death (with Bill Crider)
Freaks Must Die (with Joel Goldman)
Slaves to Evil (with Lisa Klink)
The Midnight Special (with Phoef Sutton)
The Death March (with Christa Faust)
The Black Death (with Aric Davis)

The Killing Floor (with David Tully)
Colder Than Hell (with Anthony Neil Smith)
Evil to Burn (with Lisa Klink)
Streets of Blood (with Barry Napier)
Crucible of Fire (with Mel Odom)
The Dark Need (with Stant Litore)
The Rising Dead (with Stella Green)
Reborn (with Kate Danley, Phoef Sutton, and Lisa Klink)

The Jury Series

Judgment
Adjourned
Payback
Guilty

Nonfiction

The Best TV Shows You Never Saw
Unsold Television Pilots 1955–1989
Television Fast Forward
Science Fiction Filmmaking in the 1980s (cowritten with
William Rabkin, Randy Lofficier, and Jean-Marc Lofficier)
*The Dreamweavers: Interviews with Fantasy Filmmakers of the
1980s* (cowritten with William Rabkin, Randy Lofficier,
and Jean-Marc Lofficier)
Successful Television Writing (cowritten with William Rabkin)
The Joy of Sets: Interviews on the Sets of 1980s Genre Movies
*The James Bond Films 1962–1989: Interviews with the Actors,
Writers and Directors*

DREAM TOWN

LEE GOLDBERG

THOMAS & MERCER

Published by Thomas & Mercer, Seattle

www.apub.com

Amazon, the Amazon logo, and Thomas & Mercer are trademarks of Amazon.com, Inc., or its affiliates.

ISBN-13: 9781662512346 (hardcover)
ISBN-13: 9781662512353 (paperback)
ISBN-13: 9781662512360 (digital)

Cover design by Jarrod Taylor
Cover image: © Stepanida Popozoglo / Alamy Stock Photo / Alamy

Printed in the United States of America

First edition

To Valerie & Madison, a dream come true

CHAPTER ONE

It's an age-old cliché that in the instant before you die, memories of your life flash across your mind. So Eve Ronin, the youngest homicide detective in the history of the Los Angeles County Sheriff's Department, was tempted to check her pulse as she stood outside the Rock Store, a biker hangout in the Santa Monica Mountains, and watched her life being re-created in front of her for a TV show.

A red Lamborghini Aventador roared around the tight curves on Mulholland, chased downhill by a pivoting camera that dangled from the end of a long crane mounted atop a speeding SUV. The two vehicles hugged the narrow road that snaked along the contours of the Santa Monica Mountains with jagged outcroppings on one side and a deep ravine on the other.

The Aventador blasted out of a turn and roared up behind a lone female bicyclist, then veered away at the last second, nearly shaving the woman off the road. But the bicyclist, unlike Eve, the twenty-six-year-old character she was portraying, was a trained stuntwoman who instantly regained her balance and swerved away from the camera car filming the action.

Watching the scene, Eve felt the same flash of fury she'd felt on that day a year ago, when it was actually her on the bike, wearing the same blue short-sleeved biking jersey, black cycling shorts, and wraparound racing sunglasses the stuntwoman was now. But back then, it wasn't staged and there was no camera car. It was real.

The half-a-million-dollar sports car roared down to the Rock Store, originally built with mud and lava rocks over a century ago, and came to a sudden stop. The couple inside the car immediately leaped out. The driver was a short, overly muscled man wearing a ridiculous Bengal tiger polo shirt and velvet shorts, and his passenger was a woman in a tight mini bandage dress who teetered shakily on high stiletto heels.

The man was a stunt driver portraying Blake Largo, the international movie star he'd actually doubled for in the hugely successful *Deathfist* series of action movies, and the woman was aspiring actress Shirlee Teeter, portraying herself, yet another blurring of fiction and reality that was becoming a daily, and deeply unsettling, part of Eve Ronin's life lately.

The two characters were unaware that they were being filmed by pedestrians using their phones or that the bicyclist had ridden up, too. But while the TV cameras were trained on Largo and Shirlee, the stuntwoman was swapped out for actress Erin Casey as Eve to create a seamless transition for the viewer and maintain the illusion of a single continuous shot.

Eve watched as the scene played out.

"You puked all over my Lambo," Largo said, furious with her.

"I'm sorry. All those curves made me carsick," Shirlee said. "I told you to slow down."

Largo backhanded her, nearly knocking the woman off her feet. "Nobody tells me anything."

Eve stepped between them and got in Largo's face.

"Back off," Eve said, then looked over her shoulder at Shirlee, whose nose was bleeding. "Are you okay?"

Shirlee nodded, but she was crying.

"Who gives a shit about her?" Largo said, thrusting a finger toward his car. "Look at my Lambo. There's bitch puke all over the suede dash."

"Shut up," Eve said.

Largo took a swing at her.

Eve dodged the blow, grabbed his arm, wrenched it behind his back, and forced him face-first to the ground in one fast, elegant move.

"Apologize," she said, her knee planted on his back.

"Fuck you," Largo said, spitting out the words. She twisted his arm until he winced. "I'm sorry!"

"Don't say it to me," Eve said. "Say it to her. Say it like you mean it."

He looked at Shirlee, who appeared stunned by the unexpected turn of events. His eyes became moist, his expression pleading. "I'm sorry. There's no excuse for what I did. I hope you can find it in your heart to forgive me."

"Wow," Eve said. "You're good. I almost believe it."

"You should." Shirlee wiped her nose and sniffled. "He's got an Oscar. He keeps it by his bed and stares at it while he's screwing."

"Let me up," Largo said.

"Nope," Eve said. "I smell alcohol on your breath."

"So what? You gonna write me a ticket?"

"I would but I'm off duty." She turned to see the crowd of customers behind her, filming it all, and said to nobody in particular, "Someone please call the sheriff's station. Tell them that Detective Eve Ronin is holding a man in custody for assault and possible DUI."

"Cut!" yelled Vince Nyby, the director, a white-haired man in his late seventies wearing a red blazer, paisley silk ascot, white Oxford shirt, slacks, and loafers. He sat under a picnic tent called "the video village" on a folding chair flanked by Simone Harper, the African American writer-producer of the show in the chair to his left, and Krister Ekblad, director of photography, known for his moody camera work on several Swedish crime series, in the chair to his right. All three of them faced a bank of camera monitors stacked on a rolling cart.

For the last few minutes, the cameras, lights, and crew had disappeared for Eve and all she saw was her memory come to life, but from an entirely different point of view than the one she carried in her mind.

"And that's how we ended up here today," said Duncan "Donuts" Pavone, a homicide detective who was twice as old and almost three times heavier than Eve. He stood beside her, holding a paper plate piled high with a hamburger, a steak, and fried chicken.

"That's true," Eve said. "And I still find it hard to believe."

"Did you know the catering truck serves three different options for lunch and it's all you can eat?"

She glanced at his sagging plate, which looked like it might disintegrate under the weight of all that food. "Did you leave anything for everybody else?"

Vince got up from his seat, walked over to Erin Casey, the actress playing Eve, and put his arm around her shoulder with an affection he'd never shown to the real Eve, who was his daughter.

Eve felt a pang of jealousy, which surprised and angered her, because she was sure if he dared touch her like that now, she'd knee him in the groin.

"That was a great master," Vince told Erin, whose hair was cut into a practical bob to match Eve's.

Duncan leaned close to Eve and asked, "What's a master?"

Eve had grown up around the TV industry, taking her single mother, Jen, to sets, where she toiled as a "background extra," a performer with no lines, like the ones filling the picnic tables today portraying the pedestrians at the Rock Store. So Eve was generally familiar with filmmaking terms.

She said, "It's the wide angle that establishes the geography of the scene and the characters in it, before the scene begins intercutting with two-shots and close-ups, which are known as 'coverage.'"

Vince led Erin over to the video village and said, "But now that we're into the coverage, we need to work on underscoring the key moments."

"I'm not playing moments," Erin said. "I'm playing a character."

She's playing me, Eve thought, and wondered if what she'd just seen was how people perceived her. But even if it wasn't, once this show based on her life was on the air, it was the fictional Eve, this actress in front of her now, that she would have to live up to. As if she didn't have enough pressure already.

Vince forced a smile. He wasn't used to being challenged on his direction. "That performance was fine for the master, but when the camera is tight on you, I want to see a sly smile on your face when you tell Largo to apologize. Eve knows justice is finally being served on this jerk and she's glad to be the one to do it."

"But she didn't smile," Erin said. "I've seen the original videos."

So had tens of millions of people. Once was enough for Eve. But it changed her life.

"Those videos weren't the first episode of a TV series. This is," Vince said. "And we need you to sell the moment so it pays off later."

"She didn't," Erin said.

"Actually, she did," said Simone Harper from her seat. "Eve shrewdly leveraged the popularity she achieved with that viral video to get Sheriff Lansing, desperate to shift media attention away from all of the department's embarrassing scandals, to promote her to robbery-homicide, a job she didn't deserve and was unqualified to do."

Eve whispered to Duncan, "I wouldn't put it that way."

"Because you're self-delusional and don't want to see yourself as ruthlessly ambitious, which you are," Duncan said. "But don't worry, nobody doubts you have the skills and experience now."

She certainly had the scars to prove it. Literally. It had taken her months to heal from her last big homicide case, and now she finally felt whole again. Eve was determined to stay that way by changing the way she approached the job. Otherwise, she might be dead before she reached thirty.

Simone continued to argue her point, talking about Eve as if she weren't standing right there. "That's the core conflict the series is based on and what is driving her character. Eve's constant need to prove herself."

Vince nodded and turned back to Erin. "And we need to see it now on her face. Because we're smash-cutting from your close-up to Eve at her first crime scene as a homicide detective."

Erin shook her head, still not buying it. "That may be the dramatic reason you want that grin, but it's not authentic."

"This isn't a documentary," he said. "It's entertainment."

Erin suddenly shifted her gaze to Eve. "What do you think?"

All eyes on the set turned to Eve, who stood beside Duncan behind the video village.

What Eve thought was that she wanted to be anywhere except here, watching her estranged father, a man she hated, directing the first episode of a heavily fictionalized TV series version of her recent life, which she wished she'd never agreed to do. But at the time, she'd had no choice. She'd needed the money to defend herself from what looked to be an expensive lawsuit.

If Eve said the wrong thing now, on the first shot on the first day of production, she risked undercutting her father's authority on the set for good. As much as she resented Vince for being absent in her life, for never paying child support, and for skillfully manipulating her into getting him this job, she couldn't do that to him. She'd only be hurting herself and alienating Simone, the writer and executive producer that she needed on her side.

Eve said, "I think I need to leave and let you professionals do your jobs so I can do mine."

"That doesn't answer the question," Erin said.

"Yes, it does." Simone got up from her seat. That declaration carried more impact than it otherwise would have because everybody knew that Simone, despite dressing like her favorite place to shop was T.J. Maxx, had just signed a $100 million production deal with the network. She was a powerful woman in the industry. "We need the attitude that Eve just showed us, that rigid devotion to her job, in this scene and in that smile."

Vince said, "That's why I've always called her hard-nosed. Eve has been that way since she was born."

Eve was tempted to say, *How would you know? You were never there. You were busy luring women into bed with the false promise of acting jobs, knocking them up, and running away from your responsibility, just like you did with Mom.*

But instead of saying that, she just walked away, Duncan trailing after her with his plate of food. She headed for their unmarked LASD Ford Explorer, which was parked down the road, past the long line of makeup trailers, equipment trucks, and mobile dressing rooms on the narrow shoulder.

"Why are we leaving? It was just getting exciting," Duncan said. "And we haven't tried dessert. You wouldn't believe the selection."

"Because it's unbearable."

"You don't have to choose," he said. "You can have some of everything."

"I meant watching this. I can't stand it."

"When I was a kid, there was a TV show called *Burke's Law* about a millionaire homicide detective who arrived at crime scenes in a chauffeur-driven Rolls-Royce. That could be your life."

"Never."

Duncan picked a chicken leg from his plate and reluctantly dumped the rest in a trash can. "Only because you spent your first big check on your new house, paying off your sister's nursing school debt, and setting up a college fund for your brother's little girl."

Eve had told Duncan about the down payment on her house, of course, and had invited him to her housewarming party that coming Saturday, but not the rest of her expenditures. She hadn't told anyone.

"How did you know I did that?"

"I'm a detective."

There was only one answer. "You talked to my mom."

"That's what detecting is, Eve. Talking to people. That's just one of the many incredible insights into policing viewers can learn from my character on the show."

Except that the Duncan Pavone character on the TV series had been "reimagined" as twenty years younger and 150 pounds slimmer than he was in real life.

Eve climbed into the driver's seat of the Explorer and he took the passenger side, taking a bite of the chicken leg as he got inside.

"If I'm lucky," she said, "the series will be canceled before the end of the first season."

"I hope not. I'm counting on a *Duncan P.I.* spin-off so I can retire."

"You had the opportunity to retire four months ago, and you backed out."

"Only because I wasn't a millionaire yet."

Eve grabbed the radio, notified the dispatcher that they were back on duty, and then she drove away, heading northwest on Mulholland, back toward the sheriff's department's Lost Hills station, which had law enforcement jurisdiction over an area bordered by the Santa Monica Bay to the south, Ventura County to the west and northwest, and the City of Los Angeles to the east and northeast. Within that jurisdictional island were the Santa Monica Mountains, Malibu Creek State Park, and the cities of Malibu, Agoura Hills, Westlake Village, Hidden Hills, and Calabasas, where the station was located.

They were on the road only a few minutes, driving through a canyon still dotted by trees blackened by the massive fires that had come through a year ago, when Duncan got a call on his cell phone from Captain Mel Dubois, their commanding officer. Duncan listened for a bit, then said: "Got it, sir. We'll be right there." He ended the call and looked at Eve. "A guy was hiking with his dogs and found some bones in Ahmanson Ranch."

"You mean the Preserve," she said.

It was shorthand for the Upper Las Virgenes Canyon Open Space Preserve, a state park and a vital wildlife corridor linking the Santa Monica Mountains with mountain ranges to the north. But for decades, the thousands of acres of rolling hills and native oak trees, once a sacred Chumash settlement, were known as the Ahmanson Ranch and were the setting for countless movies. During that whole time, the bank that owned the land pursued plans to build a new master-planned city on the site. The public bitterly opposed the massive development, miring the project in environmental reviews and lawsuits. The name changed when the bank finally gave up and sold the land to the state in 2003.

"The Preserve makes it sound like a jar of apricots," Duncan said, tossing his chicken leg out the window. "It's always going to be the ranch to me."

"How do we know the bones are human and not chicken drumsticks some litterbug tossed out of his car?"

"Nan was already nearby, investigating an unattended death at Mountain View Estates, so she stopped by and made a preliminary determination."

Nan Baker was head of the department's forensic unit, and knew a lot about bones, but wasn't qualified to make an official determination.

Eve sighed with frustration, but it was a performance. "So now we have to babysit the scene until a forensic anthropologist can look at the bones, make it official that they're human, and then tell us if they are ancient or recent and if we're looking at natural causes or a murder."

"If they're human, you know it's going to be another gang killing," Duncan said. "Back in the good old days, before gasoline topped six dollars a gallon, at least they had the decency to dump their dead out in the desert instead of our jurisdiction. But you're right, we could be sitting on our asses out there all day. Gosh golly, where is Nan ever going to find a bone guy willing to drop everything he's doing and schlep out here in a hurry?"

Duncan had seen right through her. She shot him a glance and saw him grinning. "Don't be a smart-ass."

Dr. Daniel Brooks was the forensic anthropologist the department usually reached out to in cases like this. When Eve left her house in Calabasas that morning, he'd been sitting at her kitchen island in his underwear, working on reports from his dig at a World War II burial site on Tarawa, where she'd spent a few weeks with him, recuperating from the injuries that she'd sustained investigating some killings in and around Malibu Creek State Park. But only Duncan knew that they were lovers.

"If we're lucky," Duncan said, "these will turn out to be ancient Chumash bones and not our problem. It will be something for the tribe or somebody else to work out. We might make it back to the *Ronin* set in time for an early dinner."

"You just ate and you're already thinking about your next meal?"

"I'm preparing to hibernate for the winter," he said.

CHAPTER TWO

The southern end of the Preserve was north of the Ventura Freeway with a tail in Crummer Canyon, between the wealthy, gated enclave of Mountain View Estates to the west and Hidden Hills to the east, and it then spread out over them like the top of a T. An asphalt road snaked through the canyon from Mureau Road to the south on up to the historic ranch house, located on a mesa several miles into the park.

Eve passed through the Mureau Road gate, following the narrow, twisting, and obviously newly laid asphalt road past gnarled, burned oaks and the thick shrubs and hills of mustard grass that had sprouted from the blackened earth left by the wildfires. It was easy to imagine they were far from an urban sprawl, even though they were right in the middle of it. She understood now why so many Hollywood westerns were shot here.

They reached the second gate, where Deputy Eddie Clayton was parked in a patrol car, securing the scene. There were two other vehicles there, the crime scene unit van and Daniel Brooks' dirty, bird-crap-covered Ford Fusion, which Eve suspected had never been washed.

Eve parked, then she and Duncan got out and approached Eddie's patrol car.

Eddie Clayton was known for rarely removing his wraparound sunglasses, whether it was day or night. He was also one of only two uniformed deputies in the sheriff's department that Eve trusted with her life.

"Good afternoon, Eddie," Eve said. "Were you the one who took the report from the hiker?"

"Yeah, but more like a dog walker than a hiker. He comes out here every week and lets his dogs run off leash. He whistles and they come back. This time they came with bones in their mouths."

Duncan spoke up. "So he doesn't know exactly where the bones were found."

Eddie nodded, then crooked a thumb over his shoulder to indicate the trail that went down the rolling hills behind him. "Nan Baker and the anthropologist are out there, where the guy says he was standing when his dogs came running back."

"That makes our crime scene the entire park," Eve said.

"That's why I'm sitting here," Eddie said, "shooing away all the hikers from this area."

"Is it exciting work?" Duncan asked.

"It's everything I dreamed of when I got my badge."

Eve and Duncan continued down the trail, where they could see Nan and Daniel standing in a meadow. Nan was impossible to miss in her bright white Tyvek jumpsuit, which practically glowed against the wide-open space behind her. And even from a distance of a hundred yards, Daniel was unmistakable in his beloved tattered Australian bush hat, khaki shirt, and cargo pants.

"I wouldn't worry about it making a case," Duncan said to Eve as they walked. "If the bones are human, we probably aren't going to find anything we can use to make an ID. That means they'll stick the bones in a bag, shelve them in a box somewhere, and we'll move on to our next case."

Eve knew the Los Angeles gangs and their families didn't usually file missing person reports on their missing and their dead, so there probably wouldn't be any dental records in the system to help identify the bones. But she hated the idea of the deaths being ignored. Everyone deserved justice.

"We can try running the DNA," she said.

"Sure we can, which will take months, if not years, for the request to be granted, since there are hundreds, if not thousands, of rape kits from the last century still waiting to be tested," Duncan said. "And if the test is ever done, the result will be worthless if the person's DNA isn't already in the system. By the time any of that happens, I'll be retired in Palm Springs, you'll be getting your star on the Hollywood Walk of Fame, and homicide investigations will be conducted by holograms."

They reached Nan and Daniel, who were huddled together, examining the bones he held in his gloved hands.

Nan was a big-boned African American woman in her forties, wearing a camera around her neck and carrying her toolbox-size evidence processing kit. Eve had never seen her without either piece of equipment and wondered if she brought them everywhere she went, whether it was grocery shopping, a dentist appointment, or a Thanksgiving dinner.

Daniel was in his early thirties, slightly pudgy, with curly brown hair. He wore rimless round-framed glasses and was deeply tanned from all the hours he spent outdoors, brushing the dirt away from buried bones. Although Eve and Daniel had been apart only a few hours, she fought the desire to greet him with a hug. It helped that he held a gnawed, sun-bleached bone in each hand, which would have made hugging awkward anyway.

Nan turned to greet them. "I see they sent the big guns."

"Likewise," Eve said.

"Luck of the draw for me," Nan said. "I happened to be next door at Mountain View Estates. A woman was found dead in her recliner by her neighbor, who came to check on her after not seeing her around for a few days."

Duncan said, "That's how I want to go, in my La-Z-Boy, a bowl of popcorn in my lap, and *Gunsmoke* on the TV. How'd she die?"

"Not by her own hand or somebody else's, if that's what you're asking," Nan said. "I'm certain it's natural causes, but I'm waiting on the ME to pin it down."

"What was she watching?"

"Fox News," she said.

Duncan nodded. "Then it was probably a stroke."

Nan gestured to Daniel. "Do you remember Dr. Brooks? He was the forensic anthropologist who consulted with us on the Bone Canyon case."

"Sure do," Duncan said. "Our very own Indiana Jones."

"He's an archaeologist," Daniel said, "not an anthropologist."

"Yes, but you're both men of action who like to dig in the dirt."

"That's true," Daniel said, then smiled at Eve, who smiled back. She said, "Good to see you again, Dr. Brooks."

"Always a pleasure, Detective Ronin."

"Enjoy it while you can," Duncan said, "because the passion will dim, and that's when things get real."

Eve looked quickly at Nan. "He's talking about the excitement you feel at the beginning of a new investigation, before it becomes hard work and drudgery."

"Oh, thanks for clearing that up," Nan said. "Because for a moment there, I thought Duncan was telling Dr. Brooks that once you two get used to the sex and calm down, you'll start seeing things about one another that irritate you, and that's when the relationship really begins."

Eve felt her face flush with embarrassment, which was so embarrassing in itself that she wondered if it was possible to double-blush. "Does everybody know about us?"

"No, but they will the instant they see you two together," she said. "Just like I did."

Daniel sighed. "That's a huge relief."

"Not to me," Eve said. "I already have enough people doubting my professionalism."

Duncan brushed away her concern.

"What do you care? You have a TV series," he said, then tipped his head toward Daniel's hands. "What have you got there, Indy?"

Daniel held up the bones. "Two human femurs that show signs of animal predation."

"You mean some coyotes or bobcats have chewed on the corpses."

"Yes. Both were adult males in their mid to late twenties, who died about two years ago," Daniel said. "They were wrapped in something and buried in shallow graves."

"You can tell all that just from looking at two bones?"

"Male and female femurs have subtle differences that indicate their sex. The coloring and condition reveals their age and what forces of erosion they've been exposed to and for how long."

"You said these bones came from two men," Eve said. "How do you know they aren't from the same guy?"

"Mammals are symmetrical and have bilateral skeletons, meaning they have two sides that are mirror images of one another. You can't have two left legs. These are two left legs."

"Were the men murdered?"

Daniel shrugged. Eve thought he was adorable when he did that. "I won't know that until we find more of their bones."

Nan said, "In the meantime, we have to treat this as a crime scene. That means locking down the perimeter and collecting evidence."

Duncan looked past her and waved his arm in an arc to illustrate the wide-open land beyond. "What perimeter?"

"The hiker told the deputy he hadn't gone much further than this spot when he whistled for the dogs, who were out of sight, meaning they were down in that canyon or beyond that hill or among those boulders or in that stand of trees." She pointed to the areas she was talking about.

Eve said, "Basically a hundred yards in each direction."

"That's our perimeter," Nan said, then looked at Daniel. "I hope you brought sunscreen, bug repellant, and hiking boots."

"No, but I brought a comfy chair, a cooler of cold drinks, and a drone."

"We need boots on the ground."

"That's the last thing we need, and especially now," he said. "The light is all wrong."

"The light?" Nan said.

"I've spent a lot of years locating and digging up graves," he said. "We need the best angle of light to see the definition between bones, twigs, and surrounding soil, and subtle changes in the terrain, like unnatural mounds and depressions. The right time of day has passed."

Duncan said, "And when is that?"

"Nine a.m.," Daniel said, then faced Nan. "I'll do an initial survey with the drone now, identify the likely areas, and then we can do a grid search on foot in the morning, when the light will be perfect."

"The bones might not be buried," Nan said. "They could be scattered all over the ground."

"That's another reason we don't want people stomping around in bad light crushing teeth and bones."

Nan's expression hardened. "My people don't stomp."

Daniel held up his hands, bones still in them, in surrender. "I meant no offense. But this is what I do, and this is how to do it right."

Eve spoke up in his defense. "Daniel just got back from several months on a Pacific Ocean atoll recovering the bones of soldiers killed in World War II."

Nan glared at her. "I'm aware of his CV, Detective. That's why I hired him." She looked at Daniel again, her expression softening a bit. "I'll stay to document your survey and lay the groundwork for tomorrow's search."

Eve said, "We'll alert the rangers to close off this section of the park until further notice and we'll keep a deputy posted at the trailhead, too."

"Which is just for show," Duncan said, "because there are a lot of other ways to get in and out of the park unnoticed. That's what makes it such a great place to dump bodies."

They discussed some more procedural details and then Eve and Duncan headed to the Lost Hills station.

CHAPTER THREE

The Lost Hills sheriff's station was a low-slung, unassuming brick-and-cinder-block building located on the south side of Agoura Road, which ran parallel to the southern side of the Ventura Freeway, and was positioned at what would have been, if this were medieval times in Europe, the imposing border wall between the kingdoms of Calabasas and Agoura. Instead of a wall, there was a man-made boulder engraved with the words WELCOME TO THE CITY OF CALABASAS erected in the grassy median, the base circled with flowers.

Eve drove through the public parking area out front into the fenced-in rear lot reserved for official vehicles, employees' cars, and the helipad tucked up against the chaparral- and oak-covered hills of Malibu Creek State Park. She pulled in beside Duncan's mint-condition Buick Regal and got out of the SUV.

They strode past her bike, which was locked to some kind of utility pipe, and went in the back entrance to the station and down the long hallway toward the squad room. Halfway there, they passed the open door of acting captain Mel Dubois' office.

Duncan stopped, leaned inside, and knocked on the open door to get Dubois' attention. Dubois waved them in. He was the fourth captain at the station in a little over a year, the third since Eve arrived, and had previously served as a lieutenant in the Court Services Division. He was a noncontroversial placeholder pick and Eve expected Lost Hills to have a new fifth captain soon.

Dubois rose from behind his freakishly tidy desk to greet them, then sat down again. With his bow-tie mustache and buzz cut, he reminded her of the cartoon character on the Pringles potato chips canisters. "Fill me in on those bones."

They did. When they were done, he said, "I'll organize a search party of reserve deputies and send them out there first thing tomorrow morning."

Eve was afraid he'd say that, forcing her into the unwanted position of disagreeing with a superior officer. "A search party is the last thing the forensic anthropologist wants."

"The reserves have done this many times before and this will speed things along," Dubois said. He prized speed over almost anything. "I don't want any portion of the park sealed off any longer than necessary."

Duncan said, "We'll be out there tomorrow, too."

Eve knew he'd spoken up quickly to prevent her from challenging Dubois, so she gave up. "In the meantime, sir, we'll see if there are any missing person reports from this area from a few years back involving men in their early twenties. Maybe that'll give us a head start on ID'ing the bodies even before the rest of the bones are found."

"They're probably gang members," Dubois said. "And there won't be any missing person reports on them."

"That's true," Duncan said, "but don't you love her optimism?"

"It's inspiring," Dubois said.

Eve wasn't happy to see the two men bonding over teasing her. "I'll take that as a compliment."

She headed for the squad room and Duncan followed.

◆ ◆ ◆

Duncan ran the scant details they had through the in-house database to see if anyone had ever walked into Lost Hills station or contacted a deputy two years ago to report a missing man in his mid to late twenties, but came up empty. He also queried the California Department of Justice Missing and Unidentified Persons Section (DOJ-MUPS), but without any identifying details besides age and sex, he hit a wall.

Meanwhile, Eve tried CLETS, the California Law Enforcement Telecommunications System, a database that combined the Department of Motor Vehicle records from multiple states with the FBI's National Crime Information Center (NCIC), which was made up of five national databases—stolen property, wants and warrants, sex offenders, missing persons (MISPER), and unidentified persons (UNID)—that were routinely updated by detectives, agents, medical examiners, and others. There were plenty of men in that age group that had gone missing nationwide two years ago, but none in Los Angeles County that were still unsolved. And without a name, description, fingerprints, dental records, X-rays, tattoos, surgical implants, or DNA to run with, they didn't have any criteria to narrow the field.

Eve and Duncan divided up the list of names anyway and hunkered down in their cubicles, looking for Los Angeles connections, but nothing stood out.

She set the list aside, leaned back in her chair, and admitted defeat. "I guess that would have been too easy."

Duncan spun around in his chair, which creaked loudly under his weight. "We've done all we can and our shift is over. The good news is we can still make it back to the *Ronin* set before they wrap."

She stood up. "No, thanks, but feel free to go without me."

"I don't understand why you aren't more excited about the show. It's your story they're telling."

"I lived it, I don't need to see it again. I'd rather go home and relax."

He looked at her in shock. "You would?"

"It's not often we actually get out of here at five. I want to take advantage of it."

Eve opened the bottom drawer of her desk and took out her bike helmet.

Duncan got up now and came over to her. "You don't want to rush out to the ranch to look for bones?"

"The bones have been sitting there for years. One more day won't change anything."

"But Daniel's there," he said.

"And it's his job to look for them, not mine. I'd just be in the way. Besides, I still have lots of things to do to get my place ready for the housewarming party on Saturday."

Duncan grabbed his coat and car keys. "But that won't get you any closer to figuring out the mystery of those bones and setting things right."

He was baiting her and she knew it.

"What's wrong with having a life outside of work?"

"Nothing," Duncan said. "It's just not who you are."

She knew that. But every time she saw the scars on her body, it was a reminder that she needed to change. "It is now."

"I hope so," he said. "I truly do."

Duncan walked her out to the parking lot. They stopped at her bike, which she unlocked, even though it would presumably be safe from theft in the employee lot of a sheriff's station. But it wasn't. She used to leave her helmet hanging from the handlebars until someone filled it with dog shit.

As she unlocked the chain, she asked Duncan, "You got plans tonight?"

"Domino's Pizza and *Diagnosis Murder*."

His abrupt decision not to retire had complicated the life-altering changes that he and his wife, Gracie, had already set in motion, including putting their home up for sale and moving to a condo they'd recently bought in Palm Springs. Gracie went to Palm Springs anyway. Duncan kept the house, living there during the week and spending his weekends in the desert. It seemed to have worked out for both of them.

"You don't miss Gracie?"

"Not really," he said. "I'll see her this weekend in Palm Springs, where she'll make me eat kale."

"It's good for you."

"Nobody likes kale. Researchers discovered we hate it even before we're born."

She climbed on her bike. "How would they know that?"

"They fed kale to pregnant women, peeked into their wombs with ultrasound, and saw the fetuses scowling in disgust," he said. "Guess what happened when the mothers ate a Domino's Pizza?"

Eve strapped on her helmet. "The fetuses did a happy dance?"

"That's right. Think about it." He ambled on to his Buick Regal.

She rode her bike east on Agoura Road to Las Virgenes, and then north across the freeway overpass toward the condo complex where she'd lived until it got firebombed. But before she got there, she made a right on Mureau Road, which paralleled the freeway, taking her past Mountain View Estates and the trailhead to the Preserve.

She resisted the almost overwhelming urge to visit the crime scene and kept on riding, past Round Meadow Elementary School and the southwest gate to Hidden Hills, following the road over the freeway again onto Calabasas Road. The zigzag journey illustrated the strange geography of Calabasas, which was bisected across the freeway and divided in half by a ridge, the top graded flat and dotted with multi-million-dollar homes in a row of gated communities.

Eve was already feeling winded as she rode past the line of German car dealerships along the hillside and turned right onto Parkway Calabasas. She used to be able to ride hard for miles without losing her breath, but that was before her injuries.

At the next corner, and to her right, a gaudy fountain that reminded Eve of champagne being poured over a stack of glasses burbled in an island in front of the gates to Oakdale, a private community of homes. Behind the fountain was a tiny guard shack, barely larger than a porta-potty, that was manned 24/7 by a uniformed private security officer. Today it was Harvey Mapes, a slim, perpetually disheveled man who always looked like he'd just rolled out of bed.

The steep hill beyond the gate was lined with small Spanish-Mediterranean homes crammed into tiny lots, built too close together and with front yards just large enough to fit a car-length driveway and postage stamp of landscaping.

The old Eve would have ridden up the hill eagerly and in stride, barely winded by the ascent. But for the new Eve, the one with a leg peppered with buckshot scars, it might as well have been Mount Everest. Tonight, she'd walk the bike up.

Eve stopped at the guardhouse, got off the bike, and smiled at Harvey as she removed her helmet. "Hey, Harvey. Would you mind opening the gate?"

Harvey smiled back at her through the open window in the door. "How come you don't drive to work?"

"I'm training for the Olympics."

Harvey hit the button, opening the ornate gate. "The Special Olympics or the Senior Games?"

"You know I'm armed, right?"

"You wouldn't shoot me." He pointed to his Big Valley Security badge. "I'm a fellow law enforcement officer."

"You obviously haven't googled me yet," she said.

"I didn't know you were famous."

"How else could a cop afford to live here?"

Harvey shrugged. "I figured they practically gave that house away after what happened in there."

That wasn't far from the truth. The house was once a bloody crime scene, and after what had happened there, nobody but the cop who'd investigated the case could be comfortable living in it. She wouldn't be haunted by the memories.

Eve walked her bike up the hill, which didn't seem to be that much easier on her knees, or her breathing, than riding it up would have been.

The house that *Ronin* bought was one of the few single-story Spanish-Mediterranean tract homes in the community and was on the northwestern edge of the ridge, facing the undeveloped, rolling hills down to Ventura Freeway, Las Virgenes Road, and the Lost Hills sheriff's station beyond, so she had a big view.

Eve had landscaped her front yard with fresh sod, which she'd laid down herself, and a stone-bordered flower garden, both of which were being ravaged by rabbits every night. A slightly curving walkway of square mocha sandstone pavers led up to her door.

She wheeled her bike up the walkway, unlocked her front door, and punched her alarm code into the keypad. She parked her bike in the marble-floored entry hall, which faced an open-concept living room and, to her right, the dining room and kitchen. To her left, a hallway went off to the three bedrooms and two baths on the other side of the house. The walls were bare, and most of her furniture, which she'd ordered online, was still waiting to be assembled or unwrapped in the center of the living room amid a few moving boxes she'd yet to unpack. There were boxes of dishes and cookware in the kitchen left to be opened and sorted, too. She had a lot of work to do before the party on Saturday.

Even so, it felt nice to have a home.

She went down the hall, undressed, and took a shower at the hottest possible temperature, then slipped into a large cotton bathrobe. Eve was drying her hair when the doorbell rang.

Since she lived in a gated community, nobody could get in to see her without a pass. So the person on her doorstep was either a neighbor or someone she'd already put on her visitor list, which held only four names: her two siblings, Duncan, and one other person.

Eve trudged barefoot to the unlocked door and opened it. Daniel, the fourth name on her visitor list, stood there in clothes covered with dirt and stained with sweat.

"You could have just come in," she said, stepping away from the door.

"You gave me a pass, but not a key," he said as he came in.

"The door was unlocked," she said.

"I didn't want to get mistaken for an intruder. A guy could get shot that way."

"Why is everybody today talking about me and guns?"

He turned to face her. "Are you packing any heat now?"

"No."

He kicked closed the floor and untied the drawstring on her robe. "Liar."

And then he kissed her, slipping his hand under her robe and doing a bit more than that. She felt her pulse quickening and drew back from him.

"Do you know what would be really sexy?"

He kept his hand where it was, doing what it was doing. "I'm a simple guy. I don't think anything could top this for me."

She began unbuttoning his shirt. "You could take a shower and help me put together some of this furniture."

"What's sexy about that?"

She kissed him and gently bit his lower lip. "You could help me break it in."

Daniel sighed. "I hope it's the couch we're building first and not the barstools."

"You'd be surprised what I can do on a barstool," she said.

CHAPTER FOUR

At a little after 9:00 a.m. on Tuesday morning, a dozen reserve deputies in matching T-shirts and four members of the CSU slowly and carefully walked side by side in a horizontal fifty-yard-long line within a delineated grid that Nan and Daniel had marked with string and stakes at the Preserve the previous day. Everyone wore rubber gloves on their hands and booties over their shoes and carried whistles around their necks that they were instructed to blow if they spotted anything resembling a bone or fragment of one.

Eve, Duncan, Daniel, and Nan walked together, performing the same tedious task as the others. It was slow going, and the first hour felt like eight. Finally, Daniel stopped.

"This has already gone on too long," he said.

Duncan stood up straight and stretched. "It's only been an hour. You're even more impatient for results than she is." He nodded at Eve.

"I didn't say anything," Eve said.

"It's not impatience, it's experience," Daniel said. "I can do this all day. Hell, I can happily do it for weeks. But you only get about forty minutes of high-quality searching from your average volunteer. Their brains get tired staring at dirt and it all blurs. They walk right over the teeth and bone we're looking for. They're finished and we've got a lot of ground to cover."

Nan put her hands on her hips, which Eve knew was the equivalent of standing her ground for the fight to come. "You're not suggesting we should already quit for the day."

"I'm saying it's time to take a piss." Daniel blew his whistle and everyone froze. He yelled, "Stand down!" Then he turned to Nan, Duncan, and Eve. "Tell the women to stay where they are, but I want the men to go pee someplace out there." He waved to the open space in front of them.

Nan stared at him. "You aren't seriously suggesting the search team should relieve themselves in shifts based on their sex."

Before Daniel could answer, Eve spoke up. "We've only got two porta-potties. The women can use those, and the men can find spots out there."

Daniel nodded. "Perfect."

"No, it's not," Nan said. "It's outrageous. You can't treat people that way. Are you trying to get us fired?"

Daniel smiled. "We have a saying in my profession: when you're answering the call of nature, watch your feet."

Duncan said, "So you won't piss on your boots?"

"So you'll find the bones you're looking for," Daniel replied. "Where do you naturally pee outdoors? Somewhere quiet and out of the way, where you won't be seen, interrupted, or vulnerable. It's instinctive."

Now Eve was seeing the logic. "It's also how people pick where to bury a body, somewhere they don't want to be seen doing it . . ."

Duncan chimed in, "And where nobody is likely to stumble across the grave later, if ever."

At first, Nan appeared unconvinced, her hands still on her hips, her feet still firmly planted in place. But then she dropped her hands. "I can't believe I'm saying this, but that actually makes some twisted sense, but you'll need to tell them why we're doing it."

"Absolutely not," Daniel said. "Maybe afterwards. But right now, I don't want them thinking about what they are doing. I want them going with their gut."

"I think you mean bladders," Duncan said.

Nan sighed. "Fine, we'll do it, but if HR comes hunting for my head, I'm bringing you to the guillotine with me."

She passed the word along the line and reminded everyone to watch where they walked—there could be bones anywhere.

A dozen men went out in different directions to relieve themselves. Eve could see the bafflement and anger on some of the women's faces. Women began to line up at the porta-potties. A few awkward minutes passed.

Nan looked out at all the men searching for discreet places to pee, some failing and flashing her with their naked butts. "This is the strangest forensic technique I've ever seen."

Eve understood how she felt. It seemed to her that almost every time she went to a homicide scene, urine became an evidentiary or investigative issue. She knew bodily fluids were always important evidence and expected that blood, saliva, and semen would figure prominently in her work. But the repeated emphasis on some aspect of piss in her cases struck her as an unusually common denominator.

Daniel said, "Surely, Nan, you've used human nature to determine where to look for evidence."

"Not like this," she said.

"Just think, Nan," Duncan said. "You could be at the forefront of a new approach to crime scene investigation. It's a lot cheaper than some of the equipment you use."

Nan glowered at him.

One of the reserve deputies whistled to get their attention, then whistled again and again to underscore the urgency.

Daniel grinned broadly and looked at Nan. "Told you."

"Incredible," she said.

They followed the sound of the whistles out toward a cluster of tangled oaks and bushes, where a reserve deputy was waving his arms above the brush.

"Over here! Over here!" he said.

They carefully approached the bushes.

"I was peeing on that bush and my gaze wandered over there . . ." The reserve deputy pointed to something white sticking out of the ground. Daniel and Nan crouched beside it.

Daniel used a brush to remove some dirt from a tiny bone.

"It's a metatarsal," he said.

Nan glanced around and spotted something else on the surface. "I've got another one over here. Looks like a phalange."

Daniel duckwalked over to her and examined what she'd unearthed. "It is."

He stood up, carefully stepped a few steps back, and crouched, looking at the lay of the land like Tiger Woods lining up a putt.

Eve crouched beside him. "What are you looking for?"

"Linear depressions. When a body decomposes, it loses all of its fluid and shrinks."

"So the ground will sink, too."

Daniel nodded. "That's why it's wise to leave mounds of dirt on a grave, so when the bodies and wooden caskets gradually collapse, the ground will become level. Most people don't know that."

Duncan said, "But no killer wants to leave a mound that screams 'body buried here.'"

"That too," Daniel said and pointed to a spot in front of him. "Up there, about ten yards to my left. That may be a depression, but I need to rake it to be sure, then do a test dig."

"I don't see it," Eve said.

"It takes a trained eye."

Nan crouched beside them and followed Daniel's line of sight. "Could be."

There was another excited whistle about ten yards away. This time it came from a nearby area surrounded by large boulders. On the way over, Eve noticed a dried pile of dog poop on the ground. It could have come from one of the hiker's dogs or one of the many others people let roam the open park.

The reserve deputy told them that while he'd been urinating, his gaze drifted, and he saw some ground that had been scratched up. He went over to look and saw what appeared to be bones.

It was clear, even to Eve, that an animal had started digging. There was a shallow hole, hidden from view by the boulders and brush, and pieces of several bones were visible in the dirt, along with bits of fabric.

Daniel crouched by the hole on one end, Nan on the other, and they both took a long look at it.

"I'll bet that this is where at least one of those leg bones came from that the dogs found," Daniel said. "We need to seal off the area around these boulders and that group of trees and send home the reserve deputies. I only want professionals here now."

"Agreed," Nan said.

Daniel got up and turned to Eve. "It's going to be slow, methodical work from here. You two might as well go, too."

"We're professionals," Eve said.

"You're detectives. This is a forensic and anthropological dig now requiring delicate work on hands and knees with trowels, brushes, and sifters."

Duncan looked at Eve. "I don't have the knees for that and neither do you."

"My knees are great."

"One of yours was nearly shot off," he said.

"And that one is still better than both of yours combined."

Daniel put his hand gently on Eve's back. "You have absolutely wonderful knees, but we've got this. Nan or I will call you if we get anything."

Eve hated to leave but knew she'd be useless here, and she didn't want Daniel saying anything else as embarrassing as what he'd just said. She walked away and Duncan joined her.

"I've never met a guy into knees before," Duncan said.

"You've never dated a forensic anthropologist. Apparently, I have incredible bone structure."

Duncan pulled a paper from inside his jacket, then consulted his watch.

Eve recognized the spreadsheet-like document in his hand. "Is that the shooting schedule for the show?"

"Yeah, I stole it from a production assistant. *Ronin* is shooting up at Gelson's supermarket. Let's stop by and take a look."

Gelson's was in the shopping center at the intersection of Mulholland Highway and Mulholland Road, which marked the eastern jurisdictional border between the Los Angeles Police Department and the Los Angeles Sheriff's Department in this corner of the county. It also represented a turning point in her life. She wasn't sure if she was ready to revisit that.

"I'd rather go back to the office and do paperwork."

"We don't have any paperwork," he said.

"I'll do somebody else's paperwork."

"Come on, it's the first day of filming with my character and I'd like to see some of it," Duncan said.

"So go."

"It's your show," he said. "It'll be better if we go together, like we just happened to be in the neighborhood and stopped by."

"You mean so it won't look like you're super excited to see yourself being portrayed by an actor that *People* magazine named one of the ten sexiest men in daytime television."

"It's perfect casting," Duncan said.

"He's at least twenty years younger and at least a hundred pounds lighter than you are."

"But he looks just like me when I was his age."

They got into their county ride and Eve called in, briefed the captain on the situation at the Preserve, and said they were taking lunch at the *Ronin* set.

Dubois said that was fine and that there was no need for her to rush back to the Preserve or the station—he'd assign her to Mulholland and Mulholland as additional security and crowd control for the production.

"You don't have to give me time to hang out at the set, sir," Eve protested. "I'd rather do my job."

"That is your job until something urgent comes up," Dubois said. "This way, I can redeploy the uniformed deputies who are sitting there now back to patrol."

"You can deploy us instead," she said.

"Enjoy the show, Eve. You've earned it."

Dubois hung up. Duncan grinned at her.

Eve scowled at him. "I liked it better when the captains at the station hated me."

"Don't worry, he probably does."

She started the Explorer and headed down the road out of the park. "He has a funny way of showing it."

"Letting you spend time watching your show being shot is an easy way to sideline you so you can't cause him any trouble," Duncan said. "And it also reinforces your image within the department as a self-obsessed media whore."

"Damn him," she said, slapping the dashboard.

"Feel better?"

"Much," she said.

CHAPTER FIVE

Eve drove herself and Duncan to the T intersection of Mulholland Highway and Mulholland Drive, just like she had done only eight months ago, the day she'd caught her first homicide case.

It was an unremarkable intersection, though it marked the crossing of two cities, two law enforcement agencies, and three neighborhoods, and a major turning point in her life three months into her new job and partnership with Duncan, who'd become like a father to her.

And if she imagined away the film crew and just focused on the pickup truck parked on the curb, the LAPD patrol car and detective division Crown Vic across the street, and the two LAPD detectives awaiting her arrival, it was the past repeating itself.

The producers, set designers, and casting directors had done an impeccable job re-creating the moment. Eve felt like an invisible time traveler, visiting her own past. It was deeply unsettling and strangely fascinating.

Eve parked at the intersection, then she and Duncan got out and approached Deputy Tom Ross, an ex-marine who did just about everything in his life with military bearing. She'd been tempted to ask her younger sister, Lisa, who was dating Tom, if that attitude also expressed itself in their love life.

Tom had protected and supported Eve within the department, and on the street, more than anyone besides Duncan. That was especially remarkable and courageous of Tom, since he had the same Great White tattoo on his leg as the members of the corrupt deputy gang with the Lost Hills station that she'd exposed and battled, almost to her death.

Today, Tom and another deputy she didn't know were handling security and traffic control for the TV shoot.

There was only light traffic at this time of day and very few pedestrians were watching the filming. Local residents were either in the entertainment industry, or tangentially related to it, or had seen so much location filming that it held little interest anymore. It was just an inconvenience. Plus, there weren't any big stars around to draw the paparazzi, who staked out the nearby Commons shopping center waiting for a celeb sighting, like a starlet buying tampons or an action hero wolfing down a cheeseburger.

Eve approached Tom. "How's it going?"

"A thrill a minute," he said.

"Are you still miffed that nobody is playing you on the show?"

"See that corpse in the pickup?" Tom ignored her question and gestured to the pickup truck parked at the curb. There was a motionless body behind the wheel. "That's a rubber doll. But he represents a real person who was killed. I doubt his family is going to like seeing his brutal murder turned into entertainment."

He had a point, Eve thought, one she hadn't considered at all. She'd only thought about how the show would impact her. But the murder happened, and it wasn't her story. How it was depicted, on this show or in some other production, was outside of her control, but she hoped the camera wouldn't linger on the body.

Eve just nodded, avoiding the issue, and wandered with Duncan up the southbound side of Mulholland Road, where the crew was setting up the next shot. The scene they were about to shoot depicted Duncan and Eve arriving to meet with the two LAPD detectives, Knobb and Prescott, and the uniformed police officer who'd found a body on the jurisdictional line between their agencies.

Erin Casey and Mick Coltrane, the actor playing Duncan, stood on their camera marks, two pieces of gaffer's tape placed on the ground, while Krister Ekblad, the director of photography, used a light meter to measure the exposure around the actors. Vince was hunched over the monitors at the video village, watching the feed as a Steadicam operator moved around the crime scene, rehearsing his shot. Simone sat in her chair, typing furiously on her MacBook.

"Okay, let's do this, picking up where we left off after Eve and Duncan got out of their car," Vince said. Ekblad took his seat, everyone got quiet, and then Vince said, "Action!"

Duncan approached the two LAPD detectives and the police officer while Eve studied the body in the pickup truck. His throat had been slit from ear to ear and gaped open like an obscene, bloody smile.

"What's the story on this dead man?" Duncan asked.

Knobb said, "A jogger spotted the body and called 911. The operator called the LAPD. This fine young patrol officer showed up, saw the guy was dead, and brought us in."

"What he failed to notice was the boulder." Prescott pointed to the median, where a boulder that read **WELCOME TO CALABASAS** *sat in a bed of flowers. "And which side of it the truck was parked on."*

"Your side," Knobb said. "So here you are. We stuck around to preserve the scene as a professional courtesy."

"Really?" Eve said, turning away from the truck. The two detectives looked at her like a misbehaving child. "Because I thought securing the scene meant making sure it wasn't disturbed."

"It doesn't look disturbed to me," Knobb said.

"The truck is covered with pine needles," Eve said. "It obviously spent the night parked under a pine tree, which is odd, since the nearest one is down the corner, in Los Angeles. You obviously moved the truck into Calabasas so we'd have to investigate the case."

"Cut and print!" Vince said. "That was excellent. We're moving inside the car now for the rest of their dialogue."

Vince and Krister headed over to the car to block out the camera moves and lighting placement. In the meantime, the actors were free to relax for a few minutes.

Mick Coltrane spotted Duncan watching and ambled over. "What did you think of my performance?"

"You're the next Clint Eastwood." Duncan reached into his coat and fumbled out his iPhone. "Can I get a selfie? It's for my wife. She'll be thrilled, seeing me before and after in one picture."

"Before and after what?"

Duncan held his phone out at arm's length, then stepped beside Mick, slipping his other arm around the actor's shoulders. "Thirty years of marriage."

They smiled into Duncan's camera. Click!

Simone waved Eve over to the video village. "How's it feel to see this?"

Eve stood beside Simone's chair. "Honestly, it's surreal watching my father directing someone pretending to be me at a place where I actually stood, doing what she's doing."

"If it feels authentic, you can thank your father. His insights into your character have been invaluable."

"He doesn't know anything about me," Eve said.

"Maybe not the real you, but he sure gets your character."

"That's nice."

"I think it will seem less surreal for you in the future," Simone said, "when the episodes are all fiction and have nothing to do with you."

"Or I'll be even more uncomfortable with it." She had nightmares about the things they might have her character doing and how it might impact her in real life.

Simone's phone rang and she looked at the screen with a scowl. "Shit. It's the network. They probably have notes on the next script. Sorry, I need to take this."

"No problem." Eve stepped away to give her some privacy and Erin immediately intercepted her, as if she'd been waiting for the chance.

"How awkward is this for you?"

"Very," Eve said. "But you were great."

"Really? It's weird playing you, especially in the place where this scene really happened, while you're watching and so are other real cops."

It hadn't occurred to her that her presence on the set might actually sabotage the actors' performances. It was a stupid oversight.

"I'm so sorry. Duncan and I will go." Eve started to turn, but Erin gently touched her arm to stop her.

"No, no . . . that's not what I meant," Erin said. "You should be here. I feel like I'm the one who doesn't belong."

"Then you're nailing it."

"What do you mean?"

Eve looked out at the fake, but eerily accurate, crime scene. All the old feelings came rushing back.

"The morning this happened, I felt the same way, that I was acting in a role I didn't know how to play, and that everybody knew it."

"So how did you get past it?"

"I looked at him." Eve pointed to the corpse in the pickup. It wasn't real, but it was still very convincing. "He was wronged. I couldn't save his life, but I could honor it by getting him justice."

"You cope by making it about the victims and not about you."

"It's a battle, though. Because they keep wanting to make it about me." Eve pointed to the actors playing the two LAPD detectives.

"Because other cops resent you for how you got the job and will never accept you, no matter how many times you prove yourself."

"Yes, but that's not entirely the reason," she said. "I also put a bunch of corrupt cops in jail, shot another one, and maybe pushed a deputy so hard that he killed himself in front of me, but that all happened after this."

Eve gestured to the scene unfolding in the intersection. But her first homicide wasn't that long ago, not even a year, though it felt like so much longer.

"That's a lot to carry," Erin said.

"Not for you, at least not yet," Eve said, forcing a smile. "It's only episode one."

But Erin didn't smile back. Her expression was grim. "Everybody in Hollywood thinks I'm too young and inexperienced to be the lead in a TV series, that I only got the role because my tits went viral and made me famous."

"I knew nothing about that," Eve said and it was the truth. Nobody had told her and she wasn't plugged into what was happening on social media, not unless it was generated by a case she was working on.

Erin explained that her iPhone had been stolen and hacked by a repairman her landlord had given access to her apartment while she wasn't there. She'd taken some topless photos for a boyfriend and never deleted them. The repairman demanded a ransom or he'd post the photos. She refused to pay, so her photos went viral. The repairman, a Russian national, disappeared and the LAPD seemed to be in no hurry to track him down. In the meantime, the photos were still on the net and had been downloaded millions of times.

"Suddenly I got offered a hundred roles that would've required me to take off my top. I turned them all down, choosing small character parts with some depth to them and no nudity," she said. "So I have to prove myself here now, too."

"No, you don't," Eve said. "You have the job, so do it and don't look back. Do it the way you believe it should be done. Don't let anybody or anything stop you. That way, if you succeed or fail, you'll know it was because of choices you made, not somebody else."

"Does that attitude work?"

"It does for me," Eve said. "And if you want to be true to my character, you'll have to adopt it, too, at least whenever you're wearing that badge." She pointed to the fake, and unrealistically large, LASD badge clipped to Erin's belt.

Erin glanced at her prop badge, then smiled at Eve. "I will. Thank you."

The assistant director yelled, "First team."

Erin gave Eve a hug, then got up and joined Mick inside the fake LASD car for the rest of their dialogue.

Eve relieved the deputies on traffic control, letting them go back to patrol, and took over the job herself, while Duncan watched the scene being shot from countless angles and sampled everything the catering truck had to offer. She'd seen enough of her life being filmed, and by directing the dribble of traffic, at least she could feel like she was doing something productive there.

During a break between scenes, her father came out to her in the intersection. There was no place for Eve to duck and hide without looking foolish, so she was forced to talk to him while she handled the traffic.

"Whatever you said to Erin took her performance to the next level, one I was struggling to get her to reach," Vince said. "Thank you."

"I had nothing to do with it," Eve said. "Whatever you saw, she found it within herself."

"I think it's great that we're working hand in hand together, enjoying the kind of father-daughter relationship I've always longed for."

"You're confusing me with the actress playing my part," she said, waving a car by. "We aren't working together and we certainly aren't bonding."

"I feel closer to you now than I have in years."

"Get any closer, and I'll push you into oncoming traffic."

At that moment, a big truck chugged by, underlining the danger of that threat.

Vince chuckled, but it felt false. "I know I wasn't the father you wanted me to be—"

Eve interrupted him. "You weren't a father at all."

"But you're an adult now and that's all in the past. I don't understand why you insist on being such a hardnose with me, especially after I did all this to make it up to you." He gestured to all the dressing rooms, makeup trailers, and equipment trucks along the street and in the Gelson's parking lot.

"You forgot I existed until I became a hero and everybody in Hollywood wanted my story," Eve said. "You told them I was your daughter and, in order to get me, they had to hire you to direct. Then you shamelessly manipulated Mom, a woman you knocked up and abandoned, into helping you coerce me into it by promising her you'd make her acting dreams come true. Which, in a sickening throwback, was the same way you seduced her the first time."

Vince shrugged. "In other words, I found a way to make amends to you both for my past mistakes. What do you have to be angry about now?"

"This isn't about us, Vince. It's about you rewriting the end of your career, going out with a hit instead of your slow, dreary fade into obscurity at the old folks' home, regaling everyone with stories from your TV past while you wait for your four p.m. dinner."

Vince sighed and looked off into the distance, which happened to be in the general direction of the Motion Picture and Television Country House and Hospital, where he lived in a bungalow. "It's true that I don't have many years left. All I want is to be in your life while I still can."

"You mean you want to direct more episodes of the show."

"If it means I can spend more time with you or help make your show a success so you can reap the benefits long after I am gone, then I'm willing to come out of retirement to do it."

Eve's cell phone vibrated in her jacket. She took it out and looked at the screen. It was Daniel. She took the call, but she would have taken a spam call, too—anything to end this conversation with her father.

Daniel said, "We've got something for you to see."

"Thank God," she said. "It's been forever."

"We haven't been apart that long."

"It's been an eternity for me."

"Miss me that much?"

"We'll be right there." Eve ended the call and moved past her dad. "I have to go. I have real police work to do."

He followed after her, careful not to get hit as a car drove slowly through the intersection, the driver looking at the production activity, perhaps hoping to glimpse a star, and not where he was going.

"Of course," Vince said. "Generating fodder for future episodes. I hope to see you back on the set this week."

"I've seen enough. I won't be back." Eve waved at Duncan, catching his eye and gesturing him to return to their car.

"Not even to support your mom in her first major speaking role?" Vince said. "That would break her heart."

It was one line, and her character didn't even have a name, but Vince was right. It was huge for her mother. Eve stopped at her car and faced her dad. "You really are a manipulative prick."

"Is that so?" He smiled at her. "Remind me, hardnose. How did you get your badge?"

Vince turned his back to her and walked away, so he didn't see her flip him off. But Duncan did as the two men passed.

"A daughter's bond with her father is so special," Duncan said to her. "It always tugs at my heart to see it."

CHAPTER SIX

The dirt had been dug away a few inches all around the male corpse, creating an earthen pedestal, which Eve noticed was slightly inclined so the lower half of the body was closer to the surface than the rest.

The corpse was wrapped like a burrito in a filthy blue tarp, which had become frayed at the bottom, as if an animal had clawed it apart, revealing some leg bones in shredded denims. Some tiny bones and fragments that Eve couldn't identify were scattered around the pedestal like a string of pearls that had broken.

A mummified head, some of the skull exposed to reveal a ragged hole in the brow, poked out of the top end of the tarp. The jaw was open, as if in a permanent scream, revealing some teeth in a mouthful of dirt.

Eve and Duncan stood at one end of the grave as Nan photographed the scene, Daniel used a brush to move dirt away from the bones, and Dr. Emilia Lopez, the deputy medical examiner, crouched over the dead man's head, examining it with a magnifying glass. Lopez was a short woman with a tendency to wear glasses that were too big for her face and made her eyes seem huge. The magnifying glass added to the effect.

Daniel stood to greet the two detectives. "What we have here is a corpse, not a skeleton."

Eve could see that. "Why isn't he, if he's been dead and buried for two years?"

"The drought," Daniel said. "Really dry soil sucks the fluids out of a body and essentially mummifies it. And this body was rolled in a tarp, which isn't porous, so all the fluid and organs were more contained."

Lopez nodded in agreement. "He's going to be gooey, so we won't open the tarp here."

Duncan said, "We deeply appreciate that."

Nan said, "We'll open it at the morgue so we're certain we can capture anything that spills out."

Duncan grimaced. "You might as well open it up here now that you've put that colorful image in my head."

"Speaking of heads," Eve said, "is that a bullet hole in his?"

Lopez peered closer at the hole. "It certainly appears to be, but I won't know for sure until I open him up. Maybe I'll find a bullet rattling around in there."

Nan straightened up. "After the body is removed, we'll sift through the dirt underneath to make sure no bullets or other evidence have been left behind."

"Can you tell us anything about him yet?" Eve asked.

Daniel said, "He's a native South American, from somewhere rural."

"How do you know?"

"A few facts, lots of past experience, and some educated guesses."

"In other words," Duncan said, "detective work."

"Walk us through it," Eve said to Daniel, which she knew he'd be delighted to do. But she didn't ask so he could show off his knowledge. She wanted to learn for herself so, in the future, she might be able to make some educated guesses.

"Sure," Daniel said, first pointing to the nasal cavity, since most of the nose was gone. "The prominent malar and intermediate nasal spine suggests that he's Hispanic. His teeth tell me rural."

Duncan said, "His teeth look like any teeth to me."

"Up close you'd see he's got shovel-shaped incisors, which is indicative of Native Americans, and more wear on them than someone who has spent his life eating at McDonald's or food from Ralphs. His teeth are almost flat."

"So," Eve said to Duncan, "teeth entirely different from yours."

Duncan ignored her comment and asked Daniel another question. "Has he been chewing on gravel?"

"No, but you're on the right track," Daniel said. "Here almost all of our food is processed, so there's no grit on the grains to sand down the teeth. But food is only semiprocessed in South America, and not at all in the rural areas, where they eat what they grow and still grind their corn with a stone, leaving grit in the flour. But we can pin down exactly where he's from, right down to the village he grew up in, with a radioactive isotope test on his teeth."

"Dental GPS," Duncan said.

"I like that," Daniel said. "I may steal it."

"You can't," Duncan said. "We're keeping it for my character in my show."

To underscore the point, he took a notepad from his back pocket and wrote the comment down so he wouldn't forget it. Eve gestured to the notepad, which was curved from being sat upon.

"Out of everything he's told us," she said, "that's what you think is important enough to write down?"

"I won't forget that forensic stuff, but I might forget this gem."

Eve gestured to the corpse. "How did the dogs get to him?"

"Remember how I told you a buried body sinks as it decays?" Daniel said. "Settling and erosion gradually loosened enough dirt from one end of the grave that a wild animal, probably coyotes, caught the scent of the body and started digging."

"Why didn't they dig up the whole body?"

Nan answered the question. "Digging a grave, particularly in dirt like this, is hard work, and people tend to make them too short and too shallow, with one end deeper than the other, like a swimming pool.

The legs of this body were at the shallow end, so the animals just started tugging."

"And popped off the legs," Eve said.

"Exactly," Daniel said. "The coyotes ran off with them, chewed on them a bit, and later the dogs found the scraps."

"This explains one leg, but you said there were two bodies," Eve said. "Where's the other?"

"We don't know yet," Daniel said. "Maybe somewhere by the bushes, where we found the metatarsal and phalange."

Nan said, "We've been concentrating on this burial site, but we'll finish it up today and search over there tomorrow. We'll also bring in some ground-penetrating radar equipment to help us."

"All right," Duncan said. "We'll see you bright and early. Thanks for the great work."

He abruptly walked away and Eve went after him. "Where are we going?"

"Back to the station to brief the captain and then home. There's nothing more we can do here and probably nothing we can do at all."

"We're homicide detectives and that man was murdered."

"We've been through this same experience a dozen times before. They're illegal immigrants, either gang members or drug cartel mules, killed in a turf war somewhere in LA and dumped here, in our backyard."

Eve knew that was true. The fire that had raged through the Santa Monica Mountains months ago had exposed the bones of many executed gang members who had been dumped in the canyons and previously hidden in the brush. But that wasn't true of all the bones that were found. It was how she'd met Daniel.

Duncan continued. "We'll use up six reams of paper writing up reports on the unidentified bodies, giving ourselves raging tendinitis, and then the gang unit will take over the investigation while we go to physical therapy for six weeks, decimating our savings to pay the deductible."

"And the killings of these men will never get solved," Eve said.

"They chose this life," Duncan said.

"I think it's more likely they were born into it and never had a chance to get out."

Duncan glanced over his shoulder at the grave behind them. A forensic team was erecting a tent over the excavation to protect the scene.

"Well," he said, "they're out of it now."

Eve rode her bike home on Tuesday night and actually managed to get halfway up the hill before she had to stop, exhausted, and walk the rest of the way.

Once home, she showered, got into her bathrobe, and unboxed some of the dishware she'd bought at Costco but hadn't used, opting instead for plastic utensils and paper plates. Around 7:00 p.m., Daniel showed up, covered in dirt, not bothering to ring the bell this time, though he did open the door very slowly, announcing himself as he came in.

"Hey, Eve, it's me."

Daniel had an apartment in West LA, close to the UCLA campus where he actually worked, but since she'd moved out of the Hilton and into the house, they'd been spending a lot more nights together in Calabasas. He didn't have any clothes at her place, which meant they'd have to do a load of laundry tonight.

He had a sheepish, apologetic look on his face, as if he knew what she was thinking.

"I have to be back at the dig early in the morning and the traffic will be hell. I figured spending the night here was more convenient than going to my place."

Eve met him in the entry hall. She didn't want him tracking dirt all over the house. "Is that the only reason you want to stay here? Or are you also here for the hot shower, the laundry service, and a hot, free meal?"

"Sure, all that's nice. But mostly it's curiosity."

"About what?"

"Last night, we built the kitchen dinette set and broke it in."

Yes, they did. Before dinner and again before breakfast. Her back was still sore from that, maybe even bruised. But it was a nice bruise, the kind that comes with a good memory.

He tugged on her sash, letting her bathrobe fall open, and said, "But you still haven't shown me what you can do on a barstool."

So she did.

◆　◆　◆

Eve was asleep in bed when her work phone started buzzing. She woke up and glanced at the time on the screen. It was 4:00 a.m. She was on call, so this could only mean one thing.

Murder.

She reached for the phone and answered it. "Ronin."

Captain Dubois said, "Sorry to wake you. Kitty Winslow has been killed in a shooting on the family compound in Hidden Hills."

Only a celebrity or major politician getting killed would merit a phone call from the captain rather than the dispatcher. That's because this homicide was going to be a media event.

Eve was on call, and she also happened to be the nearest homicide detective to Hidden Hills, which was not even a mile north of her, on the other side of the Ventura Freeway, though she'd never been beyond the gates before. But she still wondered about the political calculation that was made to send her and not another homicide detective.

"Is this a domestic situation?" she asked.

"No, it was a home invasion. It happened only within the last twenty, thirty minutes."

He gave her the address on John Chisum Road and told her the CSU and a medical examiner were on their way, but they were coming from East LA, so they were still at least forty-five minutes out. "The media will be all over this soon and I don't want you saying a word to them, understood?"

"I'll call Duncan and be there in ten minutes."

Eve hung up, bolted out of bed naked, and hurried over to a moving box to dig out a fresh set of clothes. She hadn't bought a dresser yet.

Daniel rolled over in bed and asked groggily, "What is it?"

"Kitty Winslow has been killed." Eve pulled on her panties and reached for a bra.

"I have no idea who that is."

"You're probably the only person in the world who doesn't." She put on her bra, put on a wrinkled but clean shirt, and started buttoning it up.

"What's she famous for?"

"Mostly for her beautiful face, gigantic boobs, and surgically inflated ass. But she's also a singer and model. Her father is Caleb Winslow."

"The western actor?" Daniel sat up in bed. "I didn't know he was still alive. My dad used to love him on *Saddlesore*."

She grabbed her slacks from the day before and put them on. "The Winslow family has a hit reality show about their daily life. It's made them all rich."

Eve snatched her badge off the nightstand, clipped it on her belt, and went to the closet to take her weapon out of the gun safe.

"Is their life that exciting?" he asked.

She'd never watched the show. "It was tonight."

Eve holstered her gun, leaned over the bed to give Daniel a kiss, then hurried out, giving Duncan a call on the run. He said he'd be there in thirty minutes.

CHAPTER SEVEN

The City of Hidden Hills was a modern-day Mont-Saint-Michel, an island fortress within a sea of urban sprawl. But instead of a fortress's medieval turrets, crenellated stone walls and drawbridges, there were hidden cameras, three-rail white fences, and a wooden arch over the main gate that resembled an enormous upside-down oxen yoke. In case the western theme was too subtle, a carving in the center of the arch featured a cowboy on horseback, waving his hat over his head.

It was a pastoral equestrian city without stores, restaurants, street-lights, or sidewalks, only homes and horse trails. The city contracted out its law enforcement to the Los Angeles County Sheriff's Department, though private security guards manned the main gate and two others.

To reach the Hidden Hills main gate, Eve drove across the Valley Circle overpass over the Ventura Freeway. She then made a sharp left onto Long Valley Road, which doubled as the northbound freeway on-ramp at the point where the road also curved to the right toward the entrance to the city.

It was a confusing and dangerous urban planning design failure that had vexed drivers for decades and that the City of Hidden Hills, the City of Los Angeles, and Caltrans, the state highway authority, hadn't been able to solve.

The Hidden Hills main gatehouse was centered under the oxen-yoke archway, with an exit lane on the left and dual entrance lanes on the right, one for guests and one for residents. Guests had to pass by the window of the gatehouse and show their IDs to the guards, who confirmed their invitation and gave them a printed pass to enter the city. Residents had transponders that allowed them to go through their gate.

Eve drove up to the guardhouse and held out her badge to the guard, who waved her through. She used her GPS to find the house, but it wasn't hard. The glow of lights from a single LASD patrol car, a Big Valley Security patrol car, and a Los Angeles County paramedic unit spotlighted her destination.

She grabbed a set of booties and latex gloves from her glove box, stuffed them into her coat pocket, and got out of her car, a new two-door Ford Bronco. She was met almost immediately by a stocky, middle-aged uniformed deputy, but what really stood out about him was his cowboy hat. It struck her as comical, but it fit the community's western theme. He held his hands palm out to her and blocked her path.

Eve badged him. "I'm Eve Ronin, Homicide."

But he didn't move aside. "Hold your horses, Detective. I've got things under control."

Hold your horses? she thought. *Who says that anymore?* And who did he think he was, giving her orders?

But she held her anger in check and simply asked, "Who are you?"

"Amos Tatum. I got here three minutes after the shooting, secured the scene, and called it in."

"How did you get here so fast?"

"The Winslows called me and so did their neighbors."

"They called you directly and not 911?"

"I've been the law here for a long time," he said, "and I live around the corner."

That raised a lot of questions for her, but they would have to wait. Beyond and above him, she could see an LASD helicopter streaking over the Preserve, sweeping it with a spotlight.

"Who called in the chopper?"

"I did. I also alerted the park rangers. But I'm sure the intruders are long gone now and will be on the first flight back to Chile."

Eve didn't like that he was acting as if he were in charge of the investigation. But right now what she needed was information. "Tell me what happened."

"First you need to know the lay of the land. The Winslows have a compound of two homes, a guesthouse, and a stable. The entire north end of the property backs up against the open space," he said. "Caleb and his wife, Brandy, live in the main house, that big two-story log cabin behind me, with their two teenage children, Skye and Maverick. Kitty, Caleb's eldest daughter from his first marriage, lives in the house behind that. And beyond the two homes are the guesthouse and the stable, which also has a bunkhouse."

Eve was losing patience with this man. "I can get all that off Google Earth and Zillow. I'm not interested in the real estate listing. What I need to know are the details about the killing."

Tatum's face tightened. "Three masked men broke into Kitty's house. They were ransacking her bedroom when she walked in on them from the bathroom. One of them shot her point-blank in the face and fled. Caleb ran out with his gun, saw them fleeing toward the fence to the open space, and fired off a few shots at them, but they got away. Caleb jumped on a horse and rode after them."

There were a lot of big gaps in that story that she'd have to fill. "How do you know all that?"

"I saw the body and Mrs. Winslow told me the rest," he said. "But they've got exterior cameras everywhere, so we can see for ourselves what happened outside the house."

We? She wouldn't be letting this guy anywhere near her investigation. "What about interior cameras?"

"They aren't on when they're home."

Only when they are on TV, Eve thought. "Has anybody besides the intruders, the Winslows, and you been near the body?"

"The paramedics, who got here a minute or two before you did. They are still inside with the body."

"Where's the family?"

"In the main house," he said, "but there's no reason to intrude on their grief right now."

"Except a homicide investigation," Eve said. "I have questions for them."

"There's nothing they can tell you that's relevant and there's no mystery what happened here."

"Is that so?"

He sighed. "Kitty got a big fat engagement ring yesterday and showed it off on Instagram, in a photo taken right here, with that street sign behind you in the background. Chilean gangs fly here just to pillage homes. They constantly watch social media for rich celebrities, mostly rappers and athletes, flaunting their bling."

"Everybody knows that the Winslows live in Hidden Hills."

"But not their actual address," he said. "Their homes are owned by shell companies and the family doesn't actually film their show here. They have another house in the Oaks just for that. The Chileans saw the street sign, used Google Earth to locate the house, and hit it. Case closed."

"I don't think so," Eve said. "I'm going to look at the crime scene, then talk to the Winslows."

She started to go, but Tatum stepped in front of her again, which was really starting to make her angry.

"That's pointless," he said, "but give me your questions and I'll handle it."

"I'll ask them myself," she said firmly.

Tatum sighed again, but this time he stepped to one side so she could walk past him toward the crushed-gravel motor court. "If you insist. Let's go."

"I don't need a chaperone."

"You're a stranger here," he said, keeping pace beside her. "Everybody in Hidden Hills knows I'm the law."

Eve stopped at the motor court. "Good, so you stay right there, shoo the neighbors away, and start the crime scene visitor log."

"That's a deputy's job," he said.

"Yes, it is," Eve said and continued walking across the motor court just as the team of paramedics emerged from a path alongside the main house that she assumed led to the other buildings in the compound. She knew the paramedics—Rick Gage and Jamie Dundas—from previous cases. They worked out of the Calabasas fire station.

"What can you tell me?" Eve asked, throwing the question out to both of them.

Rick answered. "She was dead before she hit the floor, but we went through the required motions. I hate this part of the job."

"I don't blame you, Rick."

Jamie said, "It's a tragedy. She just got engaged. Her ring looked like it was made with the Pink Panther diamond."

"You follow her on social media?"

"Doesn't everybody?" Jamie said and the paramedics continued on.

Eve walked down the path, noting the cameras on the eaves of the house, but also discreetly mounted on trees and light posts. Kitty's home, a contemporary log cabin with a wraparound porch, was separated from the main house across a rolling lawn and man-made creek. A small wooden bridge arched over the creek. The lights were on in the house and the front door was wide open.

She took the booties and gloves out of her pockets and put them on so she wouldn't contaminate the crime scene, then went inside the house. There was a table and chair by the front door. A set of keys were on the table and several handbags were casually stacked and draped on the chair.

The living room decor was southwestern, with lots of wooden furniture upholstered with leather, accented with rugs and pillows that reflected Native American designs. The whole place had an impersonal, interior-designer, model-home feel. Or perhaps the set of a TV sitcom. Eve pulled out her phone and documented the scene with photos.

She continued down the hall to the main bedroom. Kitty Winslow was lying face down in an unnatural position, the back of her head blown away, the stucco wall behind her spattered with blood and brain matter. She was in a nightgown and barefoot, suggesting she was either getting ready for bed or had awakened to go to the bathroom when she walked in on the burglars.

The murder angered and saddened Eve. It was such a senseless killing. Kitty was unarmed, alone, and vulnerable. They could have taken the ring without shooting her.

Or was the killing done without thinking, because whoever had the gun had been startled by her? Did he regret it the moment after it was done? Or had she said or done something that angered the intruders, provoking someone to shoot?

There was, of course, another explanation. The intruders came intending to steal her ring and kill her. If so, why? Did they resent her fame? Or was there a personal motive?

Whatever it was, Eve would find out and catch the people who did it. She made that silent promise to Kitty as she stood over her body.

Eve turned now to survey the room.

All the dresser and side table drawers had been opened and dumped, spreading clothes all over the floor, and the closet was wide open, several shoe and garment boxes tossed. Kitty's iPhone was also on the floor, in the narrow space between her nightstand and the bed.

She took more pictures, documenting everything, and walked back outside, but instead of heading back toward the main house, she walked toward the stable, which was across another wide expanse of lawn. Between Kitty's house and the stable, on the north side of the property, was the guesthouse, a small log cabin with a stone chimney, right at the fence line that separated the Winslow property from the Preserve, blocking a portion of it from view where she stood.

Eve turned and went to the main house, stepped up to the back porch, and let herself in through the french doors without knocking. She went through the huge country-style kitchen and into the two-story great room, which resembled a hunting lodge or ski resort. It was dominated by a massive stone fireplace with elk antlers above the mantel.

Brandy, Skye, and Maverick Winslow were sitting on leather couches in front of the fireplace in their pajamas. Nobody was crying, but they looked pale and nauseous, like they all had food poisoning. Eve had learned that everybody processed grief differently, and this was apparently their way.

Brandy was a tall, thin bottle-blonde, the angles of her face unnaturally squared by a scalpel held by an inarticulate hand, and her skin was as taut as a vinyl dashboard. Her breasts were high, hard, and symmetrical under her pajama blouse, and she was hugging herself.

Skye was twenty, wearing a hot-pink bathrobe that matched the color of her hair and fuzzy slippers, her knees drawn up to her chest, her eyes bloodshot. Eve could see traces in Skye's soft yet elegant face of what Brandy must have looked like before the knife. The family's plastic surgeon should be working in a meat market, Eve thought, rather than an operating room.

Maverick was an overweight eighteen, trying to hide his acne-scarred face with a patchy beard and long hair. His striped pajama top, which didn't quite cover his round tummy, made him look like an oversize infant wearing a wig.

They all looked a lot better on TV, though nobody ever looked good after seeing a loved one murdered. She felt sorry for them and hoped she could bring them some peace by finding the intruders who killed Kitty. It would never heal their heartbreak.

Eve held up her badge as she strode over to them. "I'm Detective Eve Ronin. My partner, Duncan Pavone, and I will be leading the investigation. I'm sorry for your loss."

Skye sniffled and said, "We know who you are. We don't live in a cave. I must have watched the Largo smackdown a hundred times."

"Those were some cool moves," Maverick said. "Do you have a black belt?"

"The only belts I have are from the Gap," Eve said.

Brandy got up and gestured to Eve to take a seat on a leather easy chair. "That runt Largo deserved a beating. He never met a woman he didn't feel up, including me."

Eve sat down on the edge of the chair, facing the two couches across a broad carved wooden table with some sort of tree trunk for a base.

"I know how horrified and heartbroken you are but I need to ask you some questions now while what happened is still fresh in your minds."

"It always will be," Brandy said, her voice a bit raw. "I'll never forget how my daughter was killed."

"Stepdaughter," Skye said, but then added gently, "but it's still awful."

Eve took out her notebook and pen and glanced at Brandy. "Where were you before it happened?"

"I was upstairs, asleep in bed. The gunshots woke me up."

"Me too," Skye said. "I ran into Mom in the hall."

Maverick said, "I didn't hear any of it. It was you two running down the hall that got me up."

Eve looked at him. "What time was that?"

"3:40. The time on my phone was the first thing I saw when I opened my eyes."

Brandy said, "We ran outside toward Kitty's place, and that's when we saw Caleb coming around the back of her house in his underwear, holding his gun."

"The back of the house?" Eve said. "How did he get out there before you did?"

Skye said, "Dad sleeps in the bunkhouse."

Brandy spoke up quickly, meeting Eve's gaze. "It's not what you think, Detective. We aren't separated. He just likes going to bed early and getting up before sunrise, and he doesn't want to disturb me."

"And he loves being with his horses," Maverick said.

"More than being with us," Skye said.

Maverick turned to her. "The horses don't constantly nag him for a boob job."

Skye glowered at her brother. "Not all of us were blessed with your moobs."

Brandy ignored their comments and addressed Eve. "Caleb just longs for a simpler life . . . and finds it out there."

Still, Eve thought it was strange. "So you never saw the intruders yourselves."

"No, but Caleb did," she said. "He said he shot at them as they ran off toward the fence and into the park . . . and said he was going after them. Then he asked us where Kitty was, so we all went to her house."

Brandy's voice caught as she was overcome with emotion. Skye slid across the couch to comfort her mom with a hug.

Skye said, "Dad took one look at her on the floor, ran back to the stable, saddled Wildfire, and rode off as fast as he could."

Maverick said, "It was like his opening credits shot on *Saddlesore*, except for him being in his tighty-whities. I caught myself humming the theme."

Skye glowered at her brother again. Eve suspected that glowering was her default expression when it came to Maverick. "That's a horrible thing to say."

"Why? It's true," he said. "It actually made me feel better. Like justice would be done."

"That's why I called Marshal Tatum," Skye said.

"You did?" Eve asked.

Skye pulled her phone out of her bathrobe pocket. The phone was in a fuzzy pink slipper of its own. "I have the marshal on speed dial."

The marshal? Eve wondered if that was something Tatum made everyone call him or something Skye chose to do on her own. But that wasn't the question she asked.

"You had your iPhone with you when you ran out?"

Maverick answered before his sister could. "She doesn't go anywhere without it."

"I'd rather be naked," she said.

"And taking selfies with her phone," Maverick said. "That's how her snatch 'accidentally' got all over the net."

Now Brandy glowered at her son, and Eve saw the familial resemblance on her face, despite the plastic surgery. "How can you talk that way right now? My daughter is dead."

"Stepdaughter," Maverick said. "And I wasn't talking about her snatch."

Brandy launched herself off the couch at her son, clearly with violent intent, but Eve stepped up to block her.

"You need to take it easy, Mrs. Winslow."

Brandy stopped, suddenly self-conscious, aware of what she'd been about to do. "Oh my God."

Maverick had scooted into the corner of the couch. "I'm sorry, Mom. I shouldn't have said that."

"No, no, no, I am. I can't believe what I almost did. What is wrong with me?" Brandy sat back down.

Skye cuddled up against her again. "Three assholes broke into our home and killed Kitty, that's what's wrong."

That reminded Eve that everything was on video. "Where do you keep the DVR for the security cameras?"

Brandy said, "There's a dedicated computer in a closet off the laundry room. I'll show you."

She got up, and so did Eve.

Brandy led her back toward the kitchen. "I apologize for my children. They can be crass when they're hurting. It's a defense mechanism."

"I understand." But it wasn't true. She thought it was odd.

There was a storage room off the kitchen, which was filled with bulk items from Costco, various shipping supplies, a long work counter, and a desk, where a computer, two monitors, and a digital video recording device were hooked up. The monitors were broken up into grids, each square showing a different camera angle on the property. Eve could see Tatum pacing in front of the motor court and Duncan's Buick parked behind her Bronco.

Brandy gestured to the desk. "If you want to copy the footage, all you have to do is select a time period and hit the download button, and you'll get everything from every camera. We have a bunch of empty flash drives in the desk drawer if you need one."

"You do?"

"Sometimes we use the security video in the show to give it a candid feel, a stolen glimpse of our lives, and to add to the illusion that our Oaks residence is this one."

Eve decided that she would come back and download the footage later. She wanted to meet with Duncan first.

"Please stay inside the house until the forensic crew is done with their work. The entire property outside is a crime scene. But this is the one place we know the intruders didn't go."

Brandy nodded. "We won't step outside until Amos tells us we can."

Eve noted again the casual reference to the sheriff's deputy, first by Skye as "Marshal Tatum" and now by Brandy as "Amos."

"Once the crime scene unit has let you back in Kitty's house," Eve said, "we'll need a complete inventory of everything that's missing."

"I don't know everything Kitty had. She was a raging shopaholic. I doubt even she was able to keep track of it all. But definitely her engagement ring is gone."

Eve handed Brandy her card. "Please email me a list as soon as you can. And give me a call if you have questions or if any more details occur to you."

"I will."

"How do I reach Kitty's mother?"

"A séance," Brandy said. "Or maybe a Ouija board."

"She's dead?"

Brandy looked astonished, which was an expression Eve was surprised to see, or at least recognize, considering how tight and Botox-frozen the woman's face was. "Kitty has told the story many times. You don't subscribe to *People? Us Weekly? Star?*"

"No."

"So where do you get your news?"

"CNN."

Brandy sighed, then said, "It happened one morning while Caleb was on set, shooting *Saddlesore*. Daphne was in the backyard drinking a pitcher of highballs while Kitty, who was a toddler then, played on the grass. Daphne stumbled into the pool and drowned. Kitty was out there all day alone, in a hundred-degree heat, with her mother's corpse getting ripe in the pool, until Caleb came home that night."

"That's horrible," Eve said.

"That's why there's no pool on the property," Brandy said. Eve hadn't noticed that. But it explained all the lawns. "The tragedy was the demon behind Kitty's addictions to sex, shopping, plastic surgery, and carbs. Sharing her experience with the public was how she destroyed the demon's power over her and was finally able to find . . . and love . . . herself. And now this. It's so unfair."

"Murder always is."

CHAPTER EIGHT

Eve went outside and walked to the lawn between Kitty's house and the stable just as Caleb Winslow rode up on his horse and stopped in front of Duncan, who had on latex gloves and booties, indicating that he'd just been looking at the crime scene. She knew it was Caleb because he was wearing only white briefs and held an old-fashioned six-shooter.

Caleb was in his late seventies and bone thin, with a bushy gray mustache and eyebrows, his matching hair pulled back into a ponytail that fell between his shoulder blades. His skin was like a worn saddle. He said, "The bastards got away."

Duncan badged him and introduced himself and Eve as she approached. "I need you to get off that horse, Mr. Winslow, and give me your gun."

"I was a deputy," Caleb said wistfully, "for almost twenty years."

On TV, Eve thought. *That doesn't count.*

"I know," Duncan said. "I've seen every *Saddlesore* episode a dozen times. You were great."

"I've tracked a hundred outlaws but couldn't pick up the trail on the men who gunned down my daughter."

Because that was TV, not reality. Eve wondered if he knew the difference or if he was simply in shock.

"Yeah, well, it was pretty dark out," Duncan said. "It still is."

Caleb shook his head. "It's because I wasn't a white man raised by Cherokee. I wasn't a tin-badged lawman, either. But I still feel like I lived it all, because I did, every waking hour for a quarter of my life." He handed Duncan the six-shooter, which Duncan took carefully in his gloved hand.

Eve was relieved that Caleb gave up his gun and that he could still see the line between fiction and reality, even if it had become blurry for him. She wondered, though, if it had blurred long before his daughter was killed.

Caleb said, "I don't know how I missed them, even at night and half-asleep, because they were still big targets. I thought for sure I'd find at least one of 'em on the ground or limping along. And if I did, I would have finished him off."

Eve said, "Then it's a good thing you didn't. Can you take us back to the beginning?"

Caleb leaned on his saddle horn. "I was bedding down in the bunk-house tonight. Nothing more restful than the smell of hay and the sounds of horses sighing or swishing their tails."

Duncan said, "That's so true."

"And the horses don't mind if I get up three times a night to pee."

"Is that why you were awake?"

Caleb shook his head. "Her scream woke me. I was reaching for my six-shooter under the bed when I heard the gunshot. I rushed out and saw the three bastards running from Kitty's back door."

Eve said, "Can you describe them?"

"They were all dressed in black, head to toe, like ninjas."

"And you could still see them in the darkness?"

"They ran across the lawn, along the side of her house, and some lights from the windows spilled on them," Caleb said. "That's when I fired. But they kept on going, behind the guesthouse. I couldn't see them after that, but they were obviously headed for the park, where they came from."

"Where were you standing when you shot at them?" she asked.

Caleb gestured to the ground in front of him. "Right about here. Hard to say, though, without a mark."

It took her a second to realize he was referring to the gaffer's tape that an actor stands on so he'll be well lit and in focus for the camera. "And after that?"

Caleb nodded toward the house behind Eve. "I was heading for Kitty's house when my family came running out, so we went there together . . . and saw what the outlaws had done to her."

Duncan said, "That's when you saddled your horse and went after them."

He sat up straight in his saddle and puffed out his chest. "Hell yes, I did. What else is a man supposed to do?"

Caleb didn't wait for an answer. He turned his horse and rode back to the stable. Eve and Duncan watched after him for a moment, and then she said, "How would you know if the smell of hay and the sound of horses are restful?"

"There have been many nights I've fallen asleep in my recliner, watching westerns," Duncan said. "You should do that. You'd learn a lot."

Eve briefed him on what she'd learned from the Winslows. It wasn't much.

"I got all that from Amos," Duncan said, gesturing down the path to Tatum, who was letting Nan and the three Tyvek-clad members of her forensic team pass and head their way.

Eve figured since Duncan referred to Tatum by his first name, he had more than a casual acquaintance with the deputy. "What is it with Tatum and that ridiculous cowboy hat?"

"Amos has been working in Hidden Hills for decades," Duncan said. "Officially, he's a deputy with a regular twelve-hour shift, six days on, three days off, and a patrol unit comes through here regularly when he's off duty. But unofficially, he's the city's full-time lawman."

"Is that why he wears the cowboy hat?"

"It's an equestrian community. There are horse trails everywhere and every house has to have a stable, whether they have a horse or not."

"So you're saying he does it to fit in and not because he's a nut-cake pretending to be a US Marshal in the Old West."

"Amos is not the only deputy in the department who wears a Stetson," Duncan said. "I've seen a guy in the arson squad who does, too. It's a little-known fact, but a cowboy hat has been authorized head-gear for LA County sheriff's deputies since day one."

"You love westerns, so where's yours?"

"I only wear it on special occasions, like my wedding anniversary," Duncan said.

"TMI," Eve said.

"Amos Tatum isn't a clown, Eve. He's a good cop, and he's probably right about the Chilean gangs. Kitty's bling photo was like an invitation to rob her. She wouldn't be the first celebrity that's happened to. Or even the fifteenth."

She knew he was right. Only a week earlier, a rapper had been shot during a mugging in the parking lot of a fried chicken and waffles place near the airport an hour after he'd posted a photo of himself outside the restaurant with his bling on social media.

"I know. I just don't like Tatum's attitude."

"I can see why that would bother someone as unassuming, open-minded, and nonconfrontational as you are."

They joined Nan and her team at the porch to Kitty's house.

Eve said, "Kitty Winslow's body is in there."

Nan nodded at the six-shooter in Duncan's hand. "Is that the murder weapon?"

Duncan handed the big gun to her. "No such luck. The victim's father, Caleb Winslow, used this to shoot at the escaping intruders. Caleb may have hit one of them, so this could become crucial evidence."

"We might be able to see if he got hit," Eve said. "There are cameras all over the property. We haven't watched the video yet if you want to join us for a private screening."

Nan said, "Let me see the body first and get my crew started, then we can watch it."

Thirty minutes later, the three of them went to the storage room to watch the security footage, which tracked the intruders from the moment they climbed the fence into the Winslows' property until they escaped the same way only a few minutes later.

The cameras captured the events outside from every angle. When Eve lost sight of the intruders or the family on one camera view, she could pick them up again on another camera from a new angle, or see them from the back in one camera and from the front in another. It reminded Eve of the raw footage from a TV show, the same scene shot from multiple angles, except they didn't have the master that showed the whole thing at once.

The images were so sharp, she saw a rabbit darting away, startled by the activity, as the invaders fled across the lawn from Kitty's house. She saw Caleb shooting, and it didn't look to Eve like any of the intruders got hit, but she did see them flinch when they heard the shot.

Eve saw them scale the fence, hidden from Caleb's view by the guesthouse, and drop into the high weeds in the Preserve before dashing off and becoming absorbed by the park's impenetrable darkness.

When it was over, Duncan said, "I didn't see anything we can zoom in on that will give us a lead."

Nan folded her arms under her chest and watched Caleb ride off on his horse after the invaders. "I don't either. They are wearing generic hoodies, with no visible labels, and the running shoes don't seem unique. But at least this takes the guesswork out of determining the boundaries of the crime scene and where Caleb took a shot at the assailants. We'll look for bullets, blood, footprints, anything else we can find."

Duncan said, "Maybe a matchbook from the killer's favorite bar dropped out of his pocket when he climbed over the fence into the park."

"I've seen that matchbook clue a million times on TV and not once in real life."

"Me neither," Duncan said, "but it's hope that keeps me going."

Eve checked her watch. "Speaking of the park, Daniel will be heading back out to the burial site at sunrise. He wants to get an early start."

Duncan said, "Who is he trying to impress?"

"Nobody," Eve said. "He enjoys his work." She turned to Nan. "Did you find out anything more on the body in the tarp?"

Nan shook her head. "The ME and I haven't cut it open yet. That's how I was planning to greet the day."

Duncan grimaced. "That's an awful way to start."

"Going into the office at the appointed time and doing a meticulous examination of evidence under the best possible conditions in the perfect environment—cold, well lit, sterile, and quiet, with every resource I need close at hand—is how a good day begins for me."

"How does a bad day start?" Eve asked.

"Like this," Nan said.

They made two copies of the surveillance video, using two of the thumb drives Brandy had offered them from the desk drawer. Eve took one and Nan took the other.

An assistant medical examiner removed the body at dawn. Eve and Duncan watched the crime scene unit do their work for a while, in case anything unusual came up, and then went out on the porch to see the sunrise.

Eve said, "I'm going to grab breakfast with a confidential informant who might be able to give me dirt on the Winslows."

"You do that. I'm going to grab breakfast at McDonald's with a CI who might be able to give me a lead on the elusive Hamburglar."

"The who?"

"The Hamburglar," Duncan said. "Ronald McDonald's archenemy. He steals hamburgers. Mayor McCheese wants us to crack down on it."

Eve stared at him. "You must be hungry because you're babbling incoherently. I'll meet you back at the station in an hour and we can brief the captain."

Eve and Duncan walked down the path, across the motor court, and to the street where Tatum still stood watch.

Duncan patted him warmly on the back. "We're leaving, Amos. Do you want us to send some deputies to relieve you?"

"They're already on the way. I just talked to the captain." Tatum looked pointedly at Eve. "He appreciates that I've got a town to protect . . . and that I can't do that standing here."

Eve said, "Hi-yo, Silver."

The two of them walked to their cars, Duncan stopping first at his Buick, and turned to Eve to say, "You have a real knack for making friends in the department."

"It's a gift," she said.

Duncan drove off, then made a right on Long Valley Road, heading down toward the main gate. But Eve crossed Long Valley and kept going, winding through several streets named after historical figures from the Old West, until she found Linwood Taggert's house.

She'd never been to her Hollywood agent's home before, but she knew his address and that he got up early to make calls overseas and to the East Coast. She purposely didn't call ahead, relishing the opportunity to catch him off guard and perhaps steal a glimpse of his less than perfectly coiffed persona.

His house was a sprawling single-story in the required ranch style, but with a contemporary spin, incorporating industrial elements like corrugated metal and exposed iron beams with the white shiplap and aged brick. A Range Rover was parked in the circular driveway behind the ubiquitous white three-rail fence.

Eve parked on the street, went to the huge double door, and rang the bell, smiling to the camera mounted into an eave as she did so.

Linwood answered the door in a silk smoking jacket with a velvet shawl collar and matching pajama bottoms that looked like they came from Hugh Hefner's estate sale. He was in his fifties, with bright white teeth, jet-black hair, and an airbrush-perfect tan that suggested he spent hours on the tennis court or golf course rather than in a tanning bed. He didn't seem the least bit disheveled or surprised to see her.

"Good morning, Eve," Linwood said, opening the door wide and beckoning her inside. "As soon as I heard about the Winslow shooting, I had a hunch you'd show up. You're just in time for breakfast. I've got fresh, hot scones with red currant jam and clotted cream already prepared."

She stepped in. "You do?"

He led her through the entry hall into a massive kitchen that looked as though it belonged in a restaurant, though one where very few meals were prepared. Every surface gleamed, and all the visible pots, pans, and utensils seemed more like set dressing than culinary tools. Except for the oven, which was half-open and cooling down, filling the room with the inviting smell of fresh-baked bread.

"I have the dough flown in weekly from a bakery in a small village in Warwickshire, England. All I have to do is put it in the oven." Linwood gestured to the huge center island, which was the size of a conference room table, but with a waterfall marble countertop. In the center of the island was a platter of hot scones, stacked in a small pyramid, alongside an unlabeled glass jar of jam, a butter dish, and a bowl of cream. Two plates were already set out with knives, spoons, coffee cups, and napkins. He either had a hidden guest or he really was expecting her.

"You can't find someone who makes scones here?" Eve asked.

"It's not the same without the British flour, water, and butter in the mix." Linwood sat down on a barstool at the island and Eve did the same.

"So that's how you spend my commissions."

"Your commissions wouldn't pay for the jam," he said, opening the jar and setting it in front of her. "It's from a monastery in France where the monks deseed the tiny berries by hand with the point of a goose quill."

"That's obscenely indulgent."

"Soon you can afford to be, too." He took a scone, cut it open on his plate, and began spreading jam on the two halves. "There's lots of excitement at the network about *Ronin*. They're loving the footage they've seen so far."

Eve took a hot scone for herself and also cut it in half. "That's not the show I came to talk about. What can you tell me about the Winslows?"

"An old western actor in his fifties marries a much younger, talentless lingerie model who dreams of stardom as a singer or an actress, dreams she doesn't stop pursuing, even while raising their rambunctious kids."

She spread some of the jam on her scone. "Sounds like a sitcom."

"The genius was doing it as a reality show instead."

"Who had that idea?" Eve took a bite of her scone. It was fantastic, but she tried not to show how much she liked it.

"Brandy did," Linwood said, but before he explained, he offered Eve some coffee. She asked for a Diet Coke instead. He took a Coke Zero out of the refrigerator, popped the top, and poured some in her coffee cup, then set the can in front of her. "She shot a demo herself at home and actually sold it to the USA Network. But things didn't turn out the way she expected."

"What do you mean?"

Linwood poured himself a cup of coffee from a pot on the island. "The show was supposed to make Brandy a star, but instead it was her stepdaughter, Kitty, who broke out. The release of the stolen sex tape of Kitty in a threesome with two rappers helped, of course."

That would explain Skye's naked selfies, Eve thought. She was trying to follow in her older half sister's successful footsteps. But what had worked so well for Kitty had been a nightmare for Erin Casey, the star of *Ronin*, even though it had led to more job opportunities.

"There was a time a sex tape would have destroyed a career instead of making one," Eve said.

"Same could be said of a video of a cop beating up an internationally famous movie star."

"I didn't beat him up."

He waved away her objection. "Semantics. The sex tape, and the scandal it generated, embarrassed Caleb but it brought a lot of viewers to the show, and over the years, her fame has only grown. Kitty can't sing worth shit, but she scored a Las Vegas residency. In fact, she was secretly planning to leave *Life with the Winslows* for her own reality show based on her onstage and backstage life in Sin City. I know because our agency made the deal for her."

Eve drank her cup of Coke Zero and refilled it. "Where would that have left the Winslows?"

"Canceled. Not right away, but maybe after a season or two, unless something big happened."

"Sounds like a motive for murder."

"Only if you're dumb enough to kill your golden goose."

"She wouldn't be laying eggs for them anymore." Eve took a second scone, cut it open, and spread butter on this one. She assumed the butter was outrageously expensive, too, made from the milk of Jersey cows fed only caviar and champagne or something like that, but didn't ask.

"So what?" he said. "They're already filthy rich. Besides, nothing would make Caleb happier than ending the show. He hates it. He only suffers through it for his family."

"What do you know about Kitty's fiancé? The one who gave her the Pink Panther diamond engagement ring?"

"Benji Stanet, former Disney sitcom star, who lives in terror of being typecast as wholesome and being doomed to a career doing Hallmark Christmas movies. News flash: it's too late, he already is."

Linwood licked some jam off his finger. "Word is, she had no intention of marrying him, but it's a great storyline."

"He spent a lot of money on that engagement ring," Eve said. "He might not be too happy about being humiliated."

Linwood waved that off, too. "He's already signed to be a recurring character on her show."

"A character? He's a real person."

"All reality shows are scripted. The lives of real people, even celebrities, don't generate enough twists and entertaining conflict on their own. They need a push. But you wouldn't need one if you did a reality show. You have built-in conflict."

"I've already got a show I don't want," Eve said.

"I'm your agent," he said. "It's my job to look down the road for you."

"Don't bother, it's a dead end. What do you know about Amos Tatum?"

"The marshal? He's an institution here. Everybody loves him."

"I don't," Eve said.

"Because you're too much alike. You're both cowboys, bucking the system and enforcing the law your way."

"That's not me."

Linwood pointed at her. "It's you on TV."

"It's a fictional character with my name," she said, getting up from her stool. "Thanks for the breakfast and the background."

Linwood gestured to the crumbs on her plate. "What did you think of the scones and jam?"

"You'd save a bundle if you went to Ralphs and bought Pillsbury Biscuits and Smucker's jelly instead. And it would taste the same." That was a lie, and Linwood obviously knew it, but he played along.

"You've been spending too much time with Duncan Pavone."

She smiled and found her own way out.

CHAPTER NINE

Eve stepped out of Linwood's front door to see Deputy Amos Tatum leaning against his patrol car and facing the house, arms crossed judgmentally under his chest. He kept his eyes on her as she walked up to him.

"You said you were leaving Hidden Hills," Tatum said. "And yet, here you are."

"I was having breakfast with my agent. I wasn't aware I had to clear that with you first."

"Hidden Hills is a private, gated city. There are no public streets. Nobody is allowed in without a pass to a specific residence. Nobody is allowed to roam around unless accompanied by a resident, city official, or security officer."

She took the badge off her belt and held it up in front of his face. "This is my pass. And I will go where I please."

He wasn't impressed. "Your business here is done, Detective. The nearest gate is around the corner and straight down Long Valley Road. I'll follow you out."

Eve heard a helicopter streak overhead and looked up, recognizing a television station's call letters on the side of the aircraft. She looked toward the Winslows' house and saw other choppers circling over it.

That didn't take long, she thought. Eve was tempted to go back to the Winslow house and see how Nan and her forensic team were doing, just to piss off Tatum, but she decided it was more important to brief the captain as soon as possible on the status of the investigation. She looked back at Tatum and smiled.

"Get the hell out of Dodge, is that what you're saying?"

"If you're interested in actually accomplishing something, you ought to be at LAX, looking for suspicious hombres waiting to board flights to Chile."

"Hombres," Eve said, disgusted. "That's cute. We call that racial profiling."

"I call it police work, but the difference between you and me, little lady, is that I don't have an agent and my priority is enforcing the law, not worrying about how I'll look on TV."

He got into his car. Eve got into her Bronco and drove toward the main gate, past one huge estate after another, all surprisingly visible from the street. Unlike Bel-Air, none of the homes were hidden by high walls or tall hedges. All the landscaping was lush and perfectly maintained. Even the stables and corrals were astonishingly tidy, the ground raked like golf course sand traps.

As she neared the gate, she could see TV network media vans parked outside, their satellite antennae already raised, ready to broadcast news of the celebrity death around the globe. Reporters and photographers were everywhere, clogging the road and creating a traffic nightmare for residents. Tatum would have his hands full and she was happy about that. It would keep him out of the Winslow case.

◆ ◆ ◆

Eve came into the Lost Hills squad room and saw the captain standing beside Duncan's cubicle. Dubois looked up at her.

"Perfect timing," he said. "Duncan and Tatum have briefed me on the Winslow killing."

"I wasn't aware Tatum was working homicide," Eve said.

"I agree with him that this has all the earmarks of a Chilean job," Dubois said. "Over the last few months, they've hit North Ranch in Thousand Oaks, Spanish Hills in Camarillo, and a bunch of estates in Porter Ranch and Encino. We all knew it was only a matter of time before the Chileans targeted Hidden Hills. Frankly, I'm surprised it's taken this long."

"We don't know who they are," Eve said. "Based on the evidence we have so far, there's an equal possibility they're rogue Jehovah's Witnesses."

Duncan chuckled, but Dubois wasn't amused.

"That's why you need to talk to an expert," Dubois said. "Jack Regan, from the MCU, is leading the department's task force on Chilean burglary tourism. Give him what you have and see what he says. Here's his number."

The captain dropped a piece of paper on Duncan's desk.

Duncan picked it up and glanced at the number. "Does Regan know anything about rogue Jehovah's Witnesses?"

"We have another task force for that." Dubois walked past Eve and out of the squad room.

Duncan reached for his phone and started dialing. "And they say Dubois doesn't have a sense of humor."

Eve pulled up a chair beside Duncan, who put the call on speaker while it was still ringing. After a moment, it was answered.

"Regan."

"This is Detective Duncan Pavone. I'm on the speaker with my partner, Eve Ronin. We're at Lost Hills station, working a homicide in Hidden Hills—"

Regan interrupted. "Kitty Winslow. It's all over the news. They're saying it's Chilean burglars."

Eve said, "Who is saying that?"

"The bobbleheads on TV," Regan said. "Sounds like they could be right. I want to see what you have."

She wondered who had leaked the information to the media, whether it was Tatum or the Winslows, or both.

Duncan said, "Come on up, we'll meet you at the scene and walk you through it."

"I can't. I'm on a stakeout. You'll have to come to me." Regan gave them the address of a diner in Mission Hills, at the 405 and 118 freeway interchange above the intersection of Sepulveda Boulevard and Chatsworth Street, at the north end of the San Fernando Valley.

He told them to come in one of their personal rides because unmarked cop cars didn't fool anyone. Regan said he'd be waiting in a window booth, wearing a gray polo shirt, and described himself as a guy who'd taken too many fists in his face and who'd probably be bald in five years.

At least, Eve thought, he wasn't flattering himself.

Before Regan hung up, he said, "Be sure to bring a tactical vest and spare ammo, too."

Duncan frowned at the phone. "It's a good thing I'm not about to retire anymore."

"Because you'd miss this excitement?"

"Because I'd get shot today, guaranteed."

Eve copied the security video from the thumb drive to her phone using a USB–to–lightning cable adapter, collected her tactical equipment, and stuffed everything into a gym bag that she tossed in the trunk of Duncan's Buick, beside his gun safe.

Duncan drove them out to Mission Hills, taking the Ventura Freeway east to the 405 north, also known as the San Diego Freeway.

They got off at Devonshire heading east, then turned left, heading north on Sepulveda into a dreary commercial area lined with decrepit two-star motels, auto mechanics, warehouses, fast-food places, storage units, tattoo shops, and various industrial supply stores. She and Duncan had been in the same neighborhood before on a case, searching area motels for a missing Hispanic woman who'd worked as a housekeeper in Oakdale, the gated community where Eve now lived. It hadn't ended well.

Duncan pulled into the parking lot of the diner, which was nearly under the freeway interchange and across the street from a two-story motel with a fenced-in pool that had been filled with dirt.

"Lovely area," Eve said.

"At least the freeway overpasses provide shade," he said.

They got out and went into the diner, which hadn't changed since it was built in the 1950s. The linoleum floors, vinyl booths, and walls had all been yellowed by the decades of greasy smoke that gave the interior a permanent odor of grilled fat.

Duncan said, "My kind of place."

And Eve knew he meant it. She spotted Regan right away, since there were only four patrons and his description of himself was spot-on. He sat in a window booth, with a cup of coffee and a half-eaten slice of pie, and faced the motel across the street. From the way he was looking at it, she figured the motel was the location being staked out.

They shook hands, and just as Eve and Duncan sat down across from him, the waitress came over, refilling Regan's cup and offering them coffee as well. Duncan accepted the offer and ordered a full breakfast. Eve settled for a Diet Coke.

Duncan started the conversation with a question for Regan. "Aren't you out of your jurisdiction?"

Of course, Duncan knew that Regan wasn't supposed to be working here. The LASD operated only in unincorporated areas of the county and for cities that contracted out their law enforcement.

This was deep in Los Angeles.

"The Chilean burglary tourists don't give a shit about whose jurisdiction they're in," Regan said, "so why should we?"

"What's the LAPD think of you working on their turf?"

"They're glad they don't have to work these no-win clusterfuck cases anymore. We do."

Eve asked, "How did that happen?"

"Sheriff Lansing volunteered us to take point."

"Why would he do that if these cases are complicated losers?"

Regan gave her a cynical grin. "The rich people who are getting hit by these gangs are also the deep-pocket donors who fund political campaigns."

"Lansing has presided over the department during too many scandals," Eve said. "He's not going to be reelected."

"Who says he wants to be? He's got bigger aspirations."

Duncan nodded. "Sacramento. Or DC. But how does taking this on help him?"

"The Chileans are hitting LA, Ventura, and Orange County really hard, so Lansing proposed pooling the resources of local law enforcement agencies into an interagency task force run out of his department."

"Widening his potential donor base outside of LA County," Duncan said. "Clever man."

Eve asked, "Unless he can't stop the problem. What makes these no-win clusterfuck cases?"

Before Regan answered, the waitress brought over Duncan's eggs, bacon, hash browns, toast, and pancakes, along with a bottle of maple syrup. He dug in as if he hadn't eaten in days rather than minutes. As soon as the waitress was out of earshot, Regan started talking.

"The Chileans come here on commercial flights like any other tourists, except instead of taking the Universal Studios tour, they spend a few weeks hitting a bunch of multimillion-dollar mansions, walk out with over $100,000 in goods each time, convert it all into cash that they wire home, and then they go back to Chile."

"Aren't the FBI and US Customs all over this?"

"Nope. Home burglary is a local crime. The Feds don't have authority to get involved . . . and it's small-time shit they don't care about." As Regan spoke, he did a good job balancing his attention between Eve and Duncan and the motel behind them. "They like making busts that get them on TV, like intercepting a shipment of imported toilets that are actually made out of $10 million in molded cocaine. And local cops don't have any reach into immigration or foreign affairs to force the cooperation of the Chilean government into stopping tourists with gang affiliations, criminal histories, or false identification from coming."

Duncan swallowed a mouthful of food, then said, "So the Chileans are exploiting a law enforcement dead zone and no one is going after them."

"I am," Regan said pointedly.

"How big is your task force?"

"A half dozen detectives, sometimes more, if the local agencies can spare the manpower when we need them."

That's nothing, Eve thought. But she said, "Some of the burglars must be getting caught, out of bad luck if nothing else."

"Sure they are. But they are typically in their early twenties, have no IDs or false ID, and no criminal records here. They post bail and scram. Or they stick around, get sentenced to a year or so in prison, get released after a few months for good behavior and to ease overcrowding, go back home for a while, and then come right back to the US again, but maybe to New York, Seattle, or Raleigh this time."

Duncan dabbed his mouth with a napkin, then said, "Yep, that's definitely a no-win clusterfuck. How are you going to stop them?"

"The burglars are just the manual labor. Somebody else is making the travel arrangements, picking the targets, scouting locations, fencing the goods, and moving the money. That's who I'm going after."

Eve said, "Okay, so that's the big picture. Let's go back to the burglaries. What's the MO? What tells you they were done by the Chilean crime tourists and not anyone else?"

Duncan added, "Like rogue Jehovah's Witnesses."

Regan said, "Let me see what you've got."

Eve gave him the details, then slid her phone over and showed him the security video, which he watched in silence, before handing the phone back to her.

"Some things fit," Regan said. "Some things don't."

"Like what?"

He finished his coffee and said, "What do writers say in the TV business? Show, don't tell. I'd rather show you."

"What do you know about TV writing?"

"My brother-in-law Merle is a writer on *Young Matlock*."

"I haven't seen it," she said.

"It's an HBO reboot that takes place in the 1950s, when Matlock was a law student addicted to drugs and being pressured to join the KKK."

Duncan shook his head in dismay. "What's next? Jessica Fletcher's early days as a hooker?"

Regan said, "I'd watch that. Merle says it's always better to reveal stuff by what people do, not what they say."

Eve said, "So show us."

Regan smiled at her. "You'll have to stick around for that."

She felt her pulse quicken and hoped her excitement didn't show on her face. "What's going down?"

"We tracked some Chileans who fit the profile from LAX to that motel across the street, where, it turns out, some other Chileans are staying. We're hunkered down in the motel next door to this diner. We're waiting for them to make a hit, then we'll track them to the guy who fences their stolen goods and move in. When they do, you can see exactly how they work."

Duncan pushed his empty plate away. "You just want more manpower for your stakeout."

"Sure I do. But if it was Chileans who hit the Winslows, your guys are probably across the street right now and will lead us to what they stole. You could close your case today."

That was all Eve needed to hear. "I'm in."

But the truth was, she would have agreed anyway.

"I'm out," Duncan said. "I'm too old for this shit. I'll go back to the station and check in with Nan to see what she's got from the Winslow crime scene and the Indiana Jones dig." He glanced at Regan. "Will you give Eve a ride back to Lost Hills?"

"Not only that, we'll feed her."

Duncan grinned at him. "Nice try, but I'm still out."

Eve was impressed at how sharp Regan was at reading people. He had Duncan down pat. She turned to her partner, who was sliding out of the booth.

"Can you let the captain know I'm joining the surveillance?"

Regan said, "I already cleared it with him before you got here."

"You're pretty sure of yourself."

Now Regan grinned. "No, I was sure of you, Deathfist."

Eve grabbed her bag from Duncan's trunk, then Regan took her to the crumbling two-story motel next door. He explained on the way that they had two adjoining rooms, each with two double beds, both upstairs for an unobstructed view of the motel across the street. One room was set aside for sleeping. There were three men upstairs now, and two more in cars on the street.

When they came in, Regan introduced her to the two weary Major Crime Unit team members in the room, who sat at the window beside two video cameras mounted on tripods with telephoto lenses that were focused between the barely opened slats of the venetian blinds that covered the windows. The images from the video cameras were displayed on the screens of two laptops on the table in front of the men. One image was a wide angle, the other a close-up, of the motel room occupied by the Chileans.

"This is Detective Eve Ronin," Regan said. "She's working a homicide that might be related to our Chileans, so she'll be on the team tonight. Get her a radio and anything else she needs."

They didn't seem thrilled to see her, but one of the guys handed her a radio and a set of earbuds to go with it.

Eve thanked him, then glanced around the room. There were Costco flats of bottled water and soft drinks stacked in one corner, assorted bags of chips and boxes of crackers on the dresser top, and several empty take-out pizza boxes piled on top of the tiny garbage can. Typical stakeout decor.

She tossed her bag on one of the double beds, then went over to Regan, who sat on the other double bed, which he was using for a desk. There was a laptop open on the bed amid several eight-by-ten photographs of young Chilean men and an unfolded map of the San Fernando Valley.

"These are the four men from Chile that we tracked here from LAX the other day," he said. "We've also taken photographs of maybe a half dozen more who are already here. Now we are just waiting for them to make a move."

She picked up the photos and sorted through them, while speaking to Regan in a near whisper. "I don't think the other deputies are glad to have me around."

"You should be used to that by now, considering how you got that detective badge and what you've done since."

"Why don't you have a problem with me?"

"All of my relationships, especially with women, are purely transactional."

CHAPTER TEN

Eve spent the next few hours sitting against the headboard of the double bed, watching old episodes of *Life with the Winslows* on her phone, and snacking on potato chips, which she knew was Duncan's idea of perfect relaxation.

The show was set mainly in the Winslows' fake home, when they weren't shopping on Rodeo Drive, or eating at fancy restaurants, or partying at nightclubs, or lounging around the pool in bathing suits, or flying somewhere on their private jet, or having business meetings in high-rise corner offices and conference rooms with the agents, producers, lawyers, and sponsors involved with their various entertainment and commercial ventures. Sometimes the Winslows went on location to Hawaii, New York, Las Vegas, Paris, or other places they traveled to for business and pleasure.

The episodes followed Kitty's efforts to become a rap singer, supermodel, and actress, Skye's party-going as a social-media influencer and budding fashion designer, and Maverick's attempts to find his footing as a DJ, record producer, and filmmaker. The series also explored their various romantic and business relationships, and how their individual career aspirations sometimes put them in conflict with each other.

Brandy played the role of mother, counselor, manager, producer, and strangely, sometime competitor for attention to her children as she pursued her own acting and singing career, which she'd put on the back burner while raising her kids.

Eve found the show remarkably dull. She didn't understand how anybody could believe that the situations, and the conflicts they generated, weren't staged and scripted, especially since everybody's acting was uniformly unconvincing. Most of the dialogue was clearly improvised, yet within the confines of a determined storyline and resolution for each scene.

The only Winslow who came off as authentic to her was Caleb, who rarely spoke and, when he did, was grouchy or distant. She couldn't blame him, since most of the time he was cast in the storylines as comic relief and treated by his family as a joke, though until the show came along, they were living off his celebrity and accumulated wealth from his decades on *Saddlesore* and, afterward, as a character actor in other westerns. Caleb was openly critical of his wife's plastic surgery and Kitty's butt implants, unable to comprehend why anybody would do that to themselves, which they saw as further proof he was totally out of touch with the world. He was and was glad to be.

Kitty was clearly the center of the show, and for good reason. She was beautiful, and her strong, engaging personality, sense of humor, and undeniable personal magnetism always shone through, despite the contrived situations she was often put in. It saddened and angered Eve that someone so young, with so much obvious potential, was cheated out of it all by someone with a gun.

Kitty's relationship with Benji Stanet was a big plot point in the most recent episodes, and he was portrayed as a boyish, innocent rube amid the much more shrewd and sophisticated family. Caleb thought he was nice but too soft, often telling him to man up and stop letting Kitty push him around, while Brandy, Skye, and Maverick viewed him warily, often wondering aloud among themselves if he was using Kitty to advance his own stalled acting career. But Benji seemed to Eve to be genuinely enamored with Kitty, and if he wasn't, then he was a better actor than the Winslows were giving him credit for. He seemed less like a rube, or an opportunist, to Eve than chum in a sea of sharks.

Watching *Life with the Winslows* made Eve increasingly uncomfortable. It was hard for her not to draw parallels between what she was seeing with her own life, which was sort of *Life with the Winslows* in reverse. Instead of cameras following her around, her life was being turned into a cop show, with an actress portraying her, on the actual streets where Eve did her job. She worried about how that would impact people's perceptions of her and even her view of herself.

"They're on the move," one of the deputies said, breaking the silence.

Eve and Regan got up, went to the window, and looked over the two deputies' shoulders at the camera feeds on their laptop screens. It was getting dark outside now, and the four men Eve had seen in the photos emerged from their motel room wearing hoodies and schoolyard backpacks on their shoulders. They walked to a three-year-old Audi A3 in the parking lot and got inside.

Regan said, "They took an Uber here from LAX, so someone left that car for them. And it's an Audi, something that won't stand out in an upper-class neighborhood."

Eve understood the significance. "It's evidence that someone is planning ahead for them."

"That's right. We'll run the license number, but I guarantee you that we'll discover the car was bought for cash from the owner and still has the original plates."

"Another part of the MO?"

"Show, don't tell. Now you're beginning to see it," he said. "Grab your stuff, you're with me."

Suddenly, everyone in the room was on the move, too, gathering their gear, but aware that they had to be careful leaving so they wouldn't draw attention to themselves as law enforcement to anybody who might be watching from the motel across the street.

The two manned LASD surveillance vehicles already parked on the street would do the initial tail of the Audi. Eve and the four deputies would split up into two other vehicles that would participate in a surveillance dance once they were on the road.

Regan told her that the working assumption, since the motel the Chileans picked was at the 405 and 118 interchange, was that the thieves would immediately get on one of the freeways, so the follow cars already on the street were parked near the two on-ramps.

The assumption was right.

As Eve and Regan hurried to Regan's rented Cadillac CT5 behind the motel, the deputies in the follow cars reported over the radio that the Audi was getting on the westbound on-ramp to the 118. Regan sped out, followed shortly after by the other three deputies in an Explorer.

"I'll bet you that they're headed to Porter Ranch," Regan said, driving up the 118 on-ramp. "I'm going to have one follow car speed ahead and get off at the Tampa exit. That way, we'll have one car waiting ahead of them so we can stay loose and hang back a bit."

Even with a multicar tail, Regan was worried about the Chileans discovering the surveillance. He told the other deputies his plan and they radioed back that they understood.

One car shot ahead, exited the freeway at the Tampa exit, and parked on the westbound side of Rinaldi, the major east-west thoroughfare, on the assumption that the Chileans were getting off on either Reseda, which preceded Tampa, or farther west at Porter Ranch Road. The follow cars would be able to give the car ahead enough advance warning to intercept the Audi if it took either exit.

Porter Ranch was a relatively new master-planned community of massive housing tracts carved into the foothills of the Santa Susana Mountains, north of the 118 freeway. It was the last big, undeveloped area of the San Fernando Valley and drew thousands of upper-middle-class families to the large homes. But it had lost some of its appeal eight years ago, when an underground methane storage facility in the mountains above the community sprang a leak, spewing 110,000 pounds of gas per hour into the air for five months, prompting mass evacuations and the poisoning of thousands of people. It was the worst natural gas leak in US history. The existence of a Southern California Gas Company underground storage facility so close to a residential area hadn't been mentioned in anybody's seven-figure home purchase agreement.

Eve was stunned that anyone came back or that the new houses being constructed there on what was probably heavily contaminated soil were finding eager buyers, especially since the storage facility was still in operation.

She asked, "What's in Porter Ranch besides a few thousand homes contaminated by methane gas?"

"Half of those multimillion-dollar homes are located on top of graded hillsides overlooking open space, like foothills, a golf course, a park, a schoolyard, or a vacant lot," Regan said. "That's the key target criteria of these thieves."

The Winslows' property certainly fit the criteria, Eve thought, but so did tens of thousands of other homes in Southern California. There had to be other factors at play.

"How do the Chileans pick which houses along open space to hit?"

"They scour social media, looking for rich people flaunting cash, jewels, and designer handbags," he said, "but mostly they hit wealthy Asians and Middle Easterners."

"Why those ethnic groups?"

"Because they tend to run cash businesses, so they'll have lots of money on hand, and they like to hold their wealth close, stashing it at home rather than in a bank."

"Those are racist clichés."

Regan paused before responding to her remark, listening instead to the radio chatter. The follow cars were reporting that the Chileans were getting off at Porter Ranch Road, so the waiting car on Rinaldi would pick up the surveillance there while the other cars split off east and west, but looping back if necessary.

"It's the burglars who think that way, not me," Regan said as they neared the Porter Ranch Road off-ramp. "But it's working for them, so maybe it's not a cliché."

The follow car reported that the Chileans were now heading north, up Porter Ranch Road. Regan informed the other deputies that he'd try to get ahead of the Chileans by exiting at Wilbur, the next big street heading north. He told another car to head east on Rinaldi and take Reseda north, in case the Chileans backtracked and headed east again when they got farther up Porter Ranch Road.

Eve was impressed that Regan was constantly thinking several potential moves ahead, ensuring that a follow car was always positioned to keep the Audi in sight. Things would be a lot easier, of course, if Regan had access to a chopper, but she doubted he had those resources or he'd be using them.

Regan turned left on Rinaldi, running a red light to do it, and sped past a new shopping center full of "big box" national chain stores, all designed to look like they were part of a renovated factory. It was an architectural choice that made no sense to Eve.

He made a sharp right onto Mason Avenue and raced into the hills, which were carpeted with huge tract homes, crammed closely together. His speed and the thrill of the chase were jacking up Eve's heartbeat and adrenaline.

Over the radio, the follow cars reported that they were swapping places behind the Audi, which was making a left, heading westbound on Sesnon Boulevard, cutting across the center of the residential area.

"He's heading right toward us," Regan told Eve and, simultaneously, the other deputies on the radio. They reached the intersection with Sesnon just as the Audi entered it and made a right, heading north on Mason, up into the hills alongside a gated community.

Regan turned left, continuing eastbound on Sesnon, and told the follow cars to drop their tail and find places to park, either somewhere off the southbound side of Mason or back on Porter Ranch Road.

"You're just letting him go?" Eve said.

"Mason is a dead end between two graded foothills," Regan said. "And I think I know where he's going."

He made a right into a housing development that was under construction. The hillsides had been graded into pads, streets, and cul-de-sacs. Four model homes were being framed beside a sales office trailer surrounded with colorful flags flapping in the breeze.

Regan badged the security guard manning the single unpaved road into the site and, without explaining himself, continued up, leaving a trail of dust that was unlikely to be spotted in the darkness.

He turned off his headlights and made a hard left into a cul-de-sac, driving onto the house pad at the very end that overlooked Mason Avenue and the residential community on the opposite ridge, where the hillside was sparsely planted and crisscrossed with concrete drainage swales.

"Come on." Regan got out, opened the back door, and took a small case from the back seat.

Eve got out, crept up to the edge of the lot, and saw the Audi down below, parked on Mason at the foot of the opposite hillside. She heard a buzz and turned to see a small drone rise from the ground in front of Regan's feet and disappear into the darkness. The drone's signal lights had been disabled, making it invisible.

Regan stepped up beside her, holding a gaming-style controller with two joysticks and a color view screen with a surprisingly sharp night-vision picture.

"You have nice toys," Eve said.

"I bought it myself."

She looked over his shoulder at the screen and saw three men spill out of the Audi and scramble up one of the concrete swales on the opposite hillside.

"Look how they are dressed," Regan said, tapping the screen.

"All in black, from head to toe."

"And wearing empty backpacks," he said. "That means they're hitting one of the houses on that ridge and are going to come back down again with those backpacks filled with loot. They won't take anything that they can't fit into a backpack, so no TVs, paintings, or sculptures, just cash, jewelry, handbags, watches, the kinds of things that can be easily and quickly converted to cash."

Eve realized now that none of the intruders who hit the Winslows wore a backpack. One more thing that didn't fit with the Chilean gangs.

"Isn't it early for a break-in? It's barely dark out," she said. "People aren't even having dinner yet."

"They always strike between five and eight p.m.," he said, watching them nearing the top of the ridge.

"Why?"

"They target empty homes. But in case they're wrong, and someone is at home, at this hour they'll probably discover that right away, before they break in, because they will see the residents roaming around the house, or watching TV, or whatever," Regan said. "But if they don't see anybody and go in anyway, they're less likely to wake up someone who has a shotgun under the bed. The intruders will see the residents sitting at the dinner table, or coming out of a bathroom, and bolt."

The intruders who killed Kitty came in at 3:30 a.m. and didn't flee when she walked in on them. They shot her in the face instead. One more thing that didn't match the Chilean playbook.

Eve watched the drone monitor as the Chileans scaled the wrought-iron fence and dropped into the backyard, their movements activating several motion-sensor lights mounted on the house, lighting up everything, but that didn't stop them. That surprised her.

"They aren't worried about lights or cameras?"

"Nope," Regan said. "They'll look right into cameras, maybe even give them a wave, like that guy is doing now, the cocky asshole."

He pointed at the screen to an intruder waving at something above him. Two of the intruders moved an outdoor dinette table under the deck of a second-floor bedroom, then the third man, who'd been waving at the camera, put a chair on the table.

One by one, the intruders climbed up on the table, stepped onto the chair, then heaved themselves onto the second-floor deck.

"The homeowners might as well leave a ladder outside with a ribbon tied on it," Eve said. "But why are they going to the trouble of climbing? Why not break a window on one of the patio doors on the first floor?"

"Odds are the second-floor windows won't be alarmed, or if they are, they've probably been turned off by homeowners who like fresh air at night," Regan said, "and who still cringe at the memory of opening their windows at night, forgetting that the system was armed, and setting off a shrill alarm that woke up everybody in their house and all of their neighbors. They don't want to repeat that."

One of the Chileans broke the glass on the second-floor slider with some object Eve couldn't see, then reached in and opened the door. All three of the men slipped inside what she presumed was the master bedroom.

"If we move in now," Eve said, "we can catch them in the act."

"We don't need to," Regan said. "I have them on video."

"We can't see their faces."

"We saw their faces when they left the motel and we'll see them again when we arrest them at the meet with their middleman, who handles the conversion of the stolen goods to cash and wiring their slim share of the take back to Chile."

"You're just going to watch them commit the crime?"

"That's right," he said, the drone hovering in place, still recording, on standby for the intruders to emerge again.

"What if someone is inside and there's a shooting?"

"If anyone is shot," Regan said, "it'll be one of the burglars and they'll deserve it."

"Tell that to Kitty Winslow."

"Nothing like that is going to happen here."

"How can you be sure?" Eve asked.

"Because 99 percent of the time," Regan said, "Chilean burglars don't carry guns."

"Why not?"

"Possession of a weapon means big jail time," he said. "If they get caught, they want to be charged with simple burglary. The only thing they might have on them is a screwdriver or box cutter."

"They could kill someone with those."

"They don't fight, they run."

It was one more element of the Chilean burglar tourist MO that didn't match the Winslow case, unless the gun they used belonged to Kitty. Eve made a mental note to look into that possibility. But the theory that a Chilean gang was responsible for Kitty's murder was beginning to look shaky. As she had that thought, the burglars emerged from the upstairs bedroom and began to climb down.

"That was fast," she said.

"It was slow. Ten minutes is the average. They took fifteen."

The burglars scurried down the hill, slipping and sliding in the swale. Regan brought back the drone and landed it, then they hurried back to the car, where he radioed the others that the targets were on their way out, likely back down Mason Avenue to the 118. But where the Chileans were headed after that was anybody's guess.

CHAPTER ELEVEN

The Chileans surprised Regan by not taking the freeway. Instead, they took Reseda Boulevard south into the valley. The deputies began their rotation following the Audi so the driver wouldn't see the same car behind him all the time.

As he drove, Regan used his cell phone to call a friendly judge he had on speed dial for situations like this to get a telephonic search warrant, based on the evidence they'd collected so far, that covered both the vehicle they were following and whatever destination the Audi arrived at that would allow them to search for stolen jewelry, handbags, cash, and other goods. Regan laid out the whole story for the judge, who granted the warrant, not that the conclusion was ever in doubt.

The Chileans led them south, toward the Cal State, Northridge, campus, but before getting that far, they made a right, heading westbound on Lassen, and then left into a residential neighborhood of one-story, 1960s-era birdhouse ranch homes. They were common in the valley. Eve had grown up in a house like that herself. The architectural style was marked by board-and-batten siding, brick and stone accents, and most of all, the birdhouses built as stand-alone cupolas or integrated into the eaves of the pitched roofs. Instead of attracting birds, though, they more often lured bees and rats, at least in Eve's experience.

The Audi stopped in front of a house. Regan drove past, following the curve of the street until he was out of sight, then made a sharp

U-turn and returned the way he came. He eased the car out of the curve just enough to see the four men emerge from the Audi and go into the house.

"They are delivering their stolen good with their fence," Regan said. "This is what we were waiting for."

He ordered one of the follow cars to go around the block, behind the house, and stay there in case they needed to cordon off the street, which was shaped like a horseshoe. Regan and the other two units would converge on the house from the front, boxing the Audi in, as soon as everybody was suited up and ready to go.

"Shouldn't you wait for backup?" Eve said.

"We need to catch them red-handed."

"I don't see why waiting for backup would change that."

"This isn't up for debate," Regan said, yanking the trunk release and getting out of the car.

Eve joined him at the open trunk. Regan and Eve put on their green LASD Kevlar tactical vests, slipped their radios into the designated pockets, and checked the extra magazines for their Glocks, then Regan closed the trunk and they got back into the Cadillac.

He said, "I want you to stay in the car."

"What good will I do in here?"

"Someone needs to watch the front while we move in," he said, "just like I have a man watching the back, who isn't happy about it, either."

"You're wasting my skills," she said.

"I don't know your skills," he said. "But I know what the others on the team can do. We've done this before. We have a shared understanding of who does what and when. We're a well-choreographed, practiced unit."

That made sense to her, so she just nodded. He got on the radio. Everyone reported that they were ready, so he gave the order to move in.

He hit the gas pedal and sped around the corner, coming to a stop in front of the house at the same instant as the two other cars.

Regan left his keys in the ignition and jumped out of the Cadillac, drawing his gun on the move.

Four deputies came out of the other cars, three with their guns drawn, one holding a battering ram. They rushed up to the front door.

Eve drew her own gun, got out of the car, and moved behind the Audi so she could use it for cover if necessary and watch the house.

The deputy with the battering ram smashed the cheap door open with one practiced swing and the men rushed inside, Regan announcing them as police and telling everyone not to move. Eve heard lots of yelling and commotion, but no gunshots, which she took as a good sign.

But then she saw a strange thing. The birdhouse cupola on the roof opened like the hatch of a submarine and a man in a hoodie crawled out.

Eve stood up and pointed her gun at him. "Halt! Police!"

But Hoodie ignored her, either not caring or knowing that she couldn't legally justify shooting him. He slid down the peaked roof and over the edge into the side yard, disappearing from her view.

Eve ran over to the side of the house, expecting to find him lying on the ground with a broken leg or arm, but instead was astonished to see a small trampoline there and him flipping himself over the shaky wooden fence.

She holstered her gun and, not being deft with a trampoline, hefted herself up and over the fence by hand, dropping into the next yard just in time to see him run across the patio and scramble over the next fence.

"Shit," she said, then ran across the yard herself, dodging a tricycle and chaise longue in her path. She climbed the next fence, which wobbled under her weight, and landed on the other side, barely missing a cactus garden.

Hoodie was fast, and had a good head start, but there was a tall hedge on the opposite side of the next fence, so he was forced to veer to his right, where he was blocked by a child-protective fence around a pool.

He climbed over the safety fence by the pool's shallow end at the same time that Eve climbed over the section at the deep end.

They both ran around the pool toward the back fence. Eve tried to cut him off, but he got to the fence a moment before she did, hauling himself over the top, leaving one leg dangling.

Eve grabbed for his foot and got hold of his shoe, which came off in her hand. She swore, tossed the shoe aside, and scaled the fence, breathing hard and her knee aching, and wondered how many more times she could do this.

She crested the top of the fence in time to see Hoodie running past another pool. He was nearly at the next fence when a snarling Doberman shot out of nowhere and took him down.

Eve dropped into the yard and ran toward Hoodie, who was screaming, his arm protecting his face, as the dog furiously tore at his wrist, mostly getting a mouthful of fabric.

She grabbed the Doberman by his hind legs and pulled as hard as she could. The dog let go of his prey and tried to wriggle free and bite Eve, who spun around and flung him into the swimming pool. The dog landed with a big splash.

She quickly lifted the man to his feet, yelling at him to get up, and half dragged him along the side of the home, past a doghouse, and through a minefield of feces toward the front yard.

Behind her, she could hear the dog snarling as he emerged from the pool and the sound of his claws scratching the concrete as he scrambled after them.

Eve opened the gate, pushed Hoodie onto the driveway, then pulled the gate closed, just as the Doberman slammed against the wood, barking and growling.

Hoodie lay on the ground, whimpering and clutching his bloody arm, his one shoe and his stocking-covered foot slathered with dog crap.

Eve looked down at her own feet and saw poop all over her shoes, too.

"Wonderful," she said, then used her radio to call for backup and an ambulance.

◆　◆　◆

Eve used the edge of a curb to scrape the dog crap off the bottom of her shoes, then borrowed the absent homeowner's hose to wash off the rest.

She left her Chilean prisoner with a uniformed LAPD officer and two paramedics and walked back to the house where the chase began. Her knee was killing her but she did her best not to limp or show her pain. The last thing she wanted was to be sidelined because of an injury or perceived disability.

Regan was standing at the front door of the house when she got there, talking to someone on his phone. She imagined he had a lot of jurisdictional issues to work out, since they were deep in LAPD country here.

Five Chilean men were sitting on the driveway, their hands cuffed behind their backs, glowering at her and the two deputies guarding them. She recognized four of the prisoners as the guys they'd tracked from the motel. The one she didn't recognize, and the man she'd chased, must have been in the house.

Regan ended his call, put the phone in a pocket on his tactical vest, and looked at Eve. "I heard what happened. Are you okay?"

"Yeah," she said.

"How'd you get the dog off the guy without getting bitten yourself?"

She told him.

"Wow," he said. "Where'd you learn to do that?"

"On TV once, I saw a crocodile drag a lion by the legs into the water, drown it, and eat it."

"I'm surprised you didn't go all the way," he said.

"I had a lot of potato chips today," she said. "What have you got here?"

95

"We've got the burglars, their stolen goods, their fence, and the loot from a few other robberies," he said. "Come in and take a look."

It wasn't a crime scene, in the sense that CSU would be coming down to collect forensics, so she wasn't worried about tracking any dog poop that might still be on her shoes into the house. Even so, she politely wiped her feet on the welcome mat before going in.

The place wasn't so much a house as it was a stockroom, with free-standing shelves of high-end designer handbags, coats, and shoes. At the far end was a desk with an open safe behind it filled with jewelry and stacks of cash. There were also some handguns and rifles, presumably for protection, but the residents didn't get a chance to go for them before the deputies stormed in. She also saw dozens of new burner phones in unopened packages.

"How did you get the safe open?" she asked.

"We got lucky," he said. "The guy had it open to put in the stuff these guys stole. Tell me what you see."

"Are we playing 'show, don't tell' again?"

"Yes, we are."

"Okay, I'll play along," she said. "I see jewelry, cash, and lots of designer handbags, clothes, and shoes."

"That's what these Chilean burglary tourists always take. That's their jackpot. So why'd I see an Hermès Birkin bag and a Chanel clutch in the Winslow crime scene photos? They were piled on a chair, right by her front door. Those bags are worth fifteen, twenty grand, easy, and they were left behind."

"Maybe the burglars got spooked by Kitty walking in on them."

"That's possible," he said. "But they still took the ring."

"Maybe that's all they came for," she said, though she didn't have an inventory yet of all the stolen goods.

"Then you're looking for a local gang, or it's an escalation of a personal feud or a professional rivalry," he said. "But if Kitty was a rap or hip-hop star, I'd say it could be all of the above."

"She's done rap."

Regan nodded, remembering now. "That's right, I forgot about her threesome."

"The sex tape wasn't what I was referring to," she said, "but yeah, there's also that."

"Have you seen it?"

"Nope," she said.

"Maybe you should. It isn't hard to find," he said. "If you get us the list of whatever was stolen from the Winslows, we'll go through this stuff looking for it. But I'm telling you now that we're gonna come up empty."

"Because it's not the Chileans who killed Kitty and stole her ring."

"Probably not."

"Thanks for educating me about how the Chileans work," she said. "You've been a big help."

"Not as big as you've been," he said. "If you ever want out of Lost Hills, you're welcome in the MCU."

"I wasn't aware this was a job interview."

"I'm always looking for a crocodile who isn't afraid to take on lions."

CHAPTER TWELVE

Eve didn't ask one of the LASD guys or an LAPD officer to drive her back to the Lost Hills station when they wrapped things up at the scene. Instead, she simply called an Uber. The driver kept stealing glances at her in his rearview mirror as he drove, clearly uncomfortable having a cop in the back seat, though she didn't understand why. She wondered if he had some wants or warrants and was tempted to ask him for his ID so she could run it. But she didn't. She was too tired.

She retrieved her Bronco at the station at about 9:00 p.m. and drove back home, limping in to discover Daniel in a T-shirt and sweatpants in the kitchen, unpacking dishes from her moving boxes and placing them in the cabinets.

It irritated her for a lot of reasons. First off, it felt like Daniel was invading her privacy by opening her boxes. She also thought he was out of line deciding where the dishes should go without asking her. What if she wanted them on a different shelf in a different spot? It was her house, not his.

He also hadn't asked if he could stay over—he just showed up as if he lived there. That was her fault, though. They'd fallen into an unspoken domesticity that needed to be addressed, but not now. Perhaps after he'd dug up all the bones at the Preserve. She didn't want to have a big talk or an argument tonight.

"You don't have to unpack the house for me," she said.

"It's pure selfishness," he said. "I needed the dishes to make myself dinner and I hate to leave a job half-done."

She settled onto one of the barstools at the gigantic island, which was bigger than the entire kitchen in her old condo and was topped with slabs of quartzite. There was a six-burner stove built into it, along with drawers for utensils and plates, and also a sliding-drawer microwave, a bread-warming drawer, and a small wine captain, which she kept filled with Diet Coke and bottled water. It was ridiculously huge and ostentatious, bordering on obscene, but she liked it. The reality was this island was probably where she'd be spending most of her time in the house.

The appliances throughout the kitchen were stainless steel and chef grade. The cabinets were white, with silver knobs and pulls, and the backsplash was white subway tiles arranged in a herringbone pattern. It wasn't an inviting kitchen, but Eve thought she could warm it up by adding colorful furniture, cookie and spice jars on the countertops, nice hand towels draped on the drawer pulls, and several baskets of fake fruit (because she'd forget about the real fruit and it would probably rot). French doors at the back end of the kitchen brought in plenty of sunlight and opened out to the patio, where there was a built-in barbecue and a Jacuzzi, neither of which she'd used yet, and the rabbit-ravaged lawn beyond.

Eve asked, "What did you make to eat?"

"*Oeufs brouillés avec saucisson, champignons, porc fumé, poivrons, et fromage,*" Daniel said.

"I didn't know you were a gourmet cook."

"I'm not," he said. "It's scrambled eggs with salami, mushrooms, bacon, bell peppers, and cheese."

"I didn't know you spoke French."

"I don't. I'm repeating what my mom used to say to us to make scrambled eggs sound exciting for dinner. Want me to make it for you?"

She realized now that she hadn't eaten anything that day besides the scones and a bag of potato chips. "Sure."

Daniel took the clean frying pan and a mixing bowl from the dish strainer, set the bowl on the island and the pan on the stove, turned on the flame under the pan, then opened up the Sub-Zero refrigerator to get the ingredients he needed.

"The media frenzy over the Winslow shooting is insane." Daniel laid some strips of bacon in the pan. "There were helicopters circling over Hidden Hills all day and Mureau Road was lined with satellite news trucks."

"Did the media show any interest in what you were doing?"

He began cracking some eggs into the mixing bowl. "We were under tents, and when the medical examiner came to collect the bodies, they did it in an unmarked van."

To not draw attention. Eve wondered if that was Duncan's idea or if it came from higher up. Then she realized she was focusing on the wrong details.

"Did you say *bodies*?"

He reached for the whisk in the dish strainer, then started beating the eggs. "We uncovered two more, so three total. All rural South American males in their twenties, all shot in the head."

"How do you know their age and ethnicity? Was it the teeth again?"

"I determined the age from a number of factors, like the length of their sternal rib ends and the wear on their auricular surfaces, which is part of their hip," he said, then reached for a knife from the strainer and began chopping the bell pepper. "I determined their ethnicity from their intermediate nasal spines, prominent cheekbones, and other aspects of their skulls. And, yes, they also had the same dental wear as the first victim we found."

"Excuse me for a moment." Eve took out her phone and called Regan. He answered right away and she told him about the bodies while Daniel continued preparing her meal. "What's the likelihood that a rival gang would kill Chileans they caught invading their turf?"

"Very high," Regan said.

"Is there anything I told you that pegs this as a gang killing?"

"They were all killed together execution-style, coldly and efficiently. It's something an army, or other organized group, would do."

"That's hardly conclusive."

"It also takes organization to haul three corpses to Calabasas and bury them there without being caught."

"Unless that's where they were executed," she said, watching Daniel use the spatula to mix the eggs, cheese, and vegetables in with the bacon and grease in the pan. It was a recipe for a heart attack. She could almost feel her arteries hardening in her chest.

Regan said, "Abducting three men, taking them out to Calabasas, and finding a spot to execute and bury them takes even more manpower and planning, though I doubt that's what happened. There are too many ways it could go wrong."

It made sense. "Thanks for sharing your expertise."

"Anytime, Gator."

"It was a crocodile."

"Same thing," he said and hung up.

Daniel slid the plate in front of her and handed her a fork. The eggs might have been unhealthy, but they sure looked and smelled terrific. Her stomach started to growl.

"Did you hear all that?" she asked.

Daniel nodded and watched her take her first bite. "There's one thing I should have mentioned before you made that call."

The eggs were delicious. The bacon grease was the key. "What?"

"You told him three bodies."

"That's all we have, right?" She stuffed another forkful of food into her mouth.

"For now," Daniel said. "But I think we are going to find more."

She swallowed her mouthful of food, which she washed down with some dread. "What makes you think that?"

"I've excavated a lot of burial grounds . . . in Mexico, Africa, Bosnia, Colombia, Serbia . . . recovering the remains of people who'd been summarily executed by soldiers, gangs, and drug cartels. This feels like the same," Daniel said. "So I flew my drone low over the immediate area. There are more unusual depressions that don't fit the natural topography."

"Oh joy," Eve said. "This could end up being some massive gang burial ground."

"Or not. We'll see."

She'd been up since 4:00 a.m. and by the time she finished her meal, the long day hit her like a sledgehammer.

She went to bed at ten and so did Daniel, both of them falling asleep almost instantly. But she was awakened only ninety minutes later by her ringing phone, which she grabbed and answered, thinking it was a work call.

It wasn't.

"Congratulations," Jen Ronin said, "you're a celeb!"

Eve rolled on her side so her back was to Daniel, who was snoring softly, and cupped her hand around the phone as she spoke. "Mom, it's late. Call me tomorrow."

"Are you an old lady? It's only eleven thirty and the news just ended. Did you see it?" Jen's voice, made ragged by years of smoking and drinking, gave her a distinctive rasp that men found sexy but that reminded Eve of all the mistakes her mother had made.

"No, I was asleep. I've had a very long day."

"'Celeb Killing Gets Celeb Detective,' that's what they're saying. Isn't that wonderful?"

"It's sickening, actually," Eve said.

"Your face is being paired with Kitty's on every newscast. Do you know what this means?"

"That I'm not being taken seriously as a detective and I'm just another character in a Winslow storyline."

"It's great for your brand," Jen said.

"I don't have a brand," Eve said.

"The Winslows are huge, and now their millions of followers are going to follow you."

"I'm not on social media, Mom."

"Not officially."

Eve got a very bad feeling. "Not at all."

"Your fan pages on Facebook and Twitter are going to explode," Jen said excitedly.

The bad feeling became a tightening of her shoulder muscles, which Eve knew was a reaction to Mom-stress. If her mother kept irritating her, the tightening would spread to the back of her neck and become a blasting headache.

"Since when do I have fan pages?"

"Since your TV deal was announced. It only took a few clicks and they were up in minutes."

"You did that without asking me?"

"Mothers care for their children without being asked," Jen said. "It's a primal instinct."

Her neck was getting sore now, too. "Social media isn't a primal instinct."

"It should be if you want to survive today. You know, Brandy Winslow and I are a lot alike."

She was right, Eve thought. They'd both purposely hooked up with older, successful men in the entertainment industry hoping it would lead them to stardom. But in Vince's case, he'd exploited Jen's desperation and had no intention of helping her professionally. At least Caleb had married Brandy. But Eve didn't say any of that.

Instead, she said, "You've both had plastic surgery and crave attention?"

"No, we're both gorgeous, talented performers who were impregnated by older men and are fiercely protective of our strong-willed daughters," Jen said. "Our brands are totally compatible."

"You don't have a brand, either."

Jen ignored the comment. "We should be on their show."

Eve felt the first pulses of a headache. "We?"

"As ourselves. One celeb family consoling another . . . and uniting to seek justice."

Eve sat up on the edge of the bed, dropping the hand that was cupping the phone. "Never speak of that horrible idea to anyone, understand? And I want you to delete those fan pages tonight."

"Is that snoring I hear?"

She put her pillow on Daniel's face and hoped he wouldn't suffocate. "It's my stomach."

"Oh my God, you have a man in bed. Well hell, it's about time."

The headache was here. "Good night, Mom."

"Demand your orgasm!"

"What?" Eve said.

"Don't cheat yourself and fake the orgasm, not that you'd be convincing. I got all the acting talent in this family," Jen said. "Make him do the work. You desperately need it."

If this conversation continued for another second, Eve feared she might have a stroke. "Delete those fan pages."

She ended the call and dropped her phone on the nightstand. Her head was pounding. Eve didn't know how she'd endured her childhood with her mom without turning to drugs or alcohol to relax.

From under the pillow, Daniel mumbled, "Are you going to demand an orgasm now?"

Oh God, she thought. *He heard all that.*

She lifted the pillow off his face and put it back on her side of the bed.

"No, I'm not."

"Good, because you'd have to start without me." He rolled on his side, his back to her. "I'm exhausted."

CHAPTER THIRTEEN

Detectives Wally Biddle and Stan Garvey, known at the Lost Hills station as "Crockett and Tubbs," and Duncan Pavone were working at their cubicles when Eve, carrying her bike helmet, walked into the squad room at 8:00 a.m. on Thursday morning.

"Here comes the celeb detective," Garvey said bitterly. It was no secret that the African American detective wanted to break into the entertainment industry. His cubicle was decorated with printed selfies, some of them autographed, of the celebrities he'd met while on the job and also while working private security in his off time at movie star parties and weddings. He'd watched Eve make it big in Hollywood almost from the instant she'd arrived at Lost Hills, even though she didn't want it. And, worst of all, she griped about it. He'd have gladly traded places with her.

Garvey's partner, Biddle, leaned back in his chair to get a look at Eve. "Really? She's here? Do you think I could get a selfie? What does she charge for those now?"

Biddle was an avid surfer who always looked like he'd be more comfortable in a wetsuit catching a wave than in an off-the-rack Men's Wearhouse suit at a crime scene.

She gave them both the finger as she went to her cubicle.

Garvey put a hand to his chest and turned to his partner. "I feel like I've just been blessed."

"Me too," Biddle said.

Eve opened her bottom desk drawer, dropped her bike helmet into it, then went over to see Duncan at his cluttered cubicle. Pictures of his wife, his two adult daughters, and his condo in Palm Springs decorated his partitions.

"Congratulations," Duncan said. "You're all over the news again and this time you didn't need to punch a movie star in the face or run through a raging wildfire with a child in your arms to do it."

She didn't flip him off. He'd earned the right to tease her and, she knew, there was genuine affection and respect behind it. That wasn't true with Crockett and Tubbs, who at least didn't question her investigative skills anymore.

"The captain and Lansing had to know this was going to happen the instant they assigned us, instead of them, to this case." Eve gestured to Biddle and Garvey, who were doing paperwork but still took a moment to flip her off in return.

Duncan said, "We were the detectives on call."

"Lansing did a cold calculation," Eve said. "He must think this celeb detective shit reflects well on the department. They are using me—again."

"Are you saying you don't want this case?"

"I just hate being used this way."

Biddle spoke up from his cubicle. "Unless you can find a way to leverage the publicity to get a huge promotion."

Eve turned to them. "I did that once . . . and nobody lets me forget it."

Garvey said, "It's hard to when there's a damn TV series about it."

"Nobody has seen it yet," she said.

Duncan tugged on Eve's sleeve to get her attention. "Did you learn anything on your stakeout?"

"Enough to know that we can scratch Chilean gangs off our suspect list in the Winslow killing."

Eve pulled over a chair, sat down, and told him about her night and what she'd learned about the MO of Chilean burglary tourists, and that the intruders didn't fit it.

"But that doesn't mean they aren't gang members," she said. "They could be from a local gang rather than one from Chile."

"The three who hit the Winslows probably aren't Chileans," Duncan said, "but the three guys that Indiana Jones dug up certainly are."

"*Certainly?* How do you know?"

"The medical examiner was cleaning one of the corpses with peroxide, which brightened the dark, mummified skin and raised a tattoo. Lopez took a photo of it that I sent to the gang squad. They say it's a tat from a Chilean cartel that recruits labor from rural villages."

That confirmed Daniel's observations about the corpses, but the facts still puzzled her. "They can't find manpower in Santiago?"

"I'm told by the experts in the gang squad that the poor hicks are highly trainable, will work for less money than city folk, and become intensely loyal to the cartel for plucking them from poverty, sending them on trips abroad, and making them rich."

"Is there any way to identify the victims?" Eve didn't have much sympathy for gang members, but they were still somebody's son, brother, husband, or lover and deserved justice, for themselves and their loved ones.

"Maybe the guy with the tattoo," Duncan said, "if somebody wants to go wandering around the Andes with the picture. Otherwise, no."

"The ME's office could run the radioactive isotope tests that Daniel talked about on their teeth or bones."

"Sure they could, but who is going to pay for it? Not the county. Not the state. Not the Feds. And certainly not the Chilean government," Duncan said. "This is playing out exactly the way I predicted it would, except I don't have tendinitis yet."

Yes, it was, and it was depressing Eve. "Did Nan come up with anything useful on the forensic side?"

Duncan nodded. "She found some synthetic fibers she didn't recognize in the goop that slopped out of the tarp. She's got her fiber guy looking at them."

"Did she find anything at the Winslow crime scene?"

"Footprints from three sets of generic Kirkland men's running shoes, which are sold exclusively in Costco's 840 stores worldwide. I have a pair myself." He held up his feet to prove it.

No hope there, Eve thought. "How about ballistics?"

"Kitty was shot close range with a 9mm handgun, which really narrows things down, since it's the most popular handgun on the planet," Duncan said. "The bullet was found in the wall behind her. Nan recovered the shell casing, but there were no prints."

But it was something they could use. "Maybe we can tie the bullet to other shootings that might point us to a local gang."

"We can't," he said.

"Why not?"

"Because Caleb's gun was loaded with blanks," Duncan said. "Interesting, huh? I don't think he knew it, either. Makes me wonder who did the switcheroo and why."

Eve wondered the same thing. She got up from her chair. "We need to have another talk with the Winslows."

"Yes, we do." Duncan got up, too, grabbed his jacket from the back of his chair, and walked out of the squad room with Eve.

They were going down the hall toward the exit to the parking lot when the captain stepped out of the break room, holding a mug of coffee.

"I was just about to come looking for you," Dubois said. "The sheriff is so far up my ass on the Winslow killing that I canceled my colonoscopy next week and asked Lansing if he noticed any polyps."

Eve wondered how long Dubois had been saving that colorful metaphor for the right moment. "An arrest isn't imminent, sir, if that's what you're asking."

"Any working theories?"

"Same one we had before," Eve said. "Kitty flashed her big diamond on social media and someone decided to take it. Only it wasn't the Chileans."

She quickly explained what she'd learned. When she was finished, Duncan said, "Which leaves anybody with a CompuServe account and a Glock."

Eve looked at him. "CompuServe?"

He shrugged. "Or other social media."

Eve shifted her attention back to Dubois. "We're on our way to question the Winslows again."

The captain gestured with his mug toward the front of the station. "There are reporters from all over the world outside the Hidden Hills gate demanding answers, too. We need to give them something soon or we'll look feckless. Get to it."

Dubois walked past them and on to his office.

Duncan looked at Eve. "He really means that *you* will look feckless."

"Why me?"

"You're the celeb detective."

They went outside to their plain-wrap Explorer. Now it made sense to Eve why she'd been chosen for the Winslow investigation. If things went wrong, she'd get the blame, not the department.

Duncan tossed her the keys so she could drive. She caught them and went around to the driver's side. As they got into the Explorer, she said, "I know that you know CompuServe hasn't been a thing since the 1990s."

He put on his seat belt. "I like people to underestimate me so later they'll be stunned by my brilliance. It's a trick I learned from *Columbo*."

She started up the car. "You're definitely succeeding."

◆ ◆ ◆

To avoid the media at the Hidden Hills main gate, Eve drove to the western gate, north of Mureau Road, just past Round Meadow Elementary

School. She slowed to flash her badge at the guard and, after getting a thumbs-up from him, drove through the gate.

Their drive to the Winslow house took them past a bus stop built to resemble an Old West schoolhouse with a gabled roof and bell-less bell tower. A sign out front identified it as the LITTLE RED BUS STOP, although the structure was white. Eve thought it would have fit right in at Disneyland. The only thing missing was Mickey Mouse in a cowboy hat standing out front, ready to pose for pictures with the kids.

"Is this a city, a theme park, or a movie studio back lot?" Eve asked as she drove on.

"You could ask the same question about Calabasas," Duncan said. "On one end of Calabasas Road, you've got a restored Old West town with frontier storefronts and fake hitching posts, and on the other end, you've got a shopping center that's a re-creation of an old Tuscany village with a clock tower holding the world's largest Rolex. And let's not forget the eighteenth-century-style Hindu temple on Las Virgenes Road. If you ask me, this schoolhouse fits right in. It may actually be too subtle."

She couldn't argue with that.

They were a half block away from the Winslows' compound when Eve spotted Deputy Tatum's patrol car parked in front of their house. "Oh great, it's the Lone Ranger."

"This is his beat," Duncan said. "Show the man some respect."

"I will," she said, pulling up behind his car. "But if the marshal calls me 'little lady' again, I'll deck him."

Eve got out and approached Tatum, who was leaning against his car, striking the same pose as he did outside Linwood Taggert's house. But he wasn't watching them—his gaze was up in the sky.

"I hope you haven't been standing guard here all night," she said, following his gaze and spotting a drone circling the Winslow compound.

"The guard at the Round Meadow gate notified me that you were entering the city," Tatum said. "That's why I am here. What brings you back?"

Duncan answered before Eve could. "Standard procedure, Amos. We've here to reinterview the Winslows and see if any new details have come to mind now that they've had a chance to get past the shock. Have they had any visitors?"

"Their agent, their lawyer, their publicist, their producers, and their aromatherapist all came yesterday. Here are their names and license plate numbers." Tatum handed Duncan a slip of paper.

Duncan glanced at the paper and raised an eyebrow. "An aromatherapist?"

"Lulu Lapidus. Lives up in Topanga. She's got a dozen patients in Hidden Hills, including a few horses and dogs."

Duncan put the slip of paper in his pocket. "Some people have too much money."

Tatum tipped his head toward the motor court. Eve looked and saw a black Tesla parked there.

"Benji Stanet, Kitty's fiancé, just got here," Tatum said. "That's his Tesla in the driveway."

Eve said, "Have you talked to the Winslows since we left?"

"No, I haven't, because there's no reason to intrude on their grief," Tatum said. "And they know I'm here if they need me."

"They certainly do," she said. "Does everybody in Hidden Hills have your phone number?"

"Absolutely. It's called community policing. I'm not just the law, I'm their neighbor and their friend."

That's right, she thought. He lived there, in a gated community for the ultrarich, where the teardowns started at $3 million. How was that possible? She wanted to know the answer but this wasn't the time to ask.

Duncan said, "What you're doing here is a brand of policing that's been lost today."

"And not for the better," Tatum said.

"I hear you, brother."

Tatum took what looked to Eve like a TV remote from his pocket, aimed it at the drone, and pressed a button on the device. The aircraft sputtered, spiraled out of control, and crashed into a tree, where she saw a pile of other broken drones.

She looked from the pile to Tatum and he said, "Drones aren't allowed over private property."

"I'm surprised you didn't shoot it down," Eve said.

"I don't want to disturb the peace."

Eve and Duncan turned and went to the house. She'd expected Tatum to follow, and that she'd have to put him in his place again, but instead he got into his car and drove off. She glanced at Duncan.

"Tell me you weren't serious."

"About what?" he asked.

"'I hear you, brother'?"

"Honestly, there's a part of me that envies Tatum. He's the kind of cop I set out to be, but it's just not possible anymore, at least not here, in this urban sprawl."

They went up to the front door and Duncan rang the bell. The door was opened a moment later by Brandy, who was dressed in a denim shirt, jeans, and boots.

Eve said, "Sorry to disturb you, Mrs. Winslow, but we need to ask you some more questions."

She stepped aside. "Of course, come in."

"What's that scent?" Duncan asked as they stepped into the house.

"Peace and serenity."

"I'm not familiar with that one. My wife likes Glade's Clean Linen and Hawaiian Breeze. My favorite is Meguiar's New Car Scent, but Gracie won't let me use it in the house."

"This isn't air freshener, Detective," Brandy said. "It's a prescription scent created by our aromatherapist . . . lavender, sandalwood, and jasmine. It naturally eases grief and restores emotional balance."

Duncan nodded. "Like the smell of sizzling bacon does for me. Have you tried that?"

"I'm a vegetarian," she said, then looked at Eve. "I have the list of things taken from Kitty's house. I was just about to send it to you." She took the phone out of her back pocket and hit a few keys. "There you go. It's not much . . . just the engagement ring, the jewelry that was on her dresser, and the wallet from her purse, which had her credit cards and maybe a few thousand dollars."

"But they didn't take her purse?"

Brandy shrugged. "It's one of her older Chanels."

Eve's phone dinged. She took it out and looked at the list. "Did Kitty own a gun?"

"No, why?"

"Just a question I forgot to ask before."

"Is that why you're here?"

Duncan took in the big, empty living room. "Where's everyone else?"

"Caleb is in the stable. He hasn't left there since Kitty's murder," Brandy said. "I think he doesn't want us to see him hurting. But we're broken, too, and we need his strength, now more than ever. Skye and Maverick are in the editing room with Benji, Kitty's fiancé. He just lost the love of his life and the future they were going to have together . . . so he wanted to see the proposal again, their last moment of joy together."

Of course the proposal was on film, Eve thought. It was too big of a plot point to happen off camera.

She said, "Actually, we're glad we caught you alone. We wanted to talk with you about something that's come up. Can we sit down?"

Brandy led them to the couches in the living room. Eve and Duncan sat on one, Brandy sat on the other, facing them.

"What is it?" she asked.

"The ballistics came back on Caleb's six-shooter," Eve said. "It was loaded with blanks."

Brandy didn't seem surprised at all. "Oh shit, I should have mentioned that to you before, but I wasn't thinking clearly the other night. I replaced all of the bullets in Caleb's gun with blanks for his own safety and, frankly, ours."

"Why would you do that?"

"He sometimes forgets whether he's himself or Deputy Cletus," Brandy said. "We don't want him mistaking us or the gardeners for outlaws. I sent the aromatherapist down but he threatened to shoot her."

Duncan cocked his head, bewildered. "He hasn't noticed that he's firing blanks?"

"He hasn't had an opportunity to find out," Brandy said. "Shooting firearms isn't allowed in Hidden Hills. Besides, the only weapons he's ever fired are on TV and they're given to him already loaded with dummy rounds."

"What happens if he tries to load his own gun? Won't he notice then?"

"We don't keep any real bullets on the property, only blanks," she said. "The difference between them might be obvious to you on sight, but not to him. The only experience he has with firearms is fictional. But I deeply regret what I did now."

Eve said, "Why is that?"

Brandy looked her in the eye. "Because Kitty's murderers would be dead . . . and Caleb might be able to live with himself."

"Except that he'd be doing it in prison."

"He's already in prison, one of his own making."

Eve didn't know if Brandy was talking to imaginary cameras in pithy act-break dialogue out of habit or if the cameras in the house were on, recording this conversation for a future episode. She gestured to the cameras in the house and asked, "Are these cameras off?"

Brandy seemed taken aback by the question. "Yes, why?"

"I just want to be sure our conversations won't show up on TV and compromise our investigation."

"Of course not," Brandy said. "This is our home, our private sanctuary."

Duncan looked bewildered again. "But your reality show takes place at home."

"This is our *real* home, Detective. We might occasionally use some footage from here, lifted from our security cameras, but the majority of it is shot with a full-fledged crew at our property at the Oaks. Filming isn't allowed in Hidden Hills. Besides, we can't air anything with you in it without a signed release."

"Did the guys in Kitty's sex tape sign one?"

"That was different. It was stolen from her and it wasn't broadcast on network television," Brandy said, but something occurred to her and she shifted her gaze to Eve. "Maybe I'm the one who should be worried about our conversations. Will this case become an episode of *Ronin*?"

Eve was afraid she'd get questions like this when she agreed to do the series. "The show is fiction. There's just a character with my name in it."

"And mine," Duncan added.

Brandy gave Eve a patronizing smile. "The only difference between us is that you aren't playing yourself."

"I haven't let any cameras into my life."

"Oh, honey, you let them in the day you slugged Blake Largo, only you're just letting them peek through the windows."

Duncan said, "Did Kitty have any enemies?"

"Millions. Just look at some of the comments she gets on Twitter. The world is full of haters."

"How about someone she actually knew personally?" he asked. "Any haters among them?"

"Obviously LilGlok9."

Duncan arched an eyebrow. "What do you know about the murder weapon?"

"Nothing. I was talking about the rapper," Brandy said. "LilGlok9 was one of the two men in Kitty's sex tape. He loathes her, even though I'm sure he was the one who stole the tape and leaked it."

"Didn't the tape make him famous, too?"

"Not as famous as Kitty, and he was already a celebrity at the time," Brandy said. "LilGlok9 actually believes that Kitty owes her entire career to him . . . that we *all* do. He's even trained his horse to shit on command outside our house."

"Hold on," Eve said. "He lives in Hidden Hills?"

Brandy pointed toward the back door. "Two blocks over."

Duncan glanced at Eve. "Small world."

Brandy gave them his address on Kit Carson Road and added, "It wouldn't be the first time he's killed somebody. Look at 2Fast."

"Too Fast?" Duncan asked.

Eve knew that name from old news. "2Fast was a rapper gunned down in a drive-by on the Las Vegas Strip a few years ago. The shooters were never caught."

"It was the Crips who did it," Brandy said. "And everybody knows that LilGlok9 was the shot caller. He was a Crip himself. Probably still is."

Duncan asked, "What was LilGlok9's motive?"

"LilGlok9 produced 2Fast's album for his own label," Brandy said. "But 2Fast never actually signed the contract. Instead, he took the songs to another label, LilGlok9's biggest competitor, for a lot more money. The album went platinum, and he won a Grammy. LilGlok9 was furious."

"Okay, I get that," Eve said. "But why would LilGlok9 want to kill Kitty now after all these years?"

"Jealousy," Brandy said. "He's a petty little prick, and I mean that literally, as anybody who watched the tape can tell you. He never had a song that crossed over from rap to the mainstream . . . but she just did."

"Who was the second man in the sex tape?"

Brandy looked at her in disbelief, as if she'd just asked her to name the first US president. "2Fast. It's how he got his name."

Yuck, Eve thought.

Duncan said, "Really small world. What was 2Fast's name before that?"

"Nobody."

Eve thought they'd gotten enough from Brandy for now and could always circle back to her again for more. "Can you show us to the editing room? We'd like to talk with Benji."

Brandy stood up. "Sure. Follow me."

Eve and Duncan followed her down a nearby hallway that ended in a set of double doors.

"Why do you have an editing room at home?" Eve asked.

"We shoot hundreds of hours of footage for each forty-four-minute episode. Much of that footage is raw and deeply personal, our lives laid bare," Brandy said. "Having the editors come here to cut it allows us to keep a close eye on who sees it and make sure what *isn't* used never leaves this house. We don't want that footage showing up on the internet."

Brandy opened the doors and they stepped into the darkened room.

CHAPTER FOURTEEN

The editing room resembled a small home theater, with a big screen on the far end. Except there were no theater seats. Instead, there was an editing workstation facing the screen that reminded her of the navigator's console on the starship *Enterprise*.

The workstation consisted of multiple keyboards, touchpads, and several monitors atop a half-moon-shaped table. The monitors were simultaneously playing the different shots that comprised the finished, cut-together scene that was showing on the big screen. There were four gaming chairs that looked like they belonged in race cars rather than at a workstation. A couch was up against the back wall, under a bus stop promotional poster for *Life with the Winslows* that showed the whole family around the fireplace. Off to one side of the room was a recording booth with a window so whoever was at the workstation could see whoever was recording.

Skye, Maverick, and Benji were at the workstation and didn't turn away from watching the scene to see who'd come into the editing room. They were too involved in what was happening on the screen.

The scene took place in the dining room of a fancy restaurant. Kitty and Benji were the only customers, and they'd each just been served chocolate soufflés.

Kitty cut into her soufflé, took a spoonful of the hot chocolate inside, and shrieked with delight when she saw a chocolate-covered diamond ring in her spoon.

"Chocolate and diamonds," she said. "Two of my favorite things."

Benji slid off his chair and got down on one knee beside her. "Kitty, you are the most incredible woman on earth. Nobody has more beauty, talent, or heart."

Her eyes welled up with tears. "Benji, what are you saying?"

He took her hand, the one that wasn't still holding the spoon with the diamond ring in it, which was dripping chocolate onto the white tablecloth.

"I want you in my life . . . forever," he said earnestly. "Will you marry me?"

The camera slowly pushed in on Kitty . . . intercutting with a close-up of Benji, waiting expectantly for her answer. Then the angle went back to her, the camera pushing in closer . . . then back to him . . . then back to her, even closer . . . then back to him . . . then back to her, and the camera settling tight on her face . . . What would she say?

And then Kitty looked directly into the lens and said, *"Cut."*

Maverick hit a key and the playback stopped.

Benji wiped the tears from his eyes, then turned to see who had come in the room. He fixed his gaze on Eve, who stood behind him with Duncan and Brandy.

"You're Eve Ronin," he said.

"Yes, I am, and this is my partner, Duncan Pavone."

"I auditioned to be the killer in your pilot, but my agent said you thought I was too soft." Benji sniffled. "Kurt Russell and Justin Timberlake were Disney stars. Nobody thinks they're soft. It's so unfair. I've got incredible range."

"I'm not involved in casting," she said.

Maverick turned in his chair and pointed at her. "You are now. You're looking for someone to be Kitty's killer."

"I'm looking for the *actual* killer," she said. "This is real life, not fiction."

"Sometimes it's both," he said.

Duncan gestured to the screen and the freeze-frame close-up on Kitty, looking into the camera. "So, what did Kitty say?"

"She was going to say yes, of course," Benji said, "but in next week's episode . . . which now will never be."

"We'll shoot an episode," Brandy said, "but it won't be about that. It will be about her murder."

Benji wiped away another tear. "But you'll say she said yes."

Skye shrugged. "We'll never know."

Benji shot a look at her. "She showed everyone my ring on social media. She told the world that she was engaged."

"She said she got an engagement ring," Skye said. "That's all."

"It's the same thing as a yes," Benji said. "You don't wear an engagement ring unless you're engaged."

"Or unless you're test-driving it," she said, "to see how you feel."

Brandy patted Benji's shoulder. "Don't worry, you'll be in the episode. You can share your heartbreak and the pain of never knowing her answer."

"But I do know," he said, though it sounded like more of a whine to Eve.

"When was this scene shot?" Duncan asked.

"Tuesday," Maverick said. "The same day she was killed."

Technically, she was killed very early on Wednesday morning, but they were still looking at the last thing she'd filmed before she went on social media to show off her ring, excited about her new life. Or was it an act? Was she really intending to say yes?

"Can we talk to you privately, Mr. Stanet?" she asked.

"Sure." He got up. "You can call me Benji."

They walked out of the editing room into the living room, but Eve was immediately aware of the cameras and wondered if there was a way for the family to see the feed from the editing room and hear what they were saying.

"Let's go outside," she said.

So they kept on walking right out of the house and into the motor court. But even outside, Eve was aware of the cameras.

She gestured to the Explorer. "Do you mind if we sit in the car, Benji?"

He stopped walking and stood firm, looking at her in disbelief. "Are you arresting me?"

"No, it's just the only place on the property where there aren't cameras and microphones." Eve pointed to one of the cameras mounted at the edge of the house. "Unless you want the Winslows hearing everything you say to us."

Benji shook his head. "You're paranoid."

"The Winslows are the stars of a reality show and they've used footage from these cameras before. If you feel comfortable with the possibility that anything you say to us could be on national television, then sure, let's talk here."

He thought about that for a moment, then continued walking toward the Explorer. Duncan opened the back door for him and Benji got in. Eve and Duncan got into their seats in front.

Benji sighed and said, "Okay, what do you want to know?"

Duncan adjusted the rearview mirror so he could see Benji's face. "That was a beautiful ring you gave Kitty. How much did that big rock cost you?"

"$350,000," Benji said.

Duncan said, "Wow."

"You can't propose to a woman like Kitty with a ring from Zales," Benji said. "You have to step up and prove you're serious."

"How did you swing 350K?" he asked.

"I took out a second mortgage on the house in Malibu that I bought during my Disney sitcom days."

Eve twisted in her seat so she could see Benji. "How did you feel when she didn't say yes on camera?"

"I was fine with it."

"Really?"

"I grew up in the TV business. I knew she wanted to create a cliffhanger. She'd have been crazy not to. The audience anticipation for the next episode would have been huge."

"So you were confident the answer was yes."

He held a fist to his heart. "I know it was."

"Because she signed you for her spin-off series?"

Benji's eyes went wide. "How did you know about that?"

"We're detectives," Duncan said. "Does her family know that she was planning to leave *Life with the Winslows*?"

"I don't think so," Benji said. "They just bought a $20 million home in Summerlin, so they must think they're going to Las Vegas, too."

"What about you?"

"What do you mean?"

"Did you think you were going?" Duncan asked.

"I knew I was. I signed the contract, and I signed an NDA that was thicker than a phone book," Benji said. "I'm sure the season finale would either have been a big Vegas wedding or, to create some drama, us fleeing from her family and the media to elope at one of those drive-through chapels."

Eve said, "Then why were you only signed as a recurring character?"

"That's a standard operating procedure for the networks on a series. You should know that," Benji said.

"I'm not really involved in the production of the show."

"They don't want to commit to paying a regular until they see how the character works out."

She nodded. "And if you didn't, you'd be out, and there would be no marriage, and no contract to pay off."

"It's boilerplate," he said. "I wasn't worried."

Duncan said, "Or you realized that the big season finale twist was going to be her dumping you at the altar and you didn't relish playing the fool. Except it wouldn't be a role, would it?"

"What do you think I did?" Benji said. "Hired three thugs to take my ring back and kill her?"

Duncan shrugged. "You said it, not me."

Benji leaned forward into the space between the two seats. "I loved Kitty Winslow. I wanted to spend my life with her. Why are you attacking me, someone who loved her with every molecule of his being, and not the guy who hated her, wanted her dead . . . and lives down the street?"

Eve said, "You think LilGlok9 killed Kitty just because her song is a hit?"

"Not just any song—*his* song," Benji said. "He wrote it for her when they were together and forgot all about it, until he heard her singing it on the radio. LilGlok9 told her he wanted half of everything that came from it . . . but she laughed in his face."

"How do you know?"

"I was there when it happened. He cornered her at Cardi B's VMA after-party. Kitty goes, 'Can you prove you wrote it?' So he goes, 'You know I did.' Then she goes, 'For me, and now it's mine. All mine.' And that's when he said he'd kill her."

Duncan said, "You didn't think to tell us about that until now? She was killed early Wednesday morning."

"It happened weeks ago," Benji said, defensive. "I thought she was killed by strangers who saw her flashing the ring on TikTok. It only occurred to me again just now, when you accused *me* of killing her."

Eve said, "We haven't accused you of anything."

"Then what do you call this interrogation?"

"A lively conversation," Duncan said. "We think everyone is a suspect until the evidence tells us otherwise. Speaking of which, where did you go after the proposal?"

"Back to my place in Malibu."

Duncan nodded. "Is there anybody who can corroborate that?"

"I have security cameras, so there is video, and I had to punch in my security code to get in the house. I can show it to you." He took out his phone, went to the MyADT site, and pulled up the video, which was time-stamped, showing it to them on his screen. "Can I go now?"

"Yeah," Duncan said.

Benji started to open the door, but then something occurred to him. "If you find the killer, you'll find the ring, right?"

"That's the hope," Eve said. "It would be conclusive evidence that puts the suspect at the crime scene."

"What I mean is, Kitty is dead. Who gets the ring after the trial is over?"

Duncan said, "I assume whoever she named in her will to get her estate. And if she didn't have a will, I guess her parents. But I'm not a lawyer."

"But apparently her acceptance of my engagement is in question," Benji said. "So technically, isn't the ring still mine? Shouldn't I get it back?"

Eve glanced at Duncan before answering. "You'll have to talk to a lawyer about that."

"Right, maybe I'll do that." Benji got out and closed the door.

As soon as he was gone, Eve said, "He was awfully specific about his alibi, right down to mentioning the video and time code."

"Makes sense. He's got a $350,000 motive for wanting to steal the ring from Kitty."

"You're saying he realized she wasn't going to marry him, so he sent guys there to steal the ring but not to kill her?"

"Accidents happen," Duncan said.

Eve adjusted the rearview mirror back to its original position. "I'd like to talk to LilGlok9."

"Me too. Funny how his name just happens to match what could be the murder weapon."

"Or it's his signature," she said, starting the car. "I wonder how an OG Crip like LilGlok9 got into Hidden Hills."

"I'm sure there are a lot of people here who wonder the same thing."

CHAPTER FIFTEEN

LilGlok9's mansion was in the southwestern pueblo style, with a flat roof, the rounded ends of the rough-hewn wood beams supporting it projecting out along the top of the earth-toned stucco walls above square windows and staggered setback terraces. The landscaping around the house was southwestern as well, with lots of cactuses, succulents, and sagebrush amid boulders, bleached cow skulls, and desert sand. Eve figured his water bill was almost nothing.

A Lamborghini SUV was parked in the circular driveway, which curved in front of the house. There was a white three-rail fence around the property and a buzzer with a camera in it mounted on the gatepost. She could see from the street that the house backed up to the Preserve, just like the Winslows' did.

Eve pressed the buzzer and a male voice came out of the speaker.

"Who is it? I didn't leave a pass for anybody."

She held up her badge to the lens. "We're sheriff's detectives Eve Ronin and Duncan Pavone. We'd like to talk to LilGlok9."

"Be right there."

A moment later, the front door opened and a short African American man with platinum-blond hair and a dozen gold chains around a tattooed neck bounded out in a burgundy velour Adidas track-suit and high-top white sneakers, a big grin on his face.

"This about Kitty?"

"Yes, it is," Eve said.

LilGlok9 opened the gate and let them in. His sleeves were pushed up to show off a sleeve of tattoos. "What took you so long? I was expecting you yesterday. Even had some hors d'oeuvres prepared for you."

"That would have been a first for us," Duncan said. "What did you have?"

"Shrimp tartlets, crab cakes, lobster mac-and-cheese bites," LilGlok9 said. "Very tasty, too, unless you have a fish allergy."

"No leftovers?"

"I ate them all while I was working. I've been mixing an album in my studio 24/7. You mind if we go there to talk?"

Eve said, "Anywhere is fine."

He led them down a pathway of large, flat stones that meandered past a pool and a Jacuzzi, landscaped like ponds amid a boulder-strewn oasis, and an adobe-style stable. A horse stood in the corral, watching them.

Duncan said, "This is not at all what I imagined a rap mogul's crib would look like."

"You think because I'm Black, and came up out of Compton, and am a rapper that I wouldn't have any taste?"

"Or have any horses," he said.

"That's what's wrong with cops," LilGlok9 said. "You see me, and you immediately want to fit me into a racial stereotype."

"Says the guy who is covered in gang tats and calls himself LilGlok9."

"That's my professional name. Legally, it's Charles Newton and I have an MBA from Pepperdine in entertainment, media, and sports management. Can you see Charles Newton living here?"

"Sure," Duncan said, "if Chuck wasn't a Crip."

"I'm not anymore," LilGlok9 said. "How many Crips do you know with MBAs?"

"Only one now."

They walked behind the stable, where the adobe-style studio building stood, surrounded by charred trees like those that still covered much of the Santa Monica Mountains.

Eve examined one of the trees and was surprised to see some green leaves growing on it. "Was this from the wildfire?"

LilGlok9 shook his head and tapped a code into the keypad beside the door to his studio. "Electrical fire in my man cave. This was a detached garage that I'd renovated into a recording studio. It burned to the ground two years ago," he said. "Turns out I had too much equipment plugged into an old outlet . . . and the reno wasn't exactly up to code."

"You mean not at all," she said.

LilGlok9 smiled at her. "You sound like the adjuster from the insurance company. That's the excuse they used not to cover any of my rebuilding costs." He waved his hand at the building. "This cost me $2 million to build."

"Is that why you haven't relandscaped yet?"

"That's by choice. I like the look of those burned trees. They're an art piece now." He opened the door and beckoned them inside.

It looked like a full-fledged recording studio, with enough room for an orchestra. There was a control room, several recording booths, and a full kitchen fitted with a big window that allowed anybody inside to see what was going on in the studio. All of the walls and the entire ceiling were covered with baffling that Eve assumed was for acoustics and soundproofing. He led them past the control booth, where the mixing console was covered with papers, and a trash can overflowing with beer bottles and pizza boxes.

"Sorry about the mess. My wife, Sissy K, is at Paris Fashion Week so I'm basically living in here, creating, when I'm not chillin' in the hot tub with some Dom."

They followed him into a kitchen, where he took out a bag of Ruffles potato chips, a jar of caviar, and a bowl of crème fraîche and set them on the marbled island beside a stack of plates, a pile of napkins, and a piece of pottery filled with silverware.

"All I've got is potato chips and sevruga caviar, farmed in the US."

Duncan settled onto a barstool. "That'll do."

Eve wondered what it was with Hidden Hills residents and their peculiar tastes. First Linwood with his scones and jam, now LilGlok9 with his caviar and chips.

LilGlok9 sat on a barstool across from Duncan and opened the jar of caviar. "So, Detectives, what do you want to know?"

Duncan dipped a chip into the caviar. "Is it true you trained your horse to crap in front of the Winslows' house whenever you ride past?"

LilGlok9 laughed. "Yes, it is. I didn't train the horse personally, of course—I paid some people to do it—but I'm thrilled with the results."

Duncan nodded, his mouth full, but Eve wasn't sure whether he was indicating his understanding or his approval of the chips and caviar. It may have been both.

She said, "Can you say the same about the killing of Kitty Winslow?"

"Come on," the rapper said. "Do you really think I hired some shooters to kill her?"

"Well, it wouldn't be the first time that someone you had sex with and who later betrayed you gets gunned down."

"I didn't have sex with 2Fast. I never touched him," he said, stabbing a finger at Eve. "We both did Kitty . . . and she did us."

Duncan scooped another huge dollop of caviar onto a chip. "That's sex, Chuck."

"With her," LilGlok9 insisted. "Not me with him. I'm only into women. Watch the tape, you'll see."

"I'd rather watch a colonoscopy," Duncan said, then ate his chip.

"I didn't have sex with 2Fast and I sure as hell didn't have anything to do with his killing or Kitty's." LilGlok9 used a butter knife to smear some caviar and crème fraîche on a chip and then he ate it.

Eve said, "You have to admit there's a lot of similarities between the two killings."

"I'm not admitting anything."

"Not even that you threatened to kill her?"

He held up a finger. "Okay, yeah, I said I'd kill that lying, conniving, evil bitch. But it was rhetorical. I was referring to her brand, not her."

Duncan prepared another chip for himself. "Rhetorical. I like that, Chuck. Don't hear many Crips throwing around big words like that. Maybe they didn't have your vocabulary and understand the distinction. But shooting her in the face would certainly kill her brand, too."

LilGlok9 didn't reply. Instead, he prepared another chip for himself. So Eve pressed him some more.

"Kitty stole your song and earned a fortune from it. That had to hurt."

"She stole more than that," he said. "She's a spoiled, rich, entitled white woman who appropriated our culture to enrich herself . . . and she used me to do it."

"You didn't always feel that way about her," she said, "or you wouldn't have written that song for her."

"We were using each other. I just didn't realize how much."

Duncan said, "Or how little you'd get out of it. You thought you'd humiliate her by stealing and releasing that tape and earn a rep as some kind of super stud . . . but instead it made her famous and the joke was on you."

Eve added, "And now it is again, only this time, she stole something from you."

LilGlok9 ate his chip, then dabbed at his lips with a napkin. "I didn't steal the tape. She leaked it online herself. After it went viral, who do you think made the deal to license it to a porn site and charge for downloads? I did. We both made millions of dollars from it."

"But you aren't getting a penny from the song," Eve said, "or any offers to become a Las Vegas headliner."

"Because I'm not a rich white woman with big tits and a huge ass," he said. "Besides, that pissant casino that booked her is so far off the Strip, it's got an Arizona zip code. The truth is that she owns a piece of the place. She's trying to save her investment by hiring herself as a headliner. It's a fucking scam."

Duncan used a spoon to dab some crème fraîche on a caviar-covered chip this time. "She was killed with a little Glock 9mm. It's almost like a confession."

"I'd have to be damn stupid to do that," LilGlok9 said.

"Or damn cocky." Duncan ate the chip and made a face. Apparently, he didn't like the crème fraîche. "You got any onion dip?"

"For caviar?" LilGlok9 said.

"It goes great with anything."

Eve said, "Where were you two nights ago?"

LilGlok9 looked at her. "Right here. Laying down some tracks."

"Can you prove it?"

"Nope."

"The back of the Winslow property runs along the open space," Eve said, watching Duncan prepare another chip. "So does yours."

"So do a hundred other homes in Hidden Hills." He went to the refrigerator, took out a bottle of beer, and twisted off the cap.

"But none of those homeowners have your motive or connections to the Crips," she said. "It also explains how Kitty's killers were able to jump the Winslows' fence into the open space and disappear so quickly, evading Caleb on horseback and an LASD chopper. They ran here."

"If you could prove that, you'd arrest me." He looked her in the eyes and grinned. "Are you ready to do that?"

"Not yet," she said.

"Not ever," he said, taking a drink. "Because it didn't happen. But I will say this: she got what she deserved."

Duncan swallowed his chip and wiped his mouth with a napkin. "That doesn't help you look innocent."

"I plead guilty to hating a backstabbing, talentless slut," LilGlok9 said. "But hate isn't a crime."

"It's a motive," Duncan said.

"This has been fun, but I have work to do." LilGlok9 put a plastic clip on the bag of chips and closed the lid on the caviar. "Let me know when you're coming back, and I'll have better hors d'oeuvres ready."

"That'd be nice." Duncan got off the stool. "I've never had a catered arrest."

"Can you find your way out?"

"Sure," Duncan said. "We're detectives."

They walked out of the studio and continued along the path toward the house.

Eve looked at the blackened trees, his works of art, then out at the stable. "He was right. That comment about his crib was racist."

"I wanted to get him riled up, knock him off his game," Duncan said. "I think he arranged Kitty's killing. How about you?"

"I distrust anybody who serves caviar to the police during questioning."

"And Ruffles, my favorite chip. I liked that. He was trying to knock us off *our* game. But he failed miserably. You didn't answer my question."

"It all fits . . . maybe too nicely."

"That's usually what happens when someone is guilty," Duncan said.

"If he is, and the shooters were hiding here after the murder, they could have leisurely strolled out the next morning through the ranch, the same way they came in, laughing at us all the way."

"We can't let that stand. It'd be humiliating," he said. "But the only way we're going to nail Chuck is if we find the Crips who did it and get them to talk."

"Nobody has found 2Fast's killers yet and it's been years."

"I'll reach out to the Vegas police and get the story on that drive-by. But we do have an investigatory advantage they don't have."

"What's that?" she asked.

"Kitty's $350,000 ring. Someone's got it and eventually they're gonna try to cash it in. They'll have to step out of the dark for that. Maybe it'll be Chuck."

"That'd be nice."

When they got to the front of the house, they saw Tatum's patrol car behind their Explorer. Once again, Tatum was leaning back against his car, arms folded across his chest, looking displeased.

"I don't understand what you two are still doing here. The killers are out there, not here." Tatum pointed out to the Preserve, though Eve was sure he meant outside the boundaries of Hidden Hills, not in the park.

"We're not so sure of that," she said.

"I am," Tatum said. "This is Hidden Hills. We don't have killers here."

"Did you know LilGlok9 is the prime suspect in the drive-by shooting of a rival in Las Vegas?"

"No, but that doesn't mean he's guilty, or that he had anything to do with Kitty Winslow's robbery and murder."

"Did you know LilGlok9 was one of the guys in Kitty's sex tape . . . and that he threatened to kill her?"

"No, I didn't."

Duncan spoke up. "Of course you didn't, Amos, because poking around in people's lives isn't your job. It's ours. Your job is protecting them, and you do it well."

Eve could see that Duncan was trying to make nice and she decided to follow his example, but only because she wanted something from Tatum. "And poking around is what we do well. We'd like to know if anybody else with a connection to the Winslows lives here."

Tatum considered the request for a moment, then gave a slight nod. "I can get you a list of residents."

"That would be very helpful, but I'd like more than that," Eve said. "I'd like to know about this place . . . and nobody knows it better than you. Or we could just drive around and get a feel for it ourselves."

Tatum smiled for the first time since they'd met. "If you want to understand Hidden Hills, you won't get it sitting in a car. Follow me."

He got into his patrol car. Eve and Duncan got into their Explorer and followed him through the community until they came to an Old West marshal's office, complete with a tall wooden false front, barred windows, a covered porch with a rocking chair, a hitching post, and a bulletin board for wanted posters. Behind the office were a corral and stables. And behind those structures, a long driveway curved up a grass-covered hill to an impressive antebellum estate that Eve thought Scarlett O'Hara would have been comfortable in.

Duncan said, "It looks like somebody bought the exterior set from *Gunsmoke* and put it in their front yard."

Tatum parked in a space beside the office and Eve parked out front. They got out and met the deputy on the porch.

"This is Hidden Hills sheriff station," he said, although the sign above it read **US MARSHAL**.

Eve said, "Everybody certainly knows where to find you."

"It also reminds people that there's law here."

Or a cartoon character, Eve thought, and peeked in the window. Inside it was a bit more contemporary, with a computer on top of the wooden desk and a microwave, small refrigerator, and coffee maker tucked into a back corner, as well as a half-open door leading to a bathroom. But she also saw an old-fashioned jail cell with a cot inside.

She looked at Tatum. "Is that jail cell real?"

"I have to keep prisoners somewhere until a resident or patrol car can come get them."

Duncan looked in the window, too. "What kind of prisoners do you get?"

"Sometimes drunk or disorderly residents or party guests so they don't hurt themselves or others," Tatum said. "But mostly kids who have vandalized something or played hooky and need to be scared straight.

A couple of hours behind bars, with parental consent of course, usually does the trick."

"Tough love," Duncan said, turning back from the window.

Eve knocked on the hitching post. "I can't believe the county paid for all this."

"They didn't. It belongs to Bill Crocker, the HOA president, who built it on his property and donates it for our use," Tatum said. "He was a Disney Imagineer who has worked on all their parks. He also lets us board our horse in his stable."

"You have a horse?"

"The county does. Hidden Hills is an equestrian community, with miles of horse trails alongside almost every home," Tatum said. "If you really want to patrol the city, horseback is the best way, though I also have an ATV I keep in the stable for emergencies. I called Bill on the way over, and he's lending you two of his horses. Come on, let's get you saddled up."

He headed for the stable, but Duncan held up his hands.

"Whoa, Amos," he said. "You expect us to ride around here with you on horseback?"

Tatum turned around. "You said you wanted to know Hidden Hills. This is how you do it."

"Her," Duncan said, and pointed at Eve. "Not me. I'm not getting on any horse."

"Why not?"

"I have a rule. I don't sit on animals and they don't sit on me. You can take Eve around. I'll go back to the station, make some calls to Vegas, and check in with CSU."

Duncan went back to the Explorer and got in the driver's seat before either one of them could object.

CHAPTER SIXTEEN

Tatum led Eve into the stable, where one horse was already saddled with a kit that included a rope, a rifle sheath, and a saddlebag with the Los Angeles County Sheriff's Department emblem on it.

Eve said, "There's something I don't understand. You said the guy who owns this place is the homeowners' association president, but I thought this was a city, not a neighborhood."

"It's both." He brought out one of the two other horses, brushed him down, and put a saddle blanket on him as he explained. "There's a mayor, a city manager, a city council, planning commission, the usual pack of politicians. They handle the utilities, building code enforcement, and contract with the county for law enforcement. The HOA handles parks and recreation, architectural compliance, community events, and gate security."

"Is there a lot of friction between the city and HOA?"

He hefted a saddle onto the horse and began to cinch it up. "Not really. The politicians know they work for the HOA."

"Where is city hall?" she asked.

"Outside the east gate, on Spring Valley Road, so the public can do business with the city without entering the city."

"How many residents and homes are there?"

"Eighteen hundred residents and 650 homes." He slipped his hand under the rear cinch and saddle blanket in a couple of spots to make sure the saddle fit properly on the horse, then, satisfied, offered her a stirrup and his hand. "You need a hand getting up?"

"No, thanks." Eve checked out the front and rear cinches, the blanket, and the position of the saddle herself. "What's the horse's name?"

"Blaze," he said, watching her closely.

The saddle looked good to her. She got up on the horse in one smooth, confident move and stroked the horse's neck. "Hello, Blaze."

"You've ridden before."

"I used to get horseback riding lessons when I visited my grandparents in Walla Walla. It's been some years, though."

Tatum seemed disappointed. Eve was sure he'd wanted to see her fumbling, awkward, and uncomfortable. He hefted himself up on his horse and they left the stable, where a man in his sixties was waiting for them. He wore a cowboy hat, a flannel shirt, jeans, and cowboy boots. His hair was gray, and his face was creased at the corners of his eyes and mouth from decades of repeatedly making the same expressions.

"Morning, Marshal," the man said. "You two have everything you need?"

"Thanks for lending us the horse, Bill. This is Eve Ronin, the homicide detective working the Winslow case."

Bill Crocker looked at Eve and tapped the brim of his hat. "No offense, Detective, but I'm sorry to see you here."

"I understand," she said.

"My God, a bloody home invasion in Hidden Hills," Crocker said. "Something like this would never have happened before they moved in."

"We really need to be going." Tatum started to urge his horse along.

But Eve stayed put and said, "They?"

"The Winslows," Crocker said. "And people like them."

She didn't like the sound of that and chose the least objectionable possible "them" from a long list. "Entertainment industry people?"

"Oh, no, we've always had them," Crocker said. "The first house ever sold here, back in 1950, was to actor Leo Gorcey. I'm talking about young money, people who got rich quick in their twenties, mostly rap singers, models, athletes, and 'social media influencers.'" He put air quotes around that last phrase with his fingers. "They don't share our lifestyle or our values."

She rested her hands on her saddle horn. "Which are?"

"You know Mayberry, the town in *The Andy Griffith Show*?"

"Sure." She didn't—the show was decades before her time—but she grasped the general concept. The perfect American small town, where the affable, relaxed sheriff didn't need to carry a gun. He could enforce the law with a smile, common sense, and some old-fashioned courtesy.

"Well, it's like that. A wholesome, relaxed country life, where a rooster's crow announces the new day, where kids have lemonade stands, people enjoy a pleasant evening ride on their horses, and families sit on rocking chairs on their front porches, greeting their neighbors by name with a friendly wave," Crocker said. "Where the air is redolent with hay, honey, and fresh-baked apple pie, and where modesty is a virtue and nobody flaunts their wealth."

"But Mayberry wasn't real," Eve said.

"The ideals and aspirations were," Crocker said. "We were living them here every day . . . until *they* came in."

She suspected what he meant was people of color, but again she carefully chose a less objectionable catchall: "Young and wealthy celebrities."

"They only pay lip service to our values," Crocker said. "Sure, they'll build a stable, but the only horse inside is their Ferrari, when it isn't on display in the driveway with the rest of their exotic cars. They want the roosters massacred, complain about the horse manure on the streets ruining their Louboutin boots, and they take half-naked pictures of themselves in front of their porch-less homes dripping in diamonds and waving stacks of cash in each hand. Of course it attracts crime."

Tatum said, "The gates can keep out a lot of things, but not social media."

Bill nodded in agreement. "That's the biggest danger to our community, Marshal. Look at the negative attention this crime has already received worldwide . . . That's the worst part of this."

Eve sat up in her saddle. "I thought the worst part was Kitty Winslow getting killed."

"She brought it on herself, and on all of us," Crocker said. "The people who move here strictly for the cachet, not the lifestyle and values, are the ones putting themselves and us at risk. Today it's Kitty Winslow that's dead, but tomorrow it could be our Hidden Hills way of life. You need to see what is at stake here. So please, Detective, take a good, close look at our community, then catch her killers fast."

He stepped out of their way and Tatum and Eve rode onto the street.

Tatum came up beside her. "Bill's a fine man, but he sure enjoys giving a speech."

"Makes him a good politician."

They rode along in silence for a bit, Eve looking at all the homes, most of them relatively recent, all of them massive. But she did see a couple of more modest homes, larger versions of the birdhouse ranch house that the interagency task force had raided the other night. Those old homes were like time capsules of what Hidden Hills looked like when it was founded and the HOA architectural guidelines were narrow and strictly enforced. Back then, Calabasas was "out in the country," the valley was full of farms and ranches, and the western culture was genuine.

But now? Calabasas was gated communities, faux Tuscan shopping centers, and office parks at the fringes of the Santa Monica Mountains. Was it really the new money, and the racial diversity, threatening the Hidden Hills way of life or had times simply changed, making it impossible to sustain?

She looked at Tatum. "Do you agree with Crocker?"

"I don't have his blinders on," Tatum said. "There's always been crime here, but mostly it's the kind nobody sees and that I never have to deal with."

"Rich-people crimes," she said. "Embezzlement, Ponzi schemes, securities fraud, tax evasion."

He nodded. "The kind that happen behind closed doors."

"Which also includes domestic violence, drug abuse, and sexual assault."

"I deal with some of that, but that's kept indoors and private. It's not out there on social media, reflecting on Hidden Hills."

"And nobody here sees it," she said, "or they pretend they don't."

"What's important is that the streets here are safe and clean. Women, children, and the elderly can walk alone in the darkness without any fear. You can leave your doors unlocked. We don't have burglaries or assaults."

"Then what's left for you to do?"

"Making sure it stays that way," he said. "But a crime like Kitty's murder . . . That could change things."

It could alert the Chileans, and local gangs, to the easy picking to be found behind the three-rail white fences. "Are you worried it will create more crime than you can handle?"

He gave her a hard look. "Not if it gets stomped down hard and fast . . . and everybody on both sides of these gates gets the message."

"You can do that?"

"I've been doing it," Tatum said, "almost as long as you've been alive."

◆ ◆ ◆

They continued riding, shifting between the streets and the horse trails, which were lined on each side by trees and the ubiquitous white three-rail fences. Eve understood why Tatum felt this was the only way to patrol the city. She could see into almost every property they passed. There was no privacy here, which wasn't at all what she'd expected, given the fame of the celebrities and the intensely guarded lives of the rich and powerful who lived here.

Many of the properties were lushly landscaped and incredibly lavish, with big pools, grottoes, and waterfalls, while others had elaborate stables, corrals, and even small horse arenas. Some residents actually maintained small farms, with fruit trees or vegetable gardens, while a few others, to her surprise, had terraced their land with grape vines, turning them into private vineyards. Everybody who spotted them, even major celebrities, offered a smile and a wave, which Tatum returned and, just to be sociable, so did Eve.

He led her past the community stables and riding arena, then on to the community center, which had a pool, picnic tables, barbecue grills, meeting rooms, and even an indoor theater for stage plays, concerts, and movies.

A farmers' market was being held outside the community center, with vendors selling fruit and vegetables, and several popular LA food trucks offered everything from boba and artisan grilled cheese sandwiches to tacos and Maine lobster rolls. Residents lined up to buy, wearing their cowboy hats and clutching their Gucci bags, the street clogged with parked Teslas, Bentleys, Ferraris, Range Rovers, and a smattering of golf carts, as well as a few horses tied up to fence rails.

It was a very pleasant, welcoming, clean place to be, totally free of any tension, but one only a certain socioeconomic class could afford. Eve sensed a true feeling of community on the streets, and a rhythm of life that was completely different from the world outside the gates. It was like they were under a dome, but not as if they were imprisoned. More like they were protected.

Eve felt different than she had when she arrived, and it took her a moment to realize what it was. Tranquility. Relaxation. Peace.

"I'm beginning to see the appeal of Hidden Hills," she said as they rode down another horse trail, not far from the Preserve.

"It's a very special place."

That only the richest people could enjoy. "I know what deputies earn. How can you afford to live here?"

"I rent the guesthouse on Bill Crocker's property."

"What's typical rent in Hidden Hills?"

"$10,000 a month to over $100,000," he said. "I pay $2,000."

The way she looked at it, the rent was essentially a bribe. "That's very generous of him to take such a huge loss."

"He's doing it for the community," Tatum said. "They have me 24/7."

They own you, she thought. Oakdale would be delighted if she'd do the same thing.

"What about having a life of your own?"

"This is my life," he said.

But he was alone. Eve didn't want to be alone. She wanted more in her life than just her job, even if she hadn't been able to quite manage that so far.

Something caught Tatum's attention and Eve realized he was listening to someone speaking to him in the earpiece tied to the radio in his pocket. He clicked the radio mike attached to his shoulder and said, "I'm on it."

He glanced at Eve. "That was security. A resident has reported a suspicious individual in the park, walking along the fence line."

"Isn't that public land?" Eve said.

"Yeah, but people here get nervous when anyone gets too close to their fence. They're worried about burglars casing their property or, if they're famous, paparazzi trying to take candid photos of them naked or mating."

"Mating?"

"I don't like to be crass."

The trail they were on opened into the Preserve, and as soon as they were outside Hidden Hills, they saw a man doing exactly as reported, walking along the fence line in their direction. He wore a bush hat, the kind with a flap that protected the back of the neck from getting sunburned, and a scarf over his face.

Tatum started urging his horse to pick up speed and so did Eve.

"You don't have any authority to shoo him away," she said.

"I don't want to." Tatum suddenly slowed and waved at the man, who waved back.

"You know him?"

"He's a supervisor with the weed-abatement crew that's been out here this week, cutting back flammable brush away from our fences, creating a defensible space in case another wildfire comes through here. He's just checking their work."

Eve noticed now the close-trimmed border, which resembled a path between the fence and the open space. The weeds had been cut down almost to the dirt, but they'd come back with rains, assuming there wasn't another lengthy drought. "And if he wasn't with the weed-abatement crew?"

"I'd politely remind him about penal code 647, that it's a crime to take pictures of someone on their private property without their consent or knowledge," Tatum said. "And then I'd stick to him like his shadow until he decided to enjoy the scenery elsewhere in the park."

Tatum swept his arm out to indicate the Preserve as a whole, and that's when she noticed the tents that weren't there before, the field lights set up for nightfall, the crime scene unit vehicles, and two people in white Tyvek working on their knees. She also spotted Daniel, working among them.

"Do you mind if we take a ride into my world?" Eve didn't wait for an answer and steered her horse to the dig. Tatum kept pace alongside her.

CHAPTER SEVENTEEN

Daniel looked up with surprise when he saw Eve and Tatum riding up. He ran out from under the tent, holding his hands up in a halting gesture.

"Keep back," he yelled. "I don't want you galloping on any bones that might be scattered nearby."

Eve stopped her horse, apologized, and introduced Tatum and Daniel, then asked, "Has the crime scene expanded?"

"Yes, and so has the body count," Daniel said. "We found another one. But this one's different."

"In what way?"

"I'll show you." He walked under the tent. Eve and Tatum dismounted and followed him to the excavation, where a skeleton lay atop another dirt pedestal that had been carefully dug around it.

"For starters, we've got a skeleton this time, a male in his late thirties, and he wasn't wrapped in anything when he was buried," Daniel said, "which I'm guessing was four or five years ago."

That was several years before the other three men were executed and buried, already a big difference from the previous victims. "Was he also from South America?"

"He could be, but if he is, his teeth tell us he wasn't indigenous or rural," Daniel said. "The shape and features of his skull, like his sharp nasal sill, as well as the sacral index of his pelvis, indicate he was

Caucasian, so I suppose he could be a South American of European descent. But my guess, based on the things I'm seeing, is that he wasn't. There's also bony outgrowths on his hips that indicate he engaged in a repetitive, vigorous activity like horseback riding or dirt biking."

"Cause of death?" Eve asked.

"That's an easy one." Daniel pointed to a hole, with radiating cracks, on the skull. "Blunt force trauma to the back of the skull with a hammer, crowbar, maybe a heavy flashlight. Identifying the weapon is more Nan's area of expertise."

"He doesn't fit the profile of the other killings at all," Eve said.

Tatum said, "How many other bodies have you found out here?"

He'd been so quiet, and Eve had been so focused on the skeleton, that for a moment she'd forgotten that Tatum was there.

"Three South American males," Eve said, "all shot in the head, execution-style, and buried out here about two years ago."

"Sounds like a gang killing," Tatum said.

"That's our theory, too," she said. "But this guy changes things."

Daniel said, "Those killings and this one could be totally unrelated."

"Then what's he doing out here buried with the others?" she asked.

"Could be it's just a good spot to bury a body without being seen and with little chance of it being discovered later."

Tatum looked past them to the other graves and the CSU techs working them. "Are you saying there's a popular gang burial ground two hundred yards from Hidden Hills?"

"We're still examining the topography in this area and using ground-penetrating radar to see if there are more bodies," Daniel said. "But maybe this is all of them. We don't know yet."

Tatum looked Daniel in the eyes. "You can't let word of this get out or it could have a devastating impact on the community."

"Why? The south side of Hidden Hills overlooks one of the most famous pet cemeteries in America and your residents don't seem to mind."

"This is different, Dr. Brooks, and you know it. Nobody wants to live beside a spot where killers come from all over Los Angeles to bury their dead."

"Then they'd better not live in Calabasas, Topanga, or Malibu, either," Daniel said. "Those mountains and canyons are popular body dumps, too."

Eve turned to Tatum. "The information will come out, but probably not with the spin he just gave it."

Tatum said, "The press will give it that spin."

"The press is too obsessed with Kitty Winslow's murder right now to care much about any old bones found out here anyway," she said. "They have a much more salacious story to follow."

"That's cold comfort," Tatum said.

She turned back to Daniel. "I assume you haven't found a wallet or any ID. How about his clothes?"

"He was buried naked."

That indicated to Eve that his killer was afraid the clothing might identify the victim or leave other clues. "Does he have any dental, coronary, or orthopedic implants we can trace?"

"He broke his arm at some point but didn't need any screws to repair it," Daniel said. "He has a few porcelain crowns, but they are custom-made for each individual, so they don't usually have serial numbers. But the color of them perfectly matches the enamel of his other teeth. Crowns like that aren't cheap, which means he had a great dental plan, or was reasonably well off. Odds are he was an educated professional living in the city."

"Those are good deductions," she said. "The kind a detective might make."

"You must be rubbing off on me."

The way he said that, and with his boyish grin, definitely implied a different kind of rubbing. Eve hoped Tatum didn't pick up on that grin.

"Thanks for the update, Dr. Brooks," she said. "Keep up the good work."

Daniel got the message and dropped his smile. "Will do, Detective."

Eve and Tatum climbed onto their horses and rode back toward Hidden Hills. Tatum gave her a sideways glance.

"Do you work closely with Dr. Brooks?"

"Now and then," she said, convinced he'd picked up what Nan had. She was eager to change the subject. "Dr. Brooks said the dead man could have been into horseback riding. It makes me wonder if there are any thirtysomething men in Hidden Hills who disappeared four or five years ago."

"Me too. I don't know of any, but I will definitely look into it."

"Back here would certainly be a convenient place for a Hidden Hills housewife, for example, to kill her husband and bury the body," she said. "It's like her own backyard, only it's not. She could sell her house without worrying that the new owner might decide to dig a new pool and discover her husband's body."

Eve realized that Tatum was listening not to her but to something on his radio. He grabbed his radio mike and spoke into it. "Where? I'll get him."

Eve asked, "Get who?"

Tatum listened, then said, "I'm on it." He looked at Eve. "An intruder. Security lost him on the horse trail on Ben Cartwright Way. Can you ride hard?"

"Don't worry about me."

And Tatum charged off, Eve right on his heels. The horses seemed to love it and so did Eve. It was exhilarating. They rode through several horse trails, crossed a street to another trail, then she saw a man running ahead, camera around his neck.

Tatum reached down for his rope and, to Eve's surprise, lassoed the man like a cowboy capturing a rogue steer, taking him down in a pile of horse manure, his camera flying off his neck.

They brought their horses up beside the man, who was on his knees, covered in manure and yelling obscenities, ending with "Are you fucking crazy?"

"You're trespassing," Tatum said.

The man looked around for something, then spotted his camera in pieces on the ground. "You broke my camera."

The man reached for it, but Tatum cinched the rope tight and practically yanked the man to his feet.

"Start walking," he said.

"What about my camera?"

"We'll send you the pieces."

Tatum started to go, the man trailing beside him on the rope, when Eve spoke up.

"Hold on, Tatum. What's going on here?"

But Tatum kept going, forcing Eve to trail along, too. "This guy was hiding in the back seat of a Grubhub delivery. He slipped out of the car and our security cameras caught him trying to sneak onto the Winslow property."

The man said, "Slow down, you fucking asshole. I twisted my ankle."

"That's what happens when you run on a private horse trail," Tatum said, not slowing at all as they left the trail and hit the street.

"You can't drag me through the streets covered in horse shit."

"Then you better keep up," Tatum said.

Eve came up alongside Tatum. "The man has a point."

"He should have considered the consequences before he trespassed."

Tatum rounded the corner onto Long Valley Road, the city's main street, where people were still lined up for the farmers' market. When they saw Tatum on horseback with his prisoner, they began to cheer and applaud. Many of them took photos with their phones.

The man might as well have been tarred and feathered.

Tatum took his time getting to the marshal's office, where Bill Crocker waited in a rocking chair on the porch.

"Excellent police work, Marshal," Crocker said.

"Just doing my job." Tatum tied his horse to the hitching post, climbed down, faced his prisoner, and removed the rope from around him. "Let's see some ID."

The man reached into his pocket, took out his wallet, and handed it to Tatum, who made no move to take it.

"I don't want to touch it. Show it to me."

The man sighed and flipped open his wallet, showing Tatum his license.

Tatum said, "Delano Staggs, you're under arrest for trespassing, resisting arrest, and peeping while loitering."

He went on to recite the man's rights, but Eve had the feeling Tatum was doing it for her and Crocker. She got off her horse and hitched it up, too, and Crocker headed back up to his house.

When Tatum was done, Delano Staggs said, "You attacked me, dragged me through shit, and paraded me down the street. That's police brutality."

Staggs looked at Eve. "You're a witness."

"Yes, I am, Mr. Staggs," Eve said, "and so are all the people on the street and soon everybody on Twitter or TikTok will be, too. Now you'll know what it's like to be one of the people you photograph."

Tatum gestured to the front door of his office. "Get inside."

Staggs went inside, followed by Tatum and Eve.

"Empty your pockets on the desk," Tatum said, "then get in the cell."

Staggs emptied his pockets—which included his cell phone, wallet, some loose change, and keys—onto the desk. "I want my lawyer. His card is in my wallet."

"I'll get right on it," Tatum said. "As soon as a hazmat team has disinfected your wallet."

Staggs went into the cell, Tatum locked it with a key from his pocket, then walked out again, Eve following him. He unhitched his horse and so did Eve.

"Staggs is right," Eve said. "What you did was out of line."

"How else was I supposed to catch him and restrain him?"

"You could have handcuffed him and radioed for a patrol car to pick him up," Eve said.

Tatum started to walk his horse back to the stable. Eve did the same.

"Good idea," he said. "Shame you didn't suggest it at the time. Oh well, live and learn."

She was not amused by his sarcasm. "How long do you intend to keep him in that cell?"

"Until the end of my shift. Then I'll call a patrol car over to take him to the station for booking," Tatum said. "But I'm the one paying the price. I'm going to have to hose down the cell when he's gone."

Eve's phone rang in her pocket. She took it out and looked at the screen. It was Duncan. She answered it.

"Lansing just got here," Duncan said. "He's holding a press conference today on the Winslow case and wants us to brief him first. So I'm coming to get you."

"Send a patrol car instead," Eve said, looking at Tatum as she did. "I'm bringing a prisoner back with me for booking."

"You arrested someone for the murders?" Duncan said.

"Sadly, no. A paparazzo that Tatum caught trespassing," Eve said. "And he's covered in horse manure."

"Thanks for sparing my Buick."

"What are partners for?" She ended the call.

Tatum shook his head. "You're too soft."

CHAPTER EIGHTEEN

Eve came into the squad room wondering if she smelled like horse manure or if the odor was just stuck in her nose from sharing a patrol car with Delano Staggs. She held a slim file folder that Tatum had given her.

Duncan swiveled around in his seat to greet her as she came in. "What did you learn from your patrol of Hidden Hills?"

"Nothing that will help us with the Winslow case, at least that I can tell so far, but there have been some new developments at the dig."

"I've heard. Nan gave me a call. The ME is doing the autopsies tomorrow on the other two bodies that were dug up before."

They had the room to themselves. Biddle and Garvey were out.

Eve sat down in her cubicle. Her hips and lower back were sore from riding the horse. It was the gallop after Staggs that did it. She was out of practice. "What's taking the ME so long?"

"The bodies have been in the ground for years," Duncan said. "They aren't exactly a high priority when there are fresh kills to cut up."

"I get it. So let's talk about a fresh kill: Kitty Winslow. Tatum gave me a list of all the Hidden Hills residents. There are a thousand names on this list." Eve held out the file folder to Duncan, who wheeled away from his desk to snatch it from her, then wheeled back.

"As incestuous and intertwined as Hollywood is, half of them probably have some kind of connection to the Winslows or their show."

"But probably none of them has a motive as strong as LilGlok9's for wanting Kitty dead."

"I talked to the Las Vegas police about him. They believe LilGlok9 never left the Crips. They are 175 percent certain he arranged the drive-by shooting of 2Fast, but they 100 percent can't prove it."

"That's encouraging," Eve said.

"I also reached out again to Benji Stanet, who got me a copy of the GIA certificate on the rock he gave Kitty."

"How does that help us?"

"Rocks that big, over a karat or more, are usually graded by the Gemological Institute of America, which laser-engraves them with a microscopic serial number," Duncan said. "If that rock shows up on the black market, that number is the first thing a jeweler will see when they examine it. I sent the certificate, along with pictures of the ring and Kitty's other stolen jewelry, to your good buddy Jack Regan at the MCU to run by his sources. The ring is going to solve this case. Mark my words."

"Consider them marked," Eve said. "I'm sure Lansing will be wowed by our progress."

Duncan got up from his chair and put on his jacket. "That's why I'll let you present the case to him and get all the credit."

"That's very generous of you," she said, rising from her chair with a grimace. The way her back was feeling now, she thought she might try her Jacuzzi for the first time tonight, if she could figure out how to heat it up.

"My career is over," he said, "but yours is just getting started."

"It was."

"What are you worried about? You've got a TV series," he said. "Worse comes to worse, you could always play yourself."

They left the squad room and walked down the hall to the captain's office, which was open. They could see Dubois sitting behind his desk and Sheriff Richard Lansing in the guest chair in front of it.

Dubois spotted them and waved them in. Eve and Duncan came in, and she closed the door behind them.

Lansing didn't get up. He was a square-jawed man in his late fifties, the son of a preacher who had an evangelical church out in Beaumont, though the sheriff had never struck Eve as even remotely religious, except when it came to politics. He did enjoy preaching, especially in front of the media, but God had yet to come up in one of his law-and-order sermons.

"I hope you have some good news for me, Detectives," he said. "My PIO says there's press from all over the world outside Hidden Hills, including a reporter from Tasmania. It's amazing how well known Kitty Winslow was."

Eve and Duncan sat down on the captain's vinyl couch, which reminded her of the back seat of a Chevy Impala.

"You can be, too," Duncan said. "Just shoot a sex tape."

"I don't think I'd have the same appeal," Lansing said. "Brief me on the case."

Eve talked the sheriff through their conversations with the Winslows, Benji Stanet and LilGlok9.

When she was done, Lansing said, "You believe LilGlok9 saw Kitty's post about her huge engagement ring as an opportunity to kill her for ripping him off and make it look like a home invasion robbery."

"That's one theory," Eve said.

"What's another?"

"That Benji Stanet, her would-be fiancé, realized she was going to humiliate him on TV, hired some guys to get his ring back, and things went horribly wrong."

"Or," Duncan said, "there's the obvious, simple explanation."

The captain said, "What's that?"

Duncan said, "Kitty stood outside her house, tweeted pictures of herself with a gigantic diamond ring on her finger, basically saying to the world, 'Here I am, come and get it,' and somebody did. All we really know for certain right now is that there was a home invasion, Kitty was killed, and her ring was taken."

Lansing sighed. "That's what I said in my last press conference."

Dubois leaned forward on his desk. "Would it help to release some of the security camera footage and ask for the public's help identifying the assailants?"

"That's a Hail Mary pass," Lansing said. "We'll look like we're floundering only two days into this investigation. Besides, the Winslows' lawyers have informed us that the security video is private property and we don't have the broadcast rights."

Duncan said, "Meaning the Winslows want to save it for their show."

"We'll see about that," the sheriff said. "In the meantime, good work on LilGlok9. My gut tells me he's your man. Narrow in on him."

Eve and Duncan stood, and she said, "What are you going to tell the press in the meantime?"

Lansing thought about it for a moment, then said, "That we are aggressively pursuing several promising leads and arrests are imminent but that it would jeopardize our case to share more details at this time."

"That's the truth," Dubois said.

"Except," Duncan said, "for the 'arrests are imminent' part."

Lansing said, "I am confident that's true, so you should be, too. I want to see it written all over your faces when you're both out there in front of the station with me today."

Duncan said, "You want us at the press conference?"

"Yes, I do, but I don't want you saying anything. I just want you two there, standing beside your captain, silently projecting competence, determination, and vigilance."

Oh joy, Eve thought and started to walk out with Duncan, when something occurred to her. She turned back to the sheriff.

"One more thing, sir. I've got some questions about Deputy Tatum and his situation in Hidden Hills."

Lansing chuckled, then said, "I'm sure you do. He's quite a character. The community loves him and he's kept the peace there for decades. It's his total dedication to his job, and the role he plays there, that has made him so effective. He's entitled to enjoy some eccentricity."

Duncan tugged her sleeve, trying to get her to leave. But she wasn't ready to let this go yet.

She took a step into the room. "Are you aware, sir, that he lives in a guesthouse on the HOA president's property?"

Dubois raised his eyebrows. "I didn't know that."

But Lansing did, it was clear to her by the now stony expression on his face. "He pays rent, doesn't he?"

"At far, far below the market rate," Eve said. "It's an ethical issue."

"I don't see why," Lansing said. "The city isn't paying his salary, we are. He can live anywhere he wants. He chose a guesthouse in Hidden Hills." He looked Eve in the eyes and she felt as if a spotlight had been trained on her. "It's no different than you buying a house in Calabasas that was once a crime scene that you investigated."

Dubois raised his eyebrows again. "I didn't know that, either."

Eve was surprised the sheriff did . . . and that he was keeping such a close watch on her personal life. He probably knew about Daniel, too. "It's not the same thing at all, sir."

Lansing smiled. "You got a cut rate, didn't you, far below market value?"

He obviously already knew the answer to that.

"Because nobody else would buy it," she said.

"I don't see the distinction," Lansing said. "You bought the house on the cheap so you could live in the community that you serve. Tatum is doing the same thing."

"Would you feel that way if I was living in the Calabasas mayor's guesthouse and working out of a station that she built for me in her front yard? Or would you think I was politically and ethically compromised?"

"Hidden Hills isn't Calabasas," he said. "In fact, it's like nowhere else in America."

Dubois nodded in agreement. "It's a walled city for the rich—all it needs is a castle, a moat, and a drawbridge."

Duncan added, "But that wouldn't fit with the western theme."

Lansing said, "I don't mind Tatum treating Hidden Hills like his fiefdom because, frankly, it is and it's working. The crime rate there is almost nonexistent."

"I'll tell you how he's doing it," Eve said. "Today, I saw him lasso a trespassing paparazzo, drag him through horse manure, and then parade him down their main street."

Lansing now seemed alarmed. He stood up from his seat and faced Eve. "Was the photographer white?"

"Yes," she said.

Lansing sighed with relief. "Then I wish I'd seen it."

"You still can," Eve said. "I'm sure it's on YouTube by now. You might even be asked about it at your press conference."

"I'd welcome the question . . . and I'd say that I hope it serves as a deterrent to other trespassers."

"And what if the trespasser had been black, Hispanic, or some other ethnicity?" she asked.

"I'd strongly condemn his action. But Tatum knows better than that. It's why he's remained where he is through three sheriffs . . . and probably will for one or two more before he retires."

"It was the wrong thing to do no matter what the trespasser's ethnicity is."

Lansing stepped up close to her. "The way Tatum does his job isn't what bothers you, Eve. You don't like him because you two are so much alike."

"We're nothing alike."

"You're both intent on creating your own legend. He's Marshal Tatum, the law in Hidden Hills, and you're Eve Ronin, TV detective. It's a clash of egos."

Eve could see Captain Dubois grinning at his desk and looked back to see that Duncan was grinning, too. It made her angry that she was being equated with Tatum. They weren't alike at all. She turned back to the sheriff.

"That's not who I am."

"I guess we'll find out when we watch the first episode of *Ronin*," Lansing said. "See you outside in an hour."

This time, they were clearly being dismissed. Eve and Duncan walked out. Once they were in the hall and the captain's door was closed again, Eve turned to Duncan.

"Can you believe that?"

"I think Lansing is right. You and Tatum are alike."

"I'm nothing like Tatum."

"You couldn't wait to get on that horse. Pretty soon, you'll have the hat, too. How do you want to kill the next hour?"

"I want to track down Kitty's sex tape." She felt a professional obligation to watch it. Two of the three people in the tape had been murdered. Something in the scene might prove useful in the investigation or help her understand the relationship between the two doomed participants.

They went back to the squad room, where Eve went online to find the infamous Kitty Winslow sex tape, but she didn't want to pay for it because it would mean giving her credit card or PayPal information to a porn site. Worse, it might someday get tracked back to her. Instead, she kept looking and managed to find it on a pirate site for free, where she could also find all the latest movies and TV shows. She created a fake account, downloaded the video anonymously, and hoped that opening it wouldn't release a ransomware virus on her laptop. It was only afterward that she realized the site probably recorded the IP address of her computer or the Lost Hills station. But it was too late to do anything about it, and that's when the captain leaned his head into the squad room to beckon them to the press conference.

The Lost Hills station parking lot was packed with reporters. Lansing made his remarks, but they didn't seem to go over well with the press. While he was doing that, and Eve was projecting competence, determination, and vigilance, she texted Daniel, telling him that she'd be staying late at the station. He replied that he had to go home anyway, that he couldn't keep wearing the same clothes, even if he did wash them every night. She'd been hoping he'd find an excuse to go back to his place. The casual domesticity was beginning to make her uncomfortable, though she knew she was giving him mixed signals, a reflection of her own mixed emotions about it.

After the press conference was over, she spent some time looking for missing person reports filed five years ago for any local residents who fit the loose description of the skeleton found in the Preserve but came up with nothing.

She waited until Duncan went home and there was nobody in the squad room, then watched the sex tape.

There was nothing remotely erotic about it. It was also awkward for Eve to watch LilGlok9, a guy she'd just met, having sex, but it wasn't the first time she'd experienced the same discomfort, though it involved someone else. Actor Nick Egan was a suspect once in a case, and as part of that investigation, she'd watched a sex tape of him getting a blow job from a woman in his backyard. That video, presumably shot from a window some distance away, was a major Hollywood movie directed by Steven Spielberg compared to Kitty's video.

Her sex tape was badly lit, clumsily shot, and frequently out of focus. But Kitty seemed aware of the camera, sweeping hair out of her face like a practiced porn star whenever the lens was on her. Eve realized that if you took out the sex, the video wasn't any different from the scene she'd watched in the editing room. Kitty was the one in charge, and not whatever man she shared the screen with, and she knew exactly what she was doing. Perhaps that wasn't so clear before *Life with the Winslows*, but it was now.

After watching the sex tape, she switched to the surveillance videos from the night of the robbery and murder. She studied the various angles of the intruders arriving and fleeing.

Eve watched them climb the fence, break into Kitty's house, and then race out again, getting shot at by Caleb firing blanks and scaring away a rabbit on their way back to the Preserve, where they dropped into the weeds and disappeared into the vast open space.

There was something bothering her about what she was seeing, an itch in her psyche, but whatever it was, she couldn't pinpoint it. It was hard to watch all the screens at once. She would have to watch each camera individually . . . Maybe then she'd figure out what the itch was.

At 8:00 p.m., she got on her bike and rode home. On her way to the front door, a rabbit dashed across her lawn. The way things were going, she'd have no lawn left for the housewarming party on Saturday unless she made a trip to the nursery for some pieces of sod she could use to patch the holes. She couldn't see herself doing that.

Eve made herself dinner, which meant defrosting a chicken pot pie in the microwave and eating it on the cold marble of her huge kitchen island. The house felt big and empty without Daniel in it, but it was also nice having it to herself.

Then Eve thought about Amos Tatum, eating dinner alone in his kitchen in Hidden Hills, and told herself there was no comparison between them, that she had somebody, that she had a life, but she wasn't sure it was a convincing argument.

CHAPTER NINETEEN

After her horse and bike rides on Thursday, Eve decided to drive to work on Friday morning and give her body a break. She was surprised to see a movie crew's trailers and dressing rooms lined up on the south side of Agoura Road as she approached the Lost Hills station. It wasn't until she saw the press conference podium on the front steps, and her father and his director of photography, Krister Ekblad, standing beside it that she realized this was the *Ronin* crew.

Nobody had told her the show would be shooting where she actually worked.

She drove into the restricted lot, parked her car, and immediately felt the resentment coming off the deputies she saw in the parking lot. It was worse when she got inside, everyone she passed, even the civilian clerical staff, staring at her with anger. She ran into Biddle and Garvey as they came out of the break room with cups of coffee.

"It's official," Biddle said. "We're all supporting characters in your life story."

Garvey smirked. "You just had to bring the show here, didn't you?"

"I had nothing to do with this," she said.

Biddle looked at her like she was a lying suspect. "You had nothing to do with a show called *Ronin*, about you, Eve Ronin, being shot where you work."

"This is my nightmare."

"No," Garvey said, "it's ours."

They edged past her and she went directly to the captain's office, where the door was open as usual and he was at his desk.

She leaned into the room. "Captain, did you know *Ronin* was going to shoot here?"

Dubois looked up from his paperwork. "Of course I did."

"And you didn't tell me?"

"The show is called *Ronin*. I assumed you knew."

"It's hard enough getting people here to take me seriously at the same time there's a TV show being made about me," she said. "But letting the show come here, where I work, is rubbing everyone's face in it."

"The sheriff doesn't think so. He believes the show is good PR for the department and this station."

"He could have asked me before he okayed this shoot."

Dubois set down his pen. "He doesn't need to ask your permission, Detective. He's the Los Angeles County sheriff."

Maybe he didn't, but she knew somebody who did. She left the captain and walked into the lobby and out onto the front steps, where she spotted Simone Harper sitting in the video village, which was erected on the far side of the parking lot where it wouldn't be in the shot. Simone was working on her laptop.

Eve marched over to the tent, her anger building with each step, until she stopped right in front of her. "Why didn't you tell me you were shooting here?"

Simone raised her gaze from her screen and seemed confused. "I thought it was obvious that we'd be shooting here. This is where you work."

Eve turned, glanced around for her father, and spotted him talking to Erin Casey on the steps of the dressing room trailer. "Was this his idea?"

"We all decided from the get-go to shoot as much of the show as possible on location."

"All decided?" Eve said. "You never mentioned it to me."

"You know we're shooting where the real story took place. You visited us at Mulholland and Mulholland the other day," Simone said. "We even talked about how awkward it was for you to see your past being re-created where it happened."

"I know, but it's one thing to shoot on the street," Eve said. "It's another thing for you to do it where I work."

"You worked there, too," Simone said.

"That was a crime scene." Eve pointed to the building. "This is my office."

"That's why we're on Mulholland only once this time, but we're going to be here every episode for our exteriors. All of the interiors will be on sets on our soundstage, and only because it would be a logistical, practical, and legal nightmare trying to shoot in your actual squad room."

"That's a relief," Eve said.

"Not that we didn't try," Simone continued. "The more reality we can add, the more invested the viewer becomes in the fiction. Once they accept the authenticity, they will believe anything you show them."

Eve realized that agreeing to this TV series was a huge mistake. But it was too late now to back out. All she could hope for was that *Ronin* would bomb and be canceled fast.

The parking lot was filled with fake reporters, extras hired to fill out the show, and maybe a few "day players" with lines, billed on the call sheet—the list of actors present—as Reporters #1, #2, and so on. But Eve spotted two genuine reporters. One of them was Zena Faust, an activist blogger with the *Malibu Beat*, who was easy to recognize with her bald head and multiple facial piercings. It was the investigation of the murder of Zena's lover that indirectly led to Eve getting shot in the knee and her recuperation with Daniel in Tarawa. The other real reporter was Scott Peck, who worked for *The Acorn*, the local paper covering Calabasas, Agoura, and the Conejo Valley. He was Eve's age and had big journalistic aspirations. She figured he did this to increase his visibility.

Eve said, "I see some actual reporters amid the fake ones."

Simone smiled. "It's great, isn't it? We like to get real reporters to play reporters . . . It adds one more level of authenticity. Did you see Anderson Cooper in *Batman v Superman*? Or Wolf Blitzer in *Mission: Impossible*? Wolf took off his face and it was Simon Pegg!"

Eve had no idea who Simon Pegg was and didn't care. But she couldn't believe that real reporters were participating, compromising their journalistic integrity, leveraging their hard-earned credibility, to add some credibility to fiction. She pointed to Zena Faust.

"Is she going to take off her face?"

"I hope not. I love her pierced look. It's striking and authentic," Simone said. "We took this scene almost verbatim from the actual newscasts, tightening it a bit for pacing."

Vince and Krister came over and took their seats in front of the monitors. Eve's father smiled at her.

"Glad to see you back on the set so soon, hardnose."

"It wasn't by choice."

"But here you are. And you picked a good moment, too. You've just solved the case."

"I remember," Eve said.

Vince looked at the screens, then out at the actors up on the steps.

Eve felt an odd sense of displacement, seeing herself being portrayed by Erin Casey, standing where she'd stood behind Sheriff Lansing only yesterday for another press conference.

And there, to her dismay, was Nick Egan, an actor she'd interviewed as a suspect in another homicide case, playing Sheriff Lansing.

The producers had no way of knowing Eve's history with Egan, but it was still troubling to her. They'd undoubtedly cast him because of his years on the TV series *G-Girls*, playing the tough government handler of three female FBI agents working undercover as Las Vegas strippers.

Her father directed Egan in an episode entitled "Tassels of Terror" and might even have suggested him for the part. The producers were clearly trading on Egan's established *G-Girls* persona to add gravitas to the Lansing character and she couldn't blame them for that.

Vince yelled, "Action!"

Lansing stepped up to the podium to brief the media on the successful arrest of the killer who'd massacred a family.

"Thank you all for coming today. As you know, a suspect has been arrested in the murders of the Kenworth family. The quick capture of the monster responsible for this heinous crime is due, in large measure, to the exceptional investigative work of Eve Ronin, the youngest robbery-homicide detective in the history of the Los Angeles County Sheriff's Department."

He turned and waved Eve up to the podium.

"Thank you, sir, but I'm just one of the many detectives working on this case and don't deserve the credit."

Zena Faust asked a question, and so did a couple of other reporters, and Eve got a sense of déjà vu that was so strong and disorienting, she was afraid she might need oxygen.

"Cut!" Vince yelled.

She could have hugged her father for ending the ordeal. But he didn't do it because he'd noticed her discomfort. He angrily waved over the assistant director, a shaggy-haired, perpetually stressed young man named Zach, who wore a headset and had a radio clipped to his belt that allowed him to communicate with the entire crew.

Vince said, "Zach, can we get someone to hold traffic? Some schmuck drove a Buick into the parking lot in the background and we're not going to be able to match that in coverage."

Eve knew that the schmuck was Duncan coming in to work. She got up to leave, but Vince was faster.

"Okay, let's do it again. Settle and . . . *action!*"

There was no way Eve could get back to the building without being in the shot . . . so she had to sit through it again. It was like getting a cavity filled without Novocain, not that she'd ever had the experience, but she figured it had to be just as uncomfortable.

As soon as the scene was over and they moved on to the coverage, Eve left and found Duncan at the catering truck, holding a giant breakfast burrito in one hand, a big cup of coffee in the other.

"I was about to come get you," Duncan said. "Nan just called—"

Eve interrupted, irritated, "And you thought you'd find me at the catering truck?"

He ignored her comment. "She wants us to come down to the morgue. She says there's something we have to see."

"I'll drive," she said, glad for an excuse to leave the station right away. "You eat."

"I can do both at once."

"Not if both of your hands are occupied."

"That's why God created knees," he said, but he let Eve drive anyway.

◆ ◆ ◆

It took Eve and Duncan nearly two hours in rush hour traffic to get from Lost Hills station to the Los Angeles County Medical Examiner-Coroner's office downtown at the campus of the Los Angeles County–USC Medical Center.

When they arrived at the morgue, Emilia Lopez and Nan Baker were waiting, the three mummified and eviscerated bodies laid out on the exam tables behind them. The corpses had been opened up the middle like ziplock bags, their internal organs removed and weighed as part of their autopsies.

Lopez and Nan were still in their scrubs, with caps on their heads and gloves on their hands. Nan had a camera around her neck. They'd clearly been at work before the detectives arrived, and judging by the stains on Lopez's scrubs, Eve could see it had been messy. Almost as much as Duncan's work on his breakfast burrito, which had left big stains on his shirt.

"What's the big news?" Duncan asked.

Lopez said, "First, I can tell you that all three victims are Hispanic males in their early twenties and were shot, execution-style, in the back of the head with a 9mm handgun, so these killings are linked."

That wasn't news to Eve. She'd already come to that conclusion.

Nan said, "That's not the only link. We recovered traces of polyester insulation, mineral rock board, and fiberglass from the exit wound in each victim. The specific combination of materials is used in acoustic insulation commonly found in screening rooms, soundstages, and recording studios."

Eve said, "Sounds like the men were lined up facing a soundproofed wall and then shot in the back of the head."

Nan nodded. "The bullets passed through their skulls into the wall, spraying some debris onto the victims on impact."

Duncan said, "Even as the wall was splattered with their brains."

"Evidence transfer always works both ways," Nan said.

"Were you able to identify the brand of soundproofing materials?" he asked.

"The acoustic fabric is called Guilford of Maine, the rock board is Roxul AFB, and the fiberglass is Owens Corning 703," Nan said. "The materials are too widely used to lead you to an individual suspect. But if you can find a likely wall and let me at it, I'm confident that no amount of paint or patching will entirely hide the evidence of these killings."

Duncan said, "You could have told us all that in a text but this was just the opening act for the headliner, wasn't it?"

Lopez gestured to the corpse on the nearest table. "I was examining the third victim's internal organs when I made a discovery in his stomach and immediately called in Nan to see it for herself."

Nan said, "I photographed it in situ and secured the room until you could get here."

"Meaning you stayed here protecting the scene until we walked through the door?"

"That's right," Nan said.

Duncan said, "What the hell did you find? A nuclear bomb?"

Lopez lifted up a steel pan from the autopsy table and held it out for them to see. Inside were several pearls and a ring with a huge diamond.

Eve said, "Is that Kitty's ring?"

"That would be a hell of a magic trick if it is," Duncan said. "He's been in the ground for two years."

Eve pointed at the ring. "May I look at it?"

"Go ahead," Nan said.

Eve found a box of latex gloves, pulled a pair over her hands, and then removed the ring from the pan and examined it closely.

"The stone is certainly big enough to be Kitty's," she said. "But it's an entirely different setting."

Duncan turned to Nan. "Have you looked to see if the diamond is real and engraved with a GIA serial number?"

"Not yet. I wanted you both to see it the way it was found as part of your investigation. We also need to be very careful from a chain-of-evidence standpoint with how it's handled going forward."

"And also how it's secured," Duncan said. "If that rock is a diamond and not glass, cubic zirconium, or paste, it's worth hundreds of thousands of dollars."

"Now you know why I didn't leave until two people with guns and badges got here," Nan said. "I'll go get a loupe from my truck so you can jot down the serial number if there is one, then we'll get this bagged and logged into evidence."

She left.

Duncan took the pan from Lopez and shook it, the pearls rolling around inside. "You found the ring and pearls in his stomach? What do you make of that?"

"Smuggling is my guess," she said. "I have friends at US Customs and the county jail who've caught people using their anuses and vaginas like suitcases. It's amazing what you can fit in there if you're determined and flexible."

Eve said, "I am cringing just thinking about it."

"So am I," Duncan said.

Lopez took the pan back from Duncan and held it out to Eve, who dropped the ring into it with a tiny clang. "But as far as swallowing foreign objects goes, I've only encountered a similar situation with drug smugglers, and when I have, it's because the packets of pills or coke they were carrying in their bodies burst and killed them. But I've never found jewelry in a body before."

Duncan said, "I think we're looking at a burglar who swallowed what he stole so he couldn't be caught holding the goods."

That made sense to Eve, but she saw an alternative. "Or he's a Chilean gang member who was tired of only getting a small cut of the action . . . and decided to keep the best for himself."

Duncan nodded. "That could be what got him killed."

Lopez set the pan back down on the autopsy table by the body it came from. "But he was taking a huge risk. That diamond could have created a blockage, or cut him as it went through his digestive system, causing serious internal bleeding."

Duncan said, "Not as serious as the bullet that went through his head. But the potential payoff was worth the risk."

Eve shook her head. "The problem with that theory is if his handlers knew he'd swallowed jewelry, they would have cut him open to get it back. They wouldn't have buried him with a fortune in his stomach."

"Maybe the executioner didn't know this guy had swallowed anything," he said, "and the guy didn't get a chance to say anything about it before his brains were blown out."

"Or," Eve said, "the thief thought he might still be able to walk away from the situation with his life and his bounty . . . and was wrong."

"I'm not a detective," Lopez said. "All I can tell you is that the victim swallowed the jewelry shortly before he was killed. There weren't any foreign objects in his digestive tract."

"You looked?" Duncan asked.

"Of course I did," she said. "Not only in him, but the other two as well. I like to be thorough."

Nan returned with the loupe, took the ring out of the pan, and examined the diamond. "There's a GIA number."

Duncan looked up at the ceiling. "The Gods of Evidence are smiling upon us today."

Nan read off the number and Duncan wrote it down in his notebook, then said, "I'll run this past the GIA, see if we can track down the previous owner."

He left the room to make the call. Eve stayed and filled out the evidentiary paperwork with Nan and Lopez.

Eve finished her work and asked Lopez, "Did you get anything more from the skeleton that Dr. Brooks discovered yesterday?"

"I've only read his report," she said. "I haven't had a chance yet to examine the bones myself or try for a dental match on any missing persons."

Duncan returned, a smile on his face. "This is getting interesting."

Eve said, "How could it get more interesting than a diamond found in a dead man's stomach?"

"I got a hit from the GIA. The diamond was flagged with a note to refer inquiries to NYPD detective Karl Drummond. I thought you'd like to be in on the call."

The two detectives left the morgue and went down the hall to the break room. There was a row of vending machines, as well as a sink, a strainer, and a microwave that looked as if it had never been cleaned and as if food items being heated inside had caught fire more than once. There were also three Formica-topped tables with mismatched hard plastic chairs.

They went to a table, Duncan made the call, and while it was ringing, he activated the speaker and set the phone on the tabletop between them.

Drummond answered on the fourth ring and Duncan introduced the two of them.

"We're calling regarding a diamond wedding ring we've recovered," Duncan said. "We ran the GIA number and it came back to you."

"Where did you find the ring?" Drummond had a heavy Bronx accent that bordered on caricature. Eve wondered if it was his real voice or if he was having some fun with them.

"In a dead guy's stomach," Duncan said.

"That was a twist I wasn't expecting. How long has he been dead?"

"About two years."

"Even stranger," Drummond said.

"Care to clue us in?"

"The ring was among over a million dollars in jewelry stolen from a suite at the Four Seasons Hotel in Manhattan five years ago."

"He certainly didn't swallow it then," Duncan said, "unless he's had the worst case of constipation in human history."

Eve asked, "Who were the jewels stolen from?"

"Sissy K, the rapper," Drummond said and Eve felt like she was in an elevator that had suddenly dropped two floors. "She was here for a performance at Madison Square Garden and someone burgled her room while she was onstage."

Duncan looked at Eve and asked, "Why does that name sound familiar?"

Drummond answered, "She's in some kind of feud with Cardi B or Nicki Minaj . . . or maybe it's both of them. I can't keep track."

Eve said, "Sissy K is also LilGlok9's wife."

Duncan stared at Eve and silently mouthed the words *holy shit*.

"Yeah, the little guy was here, too," Drummond said, "and accused us of slow-walking the investigation because he's black and an ex-Crip."

"Holy shit," Duncan said, aloud this time.

"What am I missing?" Drummond asked.

Eve said, "To be honest, we're not sure. Can we call you back? We need some time to think."

"Sure," Drummond said and hung up.

She turned to Duncan. "Okay, let's think this through. Five years ago, a diamond ring belonging to Sissy K, LilGlok9's wife, was stolen in New York. Now it's shown up in the mummified corpse of a guy who was executed with a 9mm handgun two years ago . . . and buried with two other men outside LilGlok9's backyard."

"And this week," Duncan continued, "Kitty Winslow, LilGlok9's ex-lover, is shot in the face with a 9mm handgun by three intruders who escaped with her diamond ring into the same open space where those bodies were buried."

Eve said, "These two robberies have too much in common not to be connected."

Duncan started ticking off the points with his fingers. "They both involve outrageously expensive diamond rings belonging to rappers that LilGlok9 was or is sleeping with."

She said, "They both involve two different groups of three men, presumably all of them gang members from here or abroad."

He said, "And both robberies in some way involve people getting shot in the head with a 9mm handgun."

She said, "Which could be a little Glock 9, which also happens to be the professional name of the one person all of these crimes have in common, who lives adjacent to both the Kitty Winslow crime scene and the burial ground."

He said, "And let's not forget the unsolved drive-by shooting of 2Fast, who was in a sex tape with LilGlok9 and Kitty Winslow. I wonder if he was shot with a nine . . . and if there were three people in the drive-by car."

"As if this wasn't convoluted enough already." Eve sighed and sat back in her chair.

"The answer is right in front of us—we just don't see it yet." Duncan got up and went over to one of the vending machines. "I see better with a Snickers bar in my hand. You will, too."

She watched him as he fished around in his pockets and came up with a couple of crumpled dollar bills, which he smoothed out on the edge of the machine and carefully fed into the cash slot. The machine spit the bills out. He smoothed them again and fed them back in. He eventually managed to get the machine to accept his money and chose two Snickers bars, which fell with a thunk into the bottom tray.

While all of that was going on, Eve thought back to their one meeting with LilGlok9. Duncan returned to the table with their candy and she saw what they were missing, and it was right there in front of them.

"The art piece," she said.

Duncan slid a Snickers over to her and kept one for himself. "What are you talking about?"

"LilGlok9 never replanted the trees that burned on his property."

"What's the significance of that?"

"It explains everything." She got out her phone, dialed a number, and put the call on speaker. It was answered in one ring.

"Amos Tatum."

"Marshal, it's Eve Ronin. I have a quick question for you."

"Okay," he said warily.

"When did LilGlok9's recording studio burn down?"

"It was about two years ago. Some sort of electrical problem," Tatum said. "We're fortunate the fire was contained on his property or it could have been a major disaster. Why do you want to know?"

Eve met Duncan's eyes and grinned. "I'll get back to you."

She ended the call. Duncan grinned back at her and tore open the wrapper on his Snickers bar. Eve could tell that now he'd put the pieces of the puzzle together, too.

"We just solved four cases at once," he said, "while sitting in the break room at the county morgue."

"We need to see the DA right away."

He wagged his candy bar at her. "First, we need to sit here for a few minutes, eating our candy bars and feeling pleased with ourselves."

"I can do that." Eve opened hers and took a bite.

They both sat there chewing their Snickers bars for a moment, the only sound the humming of the vending machines and the fluorescent lights.

Duncan said, "This is how you survive in this job."

"I'm beginning to see that," she said, taking another bite. "It's nice solving a crime without breaking any bones, getting shot, or being thrown off a cliff."

"Don't worry." Duncan took another bite of his Snickers. "There's still time for that."

CHAPTER TWENTY

Before they drove to the Hall of Justice on Temple Street, Duncan called back NYPD detective Karl Drummond to let him know his cold burglary case would soon be closed and to ask him for the name of the insurance company involved. Drummond gladly gave Duncan the information.

On their way up to Assistant District Attorney Rebecca Burnside's office, Duncan spoke to Daedalus Patrick Murphy, an investigator for the insurance company, and learned they'd paid out $1.7 million on the claim to LilGlok9 five years earlier.

As they reached Burnside's office door, Duncan told Murphy that it was a case of insurance fraud and that he'd get back to him with more information in the next day or so. He pocketed his phone and they went inside, where Burnside was waiting for them, her curiosity aroused by their call to her a half hour earlier, requesting to see her right away.

Her office was small but tidy, with a window behind her desk that gave her a view of the courthouse across the street. Eve and Duncan sat down in her two guest chairs and got right into laying out their case to her.

Burnside listened intently, her gaze never leaving the two of them, even as she scrawled notes on the yellow legal pad in front of her. She had the striking beauty of a fashion model, but the intelligence and savvy to dim her wattage with elegant office attire that muted her attractiveness without making her seem plain. Her makeup was always perfect, colors and textures that she applied with a painter's sense of light, shadow, and character to fit whatever image she wanted to project to a judge, jury, or reporter. Today it was competent, no-nonsense professional.

When they were done, she dropped her pen and leaned back in her chair.

"Let me see if I've got this straight," she said. "You believe that five years ago, Charles Newton, a.k.a. LilGlok9, faked the theft of his wife's jewelry to get the $1.7 million insurance payoff. Then, three years later, he caught some Chilean gang members burglarizing his home, executed them in his soundproofed recording studio, and buried their bodies in the Upper Las Virgenes Canyon Open Space Preserve on the other side of his fence."

Eve remembered two things Nan told them at the morgue.

Evidence transfer always works both ways.

No amount of paint or patching will entirely hide the evidence of these killings.

Eve said, "Then LilGlok9 burned his studio down to destroy any forensic evidence of the killings. But he didn't entirely succeed. We found soundproofing insulation on the bodies."

Duncan added, "Ironically, rebuilding the studio cost him all the money he got from his insurance scam."

"LilGlok9 also lost his wife's ring for real this time," Eve said. "He wasn't aware that one of the men he'd killed and buried had swallowed it and some pearls."

Duncan said, "Fate has a nasty sense of humor."

"Got it," Burnside said, who didn't seem to Eve to be as amused as Fate and Duncan were by the ironic turn of events. "So now we jump forward to earlier this week, when LilGlok9 saw Kitty Winslow, who he hated for her success and for stealing his song, showing off her big, new engagement ring on TikTok. You believe it angered him so much that he sent some Crips over to steal it from her, but things went wrong, and Kitty got killed."

"Or he intended for her to die," Duncan said. "We don't know for sure."

Burnside nodded, then said, "You think the Crips escaped from the Winslow property to LilGlok9's house, hid out there until the next morning, and then slipped away unnoticed. Is that everything?"

"Almost," Eve said. "LilGlok9 probably also killed 2Fast, the rapper who was in the Kitty Winslow sex video with him, in a Las Vegas drive-by shooting, but we can't nail him for that one . . . *yet*."

Burnside said, "What you want now is a warrant to search LilGlok9's home for Kitty Winslow's jewelry and the murder weapon, and you want the blessing of this office to arrest him on multiple counts of insurance fraud, armed robbery, and murder."

"Since you'll have him on all of that," Eve said, "maybe you can strike a deal with him and agree to take the death penalty off the table if he gives up the shooters in the 2Fast drive-by and Kitty Winslow's killing."

That made Burnside finally crack a smile. "Ambitious agenda you have there, Eve."

Duncan smiled, too. "Four cases closed all at once. It may be a department record."

"Let's not get ahead of ourselves, Duncan," Burnside said, scribbling along the bottom of her legal pad.

Eve didn't like the sound of that. "You don't seem sold."

"Not on all of it," Burnside said. "We can make the case against him for insurance fraud, and maybe even for murdering the guy with the ring in his gut, though it won't be easy since all the evidence is circumstantial. We may also have enough to convince a judge to grant us a search warrant to look around LilGlok9's home for the rest of his wife's missing jewelry. If you're lucky, the search will turn up Kitty Winslow's ring, too, because otherwise you have absolutely nothing tying him to her robbery and murder."

Eve leaned forward in her chair, trying to control her rising anger. "The killings of the three Chilean intruders tie him to it."

"I don't see how."

"Three guys robbed and killed Kitty Winslow," Eve said.

"Not the three you dug up."

"It's how he got the idea," Eve said. "He wanted to make it look like a home invasion by Chilean burglary tourists, just like the ones who hit him."

"You can't prove that," Burnside said.

"It's obvious," Eve said.

"You seem to think it's enough that LilGlok9 slept with Kitty, lives down the street from her, and another diamond ring of similar size and value was stolen from him years ago and showed up in the corpse of a dead man buried near his house."

"Yes, and a jury will think so, too."

"But not a judge, Eve. He'll throw it out before the case ever gets to them. Your case is built on pure conjecture. There's no actual evidence. So take the win you have with the insurance scam and the three executions and be happy with that. I am."

Eve glanced at Duncan, who nodded. What else could they do? It wasn't like they had any choice.

"Okay," Eve said. "How long do you think it will take to get the warrant?"

"Give me an hour or two."

The meeting was over. Eve and Duncan stood up, and he said to Burnside, "That will give us time to notify the captain and the sheriff and start planning the arrest."

Burnside stood, too. "It's not the triple play you wanted, but it's still terrific police work. Great job, Detectives."

"Thanks," Eve said and walked out with Duncan.

As soon as they were in the hallway, heading for the elevator, he said, "A *quadruple* play, that's what we wanted."

"Is that even possible in baseball?"

"It would be stretching the metaphor, but that's what would have made this arrest legendary."

"I'll take the win we've got," she said.

"You really have changed," he said. "The old Eve Ronin would have felt cheated out of greatness."

"I have faith we'll get LilGlok9 for the other crimes." She punched the call button for the elevator, maybe a little too hard. "Just not today."

"I can't believe how chill you are with this."

She wasn't. Not at all. She was using every iota of willpower she had to accept the situation. It was becoming painfully clear to her that it was going to take an enormous amount of effort to change her natural behavior . . . and do it while hiding her true feelings.

"I can't believe you just said 'chill,'" she said.

The elevator arrived, the doors opening on an empty car. They stepped inside and Duncan said, "Maybe we'll find another corpse, but this time with Kitty's ring in his gut."

Eve hit the button for the lobby. "I like your positive attitude."

It took them only an hour to get back to Lost Hills station. Eve was relieved to see the *Ronin* crew had finished filming on the front steps and had moved somewhere else. Duncan had called ahead to notify the captain of the new development, so when they got to his office, he was expecting them and already had Sheriff Lansing on speakerphone. It didn't take long for Eve and Duncan to bring them up to date on their conclusions and the warrant that Burnside was seeking.

Dubois said, "This is really exceptional work."

Lansing's disembodied voice came over the speaker. "I told you yesterday that an arrest was imminent. I obviously have more faith in you two than you two have in yourselves. Burnside needs to get some balls and charge LilGlok9 with Winslow's killing, too."

Eve said, "We couldn't convince her."

"Screw her," Lansing snapped. "I'll go over her head to the DA himself, the ambitious, craven prick."

Duncan said, "He doesn't like you much."

That's an understatement, Eve thought. The district attorney had launched several corruption probes into the LASD, and in return, Lansing had endorsed a grassroots effort to get the DA recalled for being soft on crime. It was also common knowledge that both men were considering a run for mayor.

Lansing said, "We haven't always gotten along, but closing this high-profile case in less than seventy-two hours would look good for him, too."

"Not if LilGlok9 walks on the charge," Duncan said, surprising Eve with his bluntness.

"By the time the case goes to trial, Donuts, you two will have the evidence. You might even get it today when you serve the search warrant."

"I hope you're right."

"I was before and I am now," Lansing said. "It's worth the risk."

Dubois nodded. "It will be a huge morale boost for this station and the entire department after the events of the last year."

Lansing added, "It will also go a long way, Eve, towards repairing your relationship with your fellow deputies."

"Who've repeatedly tried to kill me," she said.

"But this time you are doing something that burnishes our image rather than tearing us down," Lansing said. "And you haven't threatened to blackmail me to get what you want."

Duncan said, "The day isn't over."

Lansing ignored that remark. "Captain Dubois, what's your game plan for the arrest?"

Dubois stood up to answer, which seemed silly to Eve. "We'll position deputies in the open space outside his house and at all three Hidden Hills gates. He's just one man—I'm not expecting a firefight."

"He's a Crip," Duncan said. "He may not go down so easy . . . and he may have some of his friends at his house."

"Good point," Lansing said. "I want eyes on LilGlok9, starting now. Have Tatum keep a loose but constant watch on him."

"Will do, sir," Dubois said, sitting down again.

"Our endgame is a press conference by ten p.m. so we can hit the eleven p.m. local news."

That was the last thing on Eve's mind. They discussed a few more details on the assault, manpower, staging area, et cetera, and how to do it without alerting the media camped out in front of all three Hidden Hills gates. It was decided the strike team would enter Hidden Hills on a horse trail from the Preserve. Since it was likely that LilGlok9 had security cameras, they knew they couldn't count on catching him by surprise.

Once Lansing was off the phone, the captain said that it was time to call Tatum.

Eve said, "How much do we tell him?"

"As little as possible," Dubois replied, surprising Eve.

"I'm glad we're in agreement about that, sir," she said. "I don't want the marshal galloping over to LilGlok9's place and lassoing him before we get there."

"I don't either," Dubois said. "You make the call. If it comes from me, he'll know we're planning something big. If the call comes from you, you'll just irritate him, so status quo."

Eve and Duncan went back to the squad room to make the call on her phone. Tatum answered right away. She said, "Duncan and I need you to keep an eye on LilGlok9 without him being aware of it. Can you tell us if he's still at home?"

"It's not that simple. His car is equipped with a transponder so he can go in and out of the residence gate. We track all that activity. I'll check and see if he's left today . . . and I'll also make sure I'm immediately alerted if he leaves."

"That would be great, thank you."

"But that's hardly a foolproof method of establishing his presence," Tatum said. "He could leave in someone else's car, or hop his fence for a stroll in the park, and we wouldn't know."

"Understood."

"If you don't hear from me again," Tatum said, "you can assume he's home."

"We appreciate the assistance." Eve disconnected the call and looked at Duncan. "I bet he bit through his tongue to stop from asking me why we want to keep an eye on LilGlok9."

"You're cruel, which you've already proven today by trying to starve me to death," Duncan said. "We skipped lunch."

"How is that my fault?"

"You were driving," he said.

"We were caught up in the momentum of the case."

"He who holdeth the steering wheel decideth whether to driveth-through or not to driveth-through," Duncan said. "It's in the Bible. Or maybe it was Shakespeare. I can't remember, because I'm too hungry. We need to eat or we could faint during the arrest."

"We wouldn't want that."

They made a run to the McDonald's on Las Virgenes while they waited for Burnside to get them the warrant.

They sat facing each other in a hard plastic booth by a window eating Quarter Pounder meals with large Diet Cokes. Once Eve smelled the fries, she realized she was starving, too. It was after 3:00 p.m. and all she'd had to eat that day was a granola bar at home and the Snickers bar at the morgue. She devoured her fries before she got to her burger.

Duncan ate his hamburger first, saving his fries. "Have you given any thought to what you're serving at your housewarming party tomorrow?"

"I figured I'd order some pizzas." She'd eaten her entire meal but found herself tempted by his large order of untouched fries.

"I was afraid of that. Scrap that terrible idea. I'll bring barbecue from Bludso's. Consider it my housewarming present."

"You're coming?"

Duncan emptied his fries on the tray and drizzled them with a packet of ketchup. "Of course I am."

"But I thought your deal with Gracie is that you'd spend your weekends in Palm Springs with her." Eve stole one of his fries.

"This case is going to run into tomorrow," he said. "And what kind of partner would I be if I didn't have your back at your first housewarming party?"

"I don't need backup for a family gathering." Eve reached for more of his fries and he slapped her hand.

"You were going to serve pizza," he said. "I've already saved you from disaster. What kind of desserts do you have?"

Eve's phone rang and the caller ID read BURNSIDE. She put the phone to her ear, since she couldn't go on speaker in the McDonald's dining room with this conversation.

Burnside greeted her with, "Lansing is an asshole. He went over my head."

Eve met Duncan's eye. "Duncan and I had nothing to do with that."

Hearing her words, Eve knew that he'd deduce what had happened. He nodded and kept eating his fries.

"I know that," Burnside said. "The DA and the sheriff are mortal enemies, except when it comes to self-aggrandizement. For that, they will set all their differences aside and agree to gamble with my career."

Eve lowered her voice to a whisper. "So we're arresting LilGlok9 for Kitty's murder, too."

But it was loud enough for Duncan to hear and he did a fist pump.

"Yes," Burnside said, "but I'm praying the search warrant comes up with something more than Sissy K's jewelry."

"The judge gave us the warrant?" Eve asked that for Duncan's benefit, getting another fist pump in response.

"I'll email it to you in a moment and then I'm coming out to Lost Hills," she said. "I want to observe the search to make sure that there won't be any evidentiary issues at the trial. And I want to be there for the interrogation."

And especially for the press conference, Eve thought. Burnside also had political ambitions, which could be derailed if the Winslow case failed.

"We'll save you a seat," Eve said and hung up.

Duncan finished his fries and clapped the salt off his hands. "Sometimes politics are a good thing."

CHAPTER
TWENTY-ONE

For the second time in three days, Eve was part of an LASD team hitting a house, only now she was leading it. Eve and four uniformed deputies went to the front door with guns drawn while Duncan and four other officers peeled off to the recording studio. They all wore Kevlar vests outside their shirts that read **SHERIFF** on the back and had radio mikes on their shoulders.

Eve approached the door and knocked. "Mr. Newton, it's Eve Ronin. Open up. We have a search warrant."

There was no answer. Eve tried the doorknob. It was unlocked. Eve and the officers spilled in, each person covering a corner of the huge great room, the open-concept design giving them a wide, unobstructed view of the kitchen, too.

Eve called out again. "This is the police. Come out with your hands up."

The deputies fanned out into the house, yelling "Clear" as they reached each room. But Eve remained in the great room. The house felt still and empty when they came in, as if the air hadn't moved. She was sure nobody was there.

She picked up the mike on her shoulder. "Duncan, the house is empty. Is he at the studio?"

Duncan replied, "No. The door was unlocked and it's empty, too."

"Eddie," Eve asked, "any sign of him in the park?"

Deputy Eddie Clayton responded from his position in the Preserve. "All quiet out here. He didn't make a run for it over the fence."

A deputy came in. "His cars are in the garage."

"Look for a safe room," Eve said. "Try the master bedroom closet first. I'm going to check the grounds."

Something felt wrong. She opened the back doors and moved cautiously into the yard, her gun drawn.

"LilGlok9, are you out here?"

Eve heard the hot tub going and remembered what he'd told them about his recording studio.

I'm basically living in here, creating, when I'm not chillin' in the hot tub with some Dom.

She followed the sound of bubbling water to the pool and rocky grotto she'd spotted the other day on her walk to the recording studio.

As she crept closer, she saw a chaise longue with a towel draped on the back. On the table beside it was a silver ice bucket with a champagne bottle inside. She checked the bucket. The ice was melted.

She moved into what appeared to be a man-made cave for the hot tub. Someone was sitting in the water, his back to her, his arms outstretched on either side of him on the coping, a butcher knife gripped in his right hand.

Eve aimed her gun at him. "Police. I need you to drop the knife and get out of the hot tub. Now."

He didn't move.

As she inched forward, she smelled the stench of rotting flesh and saw that the hot, churning water was red, a champagne glass bobbing in the center of the froth. There was blood on the knife and spattered on the coping.

Eve walked slowly around the hot tub and looked at LilGlok9 from the front. His throat was slit open, creating a gaping, grotesque smile that she'd seen before, on Mulholland and Mulholland.

Death was saying hello to her again with savage glee.

Did he kill himself . . . or was it a homicide?

Eve took her radio mike off her shoulder. "I found LilGlok9. He's dead in his hot tub. We need paramedics, the ME, and CSU out here right away."

"Roger that," Deputy Clayton said.

She couldn't see LilGlok9's body below the chest, but the hot tub looked like a boiling blood gumbo and she suspected his flesh had been parboiled right off, chunks of it now floating on the surface. There were some cuts on his bloated arms with a strange white powder in them. Her stomach churned and she was afraid she might throw up.

A gruff voice said, "Jesus Christ."

Startled, Eve whirled around, gun leveled, to see Tatum standing behind her.

"Back away, Tatum," she said, swallowing back bile and lowering her gun. "You shouldn't be here. This is a crime scene."

"It looks like a titanic fuckup to me, one that could have been avoided," Tatum said. "If you'd let me handle this earlier, man-to-man, he might still be alive."

"Thanks for your input, *Deputy*," she said, but the truth was, she was grateful for his interruption—the anger it provoked had stomped down her nausea. "Now go secure the scene and get the visitor log going. You know the drill."

Tatum walked away disgusted, not so much by the corpse but with her incompetence. Duncan passed him on his way over to the hot tub.

He stepped up beside Eve and studied the scene.

"I never thought he'd off himself," Duncan said. "I had LilGlok9 pegged as a fighter, not a quitter."

"If he killed himself, wouldn't he have slit his wrists instead of his throat?"

"The throat is faster," Duncan said. "I guess he didn't want to face life in prison."

"How did he know we were coming for him?"

"Maybe he saw the dig out in the park and realized it was only a matter of time until we put the pieces together."

"And he cracked under the pressure already?"

"He wasn't wrong," Duncan said. "We're here with handcuffs, aren't we?"

Even so, it didn't feel right to her. "As soon as CSU gets here and the scene is secured, let's check out the security cameras and see what happened."

When they did, they discovered the cameras were turned off shortly after noon, about the time they were making their case to Rebecca Burnside. They didn't know it then, but the case was closed before they'd even left her office.

Eve stood with Rebecca Burnside by the pool with Nan Baker and Emilia Lopez. The body had already been taken away, the hot tub was being strained and drained for evidence, and Duncan was leading a search of the house for Kitty's ring and the murder weapon.

Burnside hit Lopez with a direct question. "Is it suicide or murder?"

"My default position is homicide until proven otherwise," Lopez said. "But I don't see any defensive wounds or other signs of a struggle."

Eve asked, "What about those cuts on his arms?"

"Those aren't linear abrasions," Lopez said. "Those are streaks of formic acid created by ants feasting on the body."

"Yuck," Burnside said.

Nan held up an evidence bag containing the butcher knife. "I can tell you that this knife came from a matching set in the kitchen. There's an empty slot in the knife block where this one fit. And the blood spatter pattern on the coping and tiles tells me his heart was still pumping when his throat was cut."

Eve thought about the champagne bottle in the ice bucket. Before the forensic team got there, she'd noticed the bottle was empty.

"That doesn't mean that he was conscious, though," she said. "It looks like he drank an entire bottle of Dom. He might not have been in any condition to put up a fight even if there was one."

Lopez nodded. "That's one of many reasons why it's necessary to do a complete autopsy and run a tox screen before assuming it's a suicide, no matter what initial observation indicates."

Eve said, "I wonder why he turned off his security cameras this afternoon."

Lopez said, "Perhaps he didn't want the video of his suicide going viral the way his sex tape did."

"You think he's been dead since noon?"

"It's going to be hard to pinpoint the exact time of death since his body was left to parboil in a hot tub. It totally throws off the key external indicators, like lividity, algor mortis, and rigor mortis. Even liver temperature will be an unreliable indicator."

Nan spoke up. "But the ants on him and the blood spatter, and the fly larvae visible near his eyes, mouth, and nostrils, tells me he's been dead for at least five or six hours."

"But insect activity isn't an exact science," Lopez countered. "The postmortem clock was destroyed by the hot tub, so picking a time of death would be pure guesswork."

Burnside frowned. "Guesswork doesn't win homicide prosecutions, so I'm hoping for a suicide."

Lopez said, "I'll get you my full report and determination on Monday."

She and Nan both walked away, but Eve and Burnside lingered by the pool.

Burnside said, "LilGlok9 essentially admitted his guilt by killing himself and saved the county the time and expense of a trial."

"He also deprived the Winslows and 2Fast's family of justice and closure."

"We don't know that yet," Burnside said.

"Their killers are still out there," Eve said. "Now we will never know who they are. LilGlok9's death is their get out of jail free card. In fact, it could be why one of the shooters might have killed him."

Duncan walked up to them. "It would explain why he turned his cameras off. He didn't want any evidence around of them coming to visit him again."

Eve asked, "Have you found anything?"

Duncan shook his head. "No luck yet."

Burnside looked back at the house thoughtfully. "We don't know how involved his wife was in his insurance scam and his other crimes. Sissy K might be able to point us to the shooters. Has she been notified yet of his death?"

"I contacted her agent," Duncan said, "who just got back to me and said he reached her in Paris. She's taking the first flight back and should get in early tomorrow morning."

"One of you should meet her at the airport and find out what she knows about her husband's activities."

Eve said, "While she's still emotionally raw, psychologically vulnerable, and physically jet-lagged."

"That tends to promote truthfulness," Burnside said.

Duncan added, "Whether they want to be or not."

That didn't sit well with Eve. "It seems to me that it's a cruel and unfair way to treat someone who just lost their spouse and isn't suspected of a crime."

"Yes," Burnside said, "but it makes it more likely that justice will prevail, and if she's innocent, doesn't that ultimately benefit both her and society?"

Duncan nodded. "A win-win."

It still felt cruel to Eve. She looked past him and saw Lou Noomis coming over in his white Tyvek jumpsuit. He was a member of Nan's CSU team, a tall, very thin man with a large Adam's apple that reminded Eve of a snake trying to digest a whole rabbit. He held a pair of bolt cutters.

"We found a fake boulder in the yard," he said, "which isn't unusual in southwestern landscaping like this. All these rocks are fake." He gestured to the grotto with his bolt cutters. "But this one was placed on top of what appears to be recent fill and that got my attention."

"In other words," Duncan said, "you're saying someone dug a hole and stuck that boulder on top."

Noomis nodded. "We started digging and found a lockbox. I thought you'd like to be there for the grand opening."

That explains the bolt cutters, Eve thought.

She, Duncan, and Burnside followed Noomis into the garden between the pool and the recording studio, where two other CSU techs leaned on their shovels on either side of a three-foot-deep hole with a rusty lockbox at the bottom. The lockbox was sealed with a padlock.

Burnside looked at Noomis, then gestured to the box. "Open it up."

Noomis glanced at one of the two techs. "Document this."

The tech put down his shovel, retrieved a camera that had been set on the fake boulder, and began filming as Noomis stepped into the hole.

Noomis snapped the padlock and then, with his gloved hands, lifted the lid on the box. Inside were several ziplock bags filled with jewelry and one that held a Glock.

Burnside glanced at Eve and Duncan. "Would you know Kitty's ring if you saw it?"

"So would nine million Instagram users," Duncan said, taking a pair of gloves from his back pocket and putting them on. Noomis held the box open in front of him, as if offering them candy.

Duncan sorted through the baggies, found one, and held it up in front of Eve and Burnside, the sunlight glimmering off the huge diamond inside.

"That's Kitty's ring," he said.

Burnside smiled and looked at Eve. "I don't think you have to worry about closure anymore."

She left, then Eve and Duncan cataloged the jewelry with photos of their own, and Duncan emailed them to Drummond, the NYPD detective, and Murphy, the insurance company investigator, to see if any of it matched what was supposedly stolen five years ago.

Noomis took the gun for fingerprint analysis and ballistic testing to see if it matched the bullet that killed Kitty Winslow. He hoped they'd have the results in the morning, but Eve felt sure that it would match. The case was truly closed.

She turned to Duncan. "Lansing is planning a press conference in a few hours. I think we owe it to the Winslows to let them know what happened before they see it on TV."

"I agree, but the captain and the sheriff probably wouldn't."

"I wasn't planning on clearing it with them first," she said.

"Let's go," he said.

CHAPTER TWENTY-TWO

Eve and Duncan walked down to the Winslows' house and, from the street, saw Caleb riding his horse in the corral. He saw them, too, and rode over to the fence to greet them. He wore a sweat-stained cowboy hat, a faded denim shirt and jeans, and leather boots. There was a scarf tied around his neck, as if he expected to herd cattle or ride hard and have to breathe with a lot of trail dust in his face. Eve wouldn't have been surprised if he'd also been wearing a gun and holster, and maybe even his *Saddlesore* deputy badge, but he wasn't.

"Lots of law enforcement activity up the street," Caleb said. "Is it another burglary?"

Duncan said, "Mr. Winslow, is your family here?"

"They're working on their show at our house in the Oaks. Have you got something to say?"

Eve and Duncan shared a look. Caleb would have to do.

She said, "There have been some major developments in our investigation. We know who killed Kitty and we wanted you to hear it from us before it hits the news tonight."

"Who was it?"

Duncan said, "Charles Newton, but you may know him as LilGlok9. He was a rap singer who lived nearby."

"I know who he is," Caleb said.

"He hated Kitty for being richer and more famous than him and for stealing his song without giving him any credit," Duncan said. "We believe he got three Crips to steal her engagement ring. We aren't entirely sure if he meant for them to kill her or if it was an accident."

Caleb frowned, studied his hands for a moment, then asked, "Where is he now?"

"The morgue," Eve said.

He looked up at her, meeting her gaze. "Did you kill him?"

"No, sir. Either he slit his own throat in his hot tub," she said, "or someone did it for him."

"Wish it was me," Caleb sighed. "I wanted to kill him after that sex tape came out, but I'd have been wrong to do it then."

"Because it's murder," Eve said.

"Because the sex tape was Kitty's idea from the start," Caleb said. "He was the dupe. She knew exactly what she was doing. I suppose she thought she did this time, too, when she put that picture of herself out there with her ring." He paused for a moment, studying his hands again, then said, "You going to catch the men who did the killing?"

Duncan said, "We're certainly going to try."

"And then you'll bring 'em back to face the law," Caleb said.

"That's our job," Eve said.

Caleb turned in his saddle and looked out at the Preserve, the hills seeming to stretch out forever.

"On *Saddlesore*, that's what the marshal and I always said we'd do, too. Very solemnlike. But we ended up killing them ourselves every time. Because when we found them, they'd always put up a fight and we'd be glad they did." He turned back to Eve. "I hope they fight you."

Eve didn't. She hoped she never would have to fire her gun again. She'd already killed one man in her short career, and that was enough. "We'll come back another time to give you and your family all the details and to return Kitty's jewelry. But for now, will you please let your family know that justice has been done?"

He gave her a little nod. "I'll tell them what happened, but there hasn't been any justice."

Caleb turned his horse and headed slowly back toward the stable.

◆ ◆ ◆

Once again, Eve found herself standing outside the Lost Hills station, in the same spot where Erin Casey, playing her, stood during a fake press conference that morning. The gaffer's tape, setting their marks for the camera, was still on the pavement.

Eve was flanked by Captain Dubois, Duncan, and Burnside, all of them standing behind Sheriff Lansing, who stood at the podium facing easily a hundred reporters and dozens of TV cameras. He had big news to share and it seemed like the whole world was waiting to hear it.

"In their investigation of Kitty Winslow's killing, and in their relentless pursuit of the truth, LASD detectives Eve Ronin and Duncan Pavone discovered this horrific home invasion was the culmination of a series of violent burglaries and brutal murders that goes back at least five years, that took place in Los Angeles, Las Vegas, and New York City, and that were all orchestrated by one man, Charles Newton, the rapper and music company executive known as LilGlok9, who was found dead this afternoon at his Hidden Hills home."

He let that revelation sink in, and Eve got the sense he enjoyed the commotion it generated in the sea of reporters.

"More details will be released soon," he said, "but I can confirm that we found Kitty Winslow's stolen jewelry at his home, as well as irrefutable evidence connecting him to the execution-style murders of three Chilean gang members, whose bodies we've unearthed in shallow graves in the Upper Las Virgenes Canyon Open Space Preserve directly behind his property. We are withholding further details at this time to avoid compromising our ongoing investigation. But the upshot is this: Kitty Winslow's killing is solved."

He turned and gestured to Eve to step forward.

"Thank you, sir." She stepped up to the podium and was hit by a wave of vertigo, a collision of reality and fantasy so jarring it almost felt like a physical shove. She gripped the podium to steady herself. She took a deep breath to clear her head and spoke.

"Although the sheriff singled out me and my partner, Duncan Pavone, for praise, I must say, with all due respect, that we don't deserve it. The investigation was a joint effort involving numerous deputies, the medical examiner's office, our crime scene investigation unit, and a forensic anthropologist who consults with us. It was their tireless work and expertise that solved this case. But there is still much more work to be done before the victims of these crimes, and their grieving families, get the justice they deserve."

It was essentially the same speech she gave here not even a year ago, and that fake Eve gave in the same spot that morning. The vertigo came back, but it was a gentler wave this time.

Lansing stepped forward. At first, Eve thought it was because he'd sensed her dislocation and wanted to help, but that misconception was quickly dispelled when he leaned into the microphone to say, "We'll now take a few questions."

Someone called out, "How did LilGlok9 die?"

Lansing stepped aside, leaving Eve in the firing line.

"This is an ongoing investigation," she said. "There are details we can't discuss for legal and investigative reasons right now."

Kate Darrow, a local TV reporter, asked, "Was it a natural death? An accidental death? A suicide? Or a police shooting?"

She'd broken the story about LASD deputies beating prisoners in the county jail, creating a huge scandal. Lansing hated her. He almost leaped for the microphone to answer her question.

"It absolutely *wasn't* a police shooting."

Another reporter asked, "Are you saying that LilGlok9 has now murdered his two lovers from his infamous ménage à trois sex tape?"

Lansing deferred to Eve, who said, "At this time, we only have evidence linking LilGlok9 to Kitty Winslow's murder."

"But the sheriff certainly implied otherwise when he mentioned Las Vegas."

Yes, he did, Eve thought.

Lansing leaned into the microphone. "We only have time for a couple more questions. Any others?"

A reporter with a British accent asked, "Did LilGlok9 personally pull the trigger in any of these killings?"

Eve leaned into the microphone. "I can't say right now."

Another reporter called out, "If LilGlok9 was one of the Winslow home invaders, who were the other two?"

"I can't comment on that, either."

Darrow said, "Meaning you still don't know who shot Kitty Winslow."

Bingo, Eve thought. Darrow wasn't stupid. She was a sharp reporter.

"I didn't say that, Kate," Eve said. "Please don't make up quotes and put them in my mouth."

That's the job of the Ronin *writers.*

Zena Faust yelled out a question. "Will this case become an episode of your TV series? And will there be any crossovers with *Life with the Winslows*?"

It was as if Faust had read her mind. "I have nothing to do with the production of the TV show."

"You were on the set today," Faust countered.

"Because they were shooting right here, where I work," Eve said. "I am a homicide detective. That's my only job."

"So this *could* become an episode," Faust said.

"I don't know, Zena. But I can assure you I won't be appearing on the Winslows' show."

"But will they be on yours?"

Lansing stepped up to the podium. "That's all the questions we have time for. Thank you for coming. We'll be handing out press releases with further details."

Eve joined Duncan in the lobby. Her heart was racing and she felt a bead of sweat trickle down her back.

She said, "Maybe you should handle the next press conference."

"It wouldn't be nearly as much fun."

"It was hell for me," she said.

"That's what made it fun."

Eve looked back outside at the reporters, who were dispersing. "Can you believe Zena Faust asking me all those loaded questions about the show? She was here this morning, standing in that same spot, asking fake me questions."

"I wonder if she knows the difference," Duncan said. "I wonder if anybody will."

"That's what scares me," she said.

"No, what scares you is that someday you might not know the difference."

Like Caleb Winslow. Like his entire family.

Before she could tumble too far down that frightening rabbit hole, Lansing came in and joined them.

"You did good, sharing the credit and deflecting specific questions," Lansing said, and then smiled. "You even got in a plug for your show."

"I wish the show hadn't come up."

Lansing dismissed her concern. "It was inevitable. The Winslows are celebrities and so are you. It's why you were the perfect detective for this case. You understand each other."

"I don't understand them at all," she said. But now her theory about why she'd been selected for this case was confirmed as fact.

"You understand more than anybody else in Lost Hills does," Lansing said. "I heard you have Nick Egan playing me. He's got a sex tape, just like Kitty Winslow."

"Who doesn't?" Duncan said.

"I have nothing to do with casting, sir," Eve said. "But if I did, I certainly wouldn't have picked him, for a variety of reasons. I'm sure it wasn't meant as a slight."

"I suppose it could be worse," Lansing said. "At least the man is hung like a horse."

Lansing walked away to confer with Captain Dubois and Rebecca Burnside. Eve looked at Duncan.

"Is that all men care about?"

"Not all men," Duncan said, "but certainly actors and politicians."

They went down the hall to the squad room, where Garvey and Biddle were on their way out the door. They congratulated Eve and Duncan on closing the case.

"It's always good when we get a win," Biddle said, as if it were necessary to make an excuse for saying something nice to Eve.

"It's a shame," Garvey said. "I loved LilGlok9's music. Now I won't be able to listen to any of it."

Crockett and Tubbs walked out together. Duncan turned to Eve.

"Sissy K's flight arrives tomorrow at LAX at eight a.m. I can go and meet her."

"I'll go, too."

"You have a housewarming party tomorrow," he said.

"Not until noon," she said. "It's a picnic in the backyard and a tour of my house. It doesn't require a lot of prep."

"Okay," he said. "I'll see you at Customs at the Tom Bradley Terminal."

Deathfist and Donuts walked out together.

Eve went from the station to the Ralphs grocery store at the Commons, where she bought soft drinks, water, big bags of chips, some packaged cookies and cakes, and a bunch of paper plates, napkins, and plastic cutlery.

She'd intended to plant some more flowers in the front yard, and maybe lay out some sod over the rabbit holes before the party, but there were no nurseries still open this late . . . and tomorrow morning, she had to go to the airport.

It reminded her that Daniel lived in West LA.

Eve went home just long enough to drop off everything she'd bought, then got back into her car.

Daniel lived on the second floor of an apartment building with outdoor walkways, like a motel, and that was arranged in a square around a central patio that had once been a swimming pool but that the landlord had long ago filled in and turned into a flower garden.

She knocked on the door of his apartment. He opened it, wearing a ratty bathrobe over a white T-shirt and pajama bottoms. His feet were in slippers lined inside with fake fur.

"This is weird," he said. "I just watched you on TV and here you are. It's almost like you stepped right off the screen into reality."

"I'm real," she said.

"So is the Eve Ronin I was watching on TV."

"I guess it depends which one of me you're looking at," she said.

"So far, it's only you," Daniel said. "I haven't seen the fictional you yet."

"Can I come in?" Eve asked.

"Oh, yes, right. Sorry." He stepped aside. "Congratulations on closing the case."

She came in and he closed the door behind her.

She said, "There's still a lot we don't know and assumptions we can't actually prove."

"Now that LilGlok9 is dead," he said, "that doesn't matter much."

"It does to me."

His apartment was a one bedroom, the living room and kitchen sharing the same space. It was clean and orderly, the shelves on one wall filled with souvenirs from his world travels digging up human bones. None of them were things that a tourist would find in a gift shop. They were all items with personal meaning to him. The monologue of a late-night TV talk show host was muted on the flat-screen TV mounted on the wall facing his leather couch.

"What brings you to my neighborhood?" Daniel asked.

"Three things," she said. "I'm meeting Sissy K, LilGlok9's widow, at LAX tomorrow at eight a.m. and your place is on my way."

"That's in nearly nine hours."

"I don't like to be late. And I wanted to personally invite you to my housewarming party tomorrow."

"Isn't it a family affair?"

"My sister, Lisa, will probably bring Tom, the deputy she's been dating. My agent is coming, and Duncan is going to be there, too."

"And you want me there?" Daniel said.

"I do. I'd miss you if you weren't," Eve said. "The fact is, I'm missing you now."

He stepped up to her. "I'm right here."

"You weren't last night."

"Since we got back from Tarawa," he said, "I've had the feeling that you think things are moving too fast . . . that I'm crowding you."

"That's true. It's how I feel."

"Yes!" Daniel smiled and raised his fists in the air, delighted. His reaction totally confused her.

"You're *happy* about that?"

"It's nice to guess right for a change . . . and because no woman has ever felt I was getting too close. Actually, the opposite," he said. "But I'm also confused, because if I'm crowding you, why are you here now and why do you want to introduce me to your family tomorrow?"

It was a hard question for her to answer, especially if she was honest. She took a deep breath and steeled herself for it.

"I want you in my life . . . I'm just not sure how that's going to work yet. But if it's going to, my life includes my family, or at least it should, so I'd like them to meet you," Eve said, certain that she'd come off as a rambling idiot. "Does that make sense?"

He shrugged. "Sure."

She loved it when he shrugged. "What about you? What do you need?"

"More conversations like this so I don't have to guess how you feel."

"Even if what I feel doesn't make any sense?"

"Two things have doomed my past relationships," Daniel said. "One, I have no idea what women are thinking, so I immediately assume it's that they want to dump me. Two, I get really into my work, to the exclusion of everything else, and I can be away on digs for months at a time, so women think I'm not that into them, which isn't true."

"You're committed to your job," Eve said.

"So are you. It's who you are," Daniel said. "I think that makes us a good fit . . . even if it's not an easy one."

"I think you're right," she said. "Does that mean you'll come tomorrow?"

"I can't wait," he said. "What's the third thing?"

"What do you mean?"

"You said there were three things you came here for. You only gave me two."

Eve put her arms around him and got very close. "I'm demanding my orgasm."

"Now?"

"This instant," she said.

"These just officially became my lucky bathrobe and slippers."

And they kissed.

CHAPTER
TWENTY-THREE

The windowless US Customs office in the basement of the Tom Bradley International Terminal at LAX resembled the morgue, except the stainless-steel tables were meant for opening up suitcases instead of corpses. There were also several desks for interviewing the travelers whose suitcases were being searched or who'd been flagged for suspicious behavior or issues with their passports.

Eve and Duncan waited at one of the desks with uniformed US Customs agent Barry Post, a man in his late twenties with naturally black hair that contrasted sharply with his pale skin. It made Eve wonder how often Post got out of this basement into the sunlight or if he was a vampire.

Post said, "Two of our agents are meeting Sharon Kirkeby Newton, a.k.a. Sissy K, on the plane and escorting her here."

"Thank you," Eve said. "We appreciate it."

"There's a considerable media contingent waiting outside the terminal for her," Post said. "If she wishes, we can escort her out another exit so she can avoid them. But you'd be surprised how often celebrities decline that offer . . . and then pretend to be surprised and upset to see the mob waiting for them."

"No, I wouldn't."

"We'll also collect her luggage for her and bring it here. Are you aware of any reason we should inspect it?"

Duncan said, "Her husband is dead and is the primary suspect in the robbery and murder of Kitty Winslow. Unless he FedEx'd the murder weapon to his wife and she brought it back in her luggage, I can't imagine there's anything in there we'd be interested in. But thanks for asking."

"I think I'll search it anyway," Post said.

Eve said, "She's a grieving widow."

"You haven't been on TikTok," he said. "There are pictures of her fingering BabyCarol, the Aussie hip-hop artist, under her skirt during the Vuitton show."

Duncan said, "Maybe that's how she grieves."

Post took out his cell phone. "Wanna see?"

"No, thanks," Duncan said.

That's when two agents came in with Sissy K, wheeling three huge, and bulging, Louis Vuitton suitcases for her. She looked like an African American version of Kitty Winslow, with the same surgically enhanced buttocks, accentuated by skintight leather pants, and enormous breasts, which were barely contained in a low-cut tank top with unusually long shoulder straps to allow for plenty of "side boob" views.

Sissy K's fingernails were polished with glitter and she wore rings on just about every finger, which Eve thought must have driven the metal detectors crazy at Charles de Gaulle Airport.

She put her hands on her substantial hips and said, "What is all this about?"

Duncan and Eve stood up and he said, "I'm Los Angeles County sheriff's detective Duncan Pavone and this my partner, Eve Ronin. We want to express our condolences on your loss."

"By dragging me off the plane like some kind of international criminal?"

Post stepped forward now. "I'm Special Agent Barry Post, US Customs and Border Protection. We thought you'd appreciate a private, expedited customs screening to avoid the crowds and attention during this difficult time."

"In a windowless pit?" she said. "Don't you have a VIP section with some decor?"

Post nodded to the two agents, who wheeled her suitcases to one of the stainless-steel tables, and then held out his hand to Sissy K. "May I see your passport?"

She reached into her Hermès bag, pulled out her passport, and handed it to him. "Some service."

Eve said, "We also have some important questions we need to ask you."

Sissy K watched Post take her passport back to the desk and sit down to go through it. "You can answer mine first. Who killed my husband . . . and why?"

Eve said, "Right now, we aren't certain if he was killed or if he committed suicide."

Post stamped her passport, got up, and returned it to her.

Sissy K shoved the passport back into her purse. "Of course he was murdered. Why would he kill himself?"

"We were about to arrest him on multiple counts of robbery and murder."

"He'd welcome that," Sissy K said. "It would only add to his street cred to be considered that dangerous, especially now that he's rich, fat, and happy in Hidden Hills."

"He was that dangerous," Duncan said. "Two years ago, he executed three men in his recording studio, buried them behind your house, then burned the studio to the ground."

"That's ridiculous," she said. "Why would he do that?"

"Because he caught them stealing your jewelry," Duncan said. "The jewelry you reported stolen five years ago at the Four Seasons in New York."

Duncan took out his phone and showed her a photo of the ring. Her eyes widened in surprise. She definitely recognized it.

"That's my wedding ring," she said. "Where did you find that?"

"In the stomach of one of the men your husband killed."

Sissy K sat down in one of the chairs, leaning one hand on the desk for support. Agent Post hurried over to her.

"Can I get you something to drink?" he asked.

Sissy K nodded. "Vodka tonic, no ice."

"I was thinking more along the lines of a bottle of water or a Coke."

"Coke," she said.

Post went off to get it. Duncan sat down in the chair in front of her and Eve remained standing.

Eve said, "We also believe he killed Kitty Winslow and took her engagement ring."

"I heard that part before I left Paris," Sissy K said. "It's horseshit."

Duncan said, "Which he trained his horse to leave each day on her front porch."

She grinned at that, and it also drew a tear. "He loved that. He had such a great sense of humor."

Sissy K wiped the tear away and Post brought her a can of Coke.

"Thanks, Barry." She popped the top open and took a big sip.

"Agent Post," he said and walked away, but not so far that he couldn't eavesdrop on the conversation.

Eve was feeling less sympathy for Sissy K with each passing moment. "You were quick to say he didn't kill Kitty, but you didn't jump to his defense over your ring or the executions."

"Because now a lot of things make sense." She reached into her purse and pulled out a tiny bottle of vodka, probably given to her on the plane.

"Like what?"

Sissy K opened the bottle and poured some of it into the Coke can, then set the bottle on the table. "My husband was a Crip and he wanted out. But there's only two ways to leave. One is in a pine box. The other . . ."

"Is to buy your way out," Duncan said. "How much did they want?"

"Two million, which is pocket change now but we didn't have it then. I always wondered where he got it. Now I know." She took another drink of her Coke and vodka. "Anyone have a lime?"

Eve said, "You had no idea the theft of your jewelry was an insurance scam and that he had it all the time?"

Sissy K pinned her with a look. "Do you really think I'd tell you if I did?"

"Was your husband responsible for the drive-by shooting of 2Fast in Las Vegas?"

"He left the Crips," Sissy K said, "but they still owed him some favors."

"Is that a yes?" Eve asked.

Sissy K shrugged. "It's an informed opinion. Knowing about a homicide and not informing the police would be a felony. I could be charged as some kind of accomplice, couldn't I?"

"You sound familiar with the criminal law."

"I spoke to a lawyer who is," she said. "He's waiting for me outside. Should we invite him in?"

"That's up to you," Eve said.

Duncan said, "Did the Crips still owe Chuck any more favors?"

Sissy K looked at him. "You mean did the Crips take that bitch Kitty's ring and shoot her in the face for him?"

"Yes."

"No, they didn't do that."

"How can you be certain?"

"Because if they did," Sissy K said, "they'd have the ring, not my husband. They'd have kept it and screwed him over. What could he have done about it? Sue them? It would be part of the price for the hit."

That was a good point, Eve thought. She glanced at Duncan and saw that he felt the same way. The interview was over. Post sensed it and stepped forward. It was his turn at Sissy K now.

"You are allowed to bring back up to $1,600 in goods duty-free," he said. "Do you have anything to declare?"

Sissy finished her drink and set the can on the table. "Nope."

"Then you won't mind if we take a look at your bags."

Sissy gave him a wave, as if he really needed her permission. Post nodded at the two agents, who hefted her suitcases onto the table and unzipped them. The suitcases were filled with designer handbags.

Eve and Duncan got up, and she said, "Thank you for your time and, again, we're sorry for your loss."

Sissy K scowled at her. "How can you be sorry if you thought he was a murderer?"

"Because you loved him and now you've lost him." Eve handed her a card. "Feel free to contact us if you have any further questions but I'm sure we'll be in touch."

The two detectives walked to the door. Post confronted Sissy K and pointed to the suitcases on the table.

"Are you sure you have nothing to declare? Each one of those designer handbags is probably worth at least $5,000."

"More than that, sweetie. I brought them all with me."

"Come on," Post said. "There must be two dozen here, all in mint condition, as if they'd never been used."

"I take very good care of my bags and I wear a different one each day."

"I find that hard to believe," Post said.

Sissy K smiled at him. "You change your underwear every day, don't you, Barry?"

Eve and Duncan walked out of the room and into the hallway.

Duncan said, "Now we know the full story behind the insurance scam. Detective Drummond owes us dinner if we're ever in the Big Apple."

"She made a good point about Kitty's ring."

They walked down the hall to the elevator and Eve hit the call button.

"If the guys he used for the job were Crips," Duncan said. "Maybe they weren't. We may never know who killed 2Fast or Kitty, but at least we know who gave the order. Not every case can be wrapped up in a nice little bow. But the good news is, it will be on your show."

"I feel so much better now," she said. They got into the elevator and rode it up to street level.

"You're fortunate you get a chance to rewrite your cases the way you wanted them to turn out."

"I'm not doing any writing or suggesting any stories for the show," Eve said and they stepped off the elevator into the far end of the packed arrivals lobby, crammed with family members and drivers waiting to pick up international travelers. There were also a lot more paparazzi than usual waiting for celebrities to show up, obviously because they'd been tipped off that Sissy K was arriving.

"Are you picking up the barbecue now?" she asked.

"Change of plans. Since we're out this way, we're taking advantage of the culinary opportunity," he said. "Roscoe's House of Chicken and Waffles is close by, right on Manchester, so you're picking up chicken, biscuits, and all the fixins'."

"I am?"

"Don't skimp on the biscuits," he said. "You want a pile of them . . . and buckets of gravy."

"Buckets?"

"And while you're doing that, I'll stop at Randy's Donuts, also on Manchester, and get a wide assortment of goodies, but definitely some Bacon Maple Long Johns, Raised Roasted Coconuts, and Lemon-Frosted Old-Fashioneds. How many people are coming?"

"A dozen," she said.

"We need at least forty-eight donuts."

"Why?" she said. "Nobody but you is going to eat four donuts."

"Three of your guests are cops," he said. "Four is the bare minimum they're each gonna eat. But don't worry—if there are any leftovers, I'll take them."

"I appreciate the sacrifice," Eve said. "See you at my place."

CHAPTER TWENTY-FOUR

The weather was cooperating. It was a bright, sunny day with clear blue skies. Eve and Daniel had brought the dining room table outside, put a tablecloth on it, and laid out all the food and silverware. Duncan had carefully arranged the donuts on a platter. All the drinks were in an icebox by the kitchen door, nice and chilled. There was nothing to do now but wait for the guests to arrive.

Daniel came outside, wearing a polo shirt, shorts, and sandals. Eve stood outside in a V-neck top and jeans, surveying the table one more time. He slipped his arm around her waist. It felt good.

"Are you nervous?" he asked.

"I was calmer when my car went off a cliff."

"How could this be any worse?"

"My mother wasn't there," she said. "And neither were you."

"If you survived that, you can certainly survive this."

"It's not me I'm worried about," she said, giving him a smile.

"She's not going to scare me away," Daniel said.

Duncan came out of the house eating a maple bar. It was his second. Or maybe his third. "I hope you don't mind, but I gave myself a tour. I love what you've done with the place."

"Thank you," she said.

"You've been here before?" Daniel asked.

"Yeah," Duncan said. "But there was a lot more blood last time."

"This was a crime scene?" Daniel said.

Shit, Eve thought.

Duncan looked at her. "You didn't tell him?"

"Actually, I haven't told anybody."

"It's hardly a secret," Duncan said. "Everybody in Oakdale knows."

"But very few outside the gates and nobody in my family," Eve said. "I don't know how it would go over with them, especially my niece. So please don't mention it."

"You've got it. I won't bring up the dead baby," Duncan said, then walked away after lobbing that grenade.

Daniel faced Eve. "There was a dead baby?"

"I don't want to get into it," Eve said. "Are you going to have a problem staying here now?"

"No, of course not. I spend my days in graves. I just haven't slept in any before, that's all."

"My bed is not a grave," she said.

"No, of course it's not, it's very lively, no death there," Daniel said. "I'm going to go put something glazed in my mouth instead of my foot."

He made an abrupt about-face and headed for the donuts.

The party is off to a great start, she thought.

The doorbell rang. Eve went to the front door and opened it. Her sister, Lisa, stood there, holding hands with Tom Ross.

"Come on in," Eve said, stepping aside.

Lisa walked past her into the entry hall. She had naturally curly black hair and was three years younger and a few inches shorter than Eve. They shared their mother's piercing blue eyes, but that was where the physical similarities ended because they had different absentee fathers. Lisa's father was a grip—part of the crew responsible for laying camera track, building scaffolding, and putting together sets—who'd dated Jen for a few weeks and then disappeared.

"My God," Lisa said. "It's a mansion."

"Any place would seem big compared to my old condo."

Lisa moved off toward the kitchen and gasped when she saw the massive island.

Tom glanced around the room, then said to Eve, "Wasn't this a crime scene?"

Oh, shit. She forgot that Tom had been in the house before and so had Eddie Clayton, who she'd also invited to the party. She hoped Lisa hadn't heard Tom.

Eve pulled Tom aside. "It's a tract home. There are fifty other houses here with the same floor plan. You're thinking of one of the others, up the street." Then, in a lower voice, she said, "You should text Eddie so he doesn't make the same mistake."

Tom got the message. "Got it. I'll do that. Right now."

He took out his phone and Eve went into the kitchen to join Lisa, who was standing at the french doors, looking out at the backyard and hills beyond.

"I love the view," Lisa said.

"So do I. It makes the backyard seem like it goes on forever. It also gives me privacy."

"Who is that with Duncan?" Lisa nodded toward Daniel, who was chatting with Duncan over the donuts. It appeared that Duncan was giving some sort of donut lecture.

Eve took a deep breath. "That's Daniel Brooks."

"The man you went off to see for your South Seas sexcation?"

"It was a medical leave," Eve said. "I was recuperating from a gunshot wound."

"I know that. I'm a nurse. Nonstop sex is frequently prescribed as physical therapy for an injured knee. But I thought the PT was finished."

"It is," Eve said. "I think he's become my boyfriend."

"You *think*?"

"This is the first time the word 'boyfriend' has come out of my mouth in a long, long time."

"I want to meet him," Lisa said.

Eve led her sister outside and over to the table. But before she could say anything, Duncan smiled and gave Lisa a hug.

"Lisa! So good to see you," he said, then took a step back to get a look at her. "This may be the first time I've seen you out of a nurse's uniform."

"And I'm finally seeing how you earned your nickname."

Daniel said, "What's his nickname?"

Eve said, "Donuts."

"Duncan Donuts," Daniel said with a big grin. "That's great."

Duncan said, "Nobody asked me if I liked it."

"I'm not wild about Deathfist, either," Eve said.

"At least it's tough," Duncan said.

Lisa held out her hand to Daniel. "You must be Daniel. I'm Eve's sister. I've heard so much about you."

He shook her hand. "You have?"

"Eve tells me everything."

"Good, then maybe you can fill me in," he said. "How am I doing with her?"

"She hasn't shot you yet," Lisa said. "That's a good sign."

The doorbell rang again. Eve ran inside to answer the door, though she was worried what Lisa might say in her absence. She opened the door and saw her younger brother, Kenny, his wife, Rachel, and their five-year-old daughter, Cassie, who was holding a lopsided, squarish chocolate cake. She held it out to Eve.

"I baked you a cake," Cassie said. "It's a house."

Eve squatted down to take the tray from her and gave her a kiss on the cheek. "It's wonderful, thank you. It's so beautiful that I am going to feel bad eating it."

"I won't. It's chocolate."

Eve stood up and led them all to the kitchen. Kenny was five years younger than Eve and, like Lisa, had a different father, a struggling actor who eventually gave up and moved back to Wisconsin.

She set the cake on the island. Kenny and Rachel went to the french doors to look out at the view.

Rachel was impressed. "You've got a huge backyard."

"It's an illusion created by the view," Eve said. "Your yard is actually bigger."

"The Jacuzzi is nice," Kenny said. "But you need a pool."

"Why?"

"So I can clean it. I want to expand my business into the West Valley," Kenny said. "Your neighbors will see my truck and hire me to clean their pools. That's how it works."

"You could just come here once a week and park your truck out front for a half hour," Eve said.

"Good idea."

"You can plant some flowers and lay some sod while you're at it," Eve said, "so you have something to do."

Rachel said, "Not until he does the gardening in our yard."

"Do you want the grand tour?" Eve asked.

"Absolutely!"

Eve took them around the house and was showing Cassie the empty bedroom that she'd set aside just for her visits when she heard Jen's unmistakably smoky voice, coming from the living room.

She left Cassie with her parents and went down the hall to find Jen at the open french doors, looking at the view. Everyone seemed drawn to it. Jen was in a loudly colorful, busy blouse and a pair of capri pants, an outfit that evoked a young Ann-Margret, which was exactly the effect she was going for because she still had the body, with the help of some plastic surgery, to pull it off. As Eve approached, she followed Jen's gaze and saw Vince Nyby chatting with Daniel.

What the hell? Eve marched up to her mom. "You brought Vince?"

"Your father didn't get an invitation," Jen said.

"On purpose," Eve said tightly, trying to control her rising anger. "He's one of the reasons why I live behind a gate. I don't want him ever showing up at my door . . . and yet, here he is."

"He hasn't been to a family gathering in years."

"Because he was an absentee father."

Jen gestured to the kitchen counter, where there was a gift-wrapped box with a ribbon on it. "He brought you a toaster oven."

"It's the first gift he's given me that isn't a Barbie doll."

"I think that was very sweet of him," Jen said. "He's trying to make amends. You could try putting the past behind you, where it belongs."

"You're just sucking up to him to get more screen time," Eve said. "Have you forgotten how that worked out for you before?"

"How can I? You're standing right in front of me in this spectacular house." Jen glanced around the large room. "Speaking of which, how much did you pay for this place?"

"That's an inappropriate question," Eve said.

"I'll just look it up on Zillow. Which one of the bedrooms is mine?"

"You don't have one because you're not living here."

"Not now, of course. I lead a very active life and cherish my independence," Jen said. "But it will be nice to have a place to stay in the valley so I can spend more time with my grandchildren."

"You only have one," Eve said.

"I might have more soon, especially if you aren't using protection. Is your lover here or was it a one-night stand?"

"He's over there, talking to Vince. His name is Daniel," Eve said. "Don't embarrass me."

"If I'd known he'd be here, I would have brought him a copy of *Becoming Cliterate*, which should be required reading for all men."

"Now you know why I didn't tell you."

"Come to think of it," Jen said, "I may have a copy in my car."

"Why would you?"

"In case of a roadside emergency."

There was a knock at the door. Eve left her mother to see who was there. It was Eddie, and he brought a six-pack of Coors, which he held out as an offering.

"These are for you. I hope you aren't one of those craft beer people."

"I'm old-school. Budweiser and Coors." Eve took the six-pack. "Thanks."

Eddie stepped inside, took the place in with a look, and nodded his approval. "It looks much better without the body bag in the living room."

Eve looked to see if her mom had heard, but thankfully she was busy hugging Cassie. "Didn't Tom text you?"

Eddie grinned. "Yeah, but I wanted to see you rattled. It's a first. Can I take a picture?"

Eve shoved him toward the backyard. "Go eat a donut."

Eddie went out to the backyard and Eve turned to see Linwood strolling through the open front door, carrying a Harrods canvas grocery bag.

He smiled when he saw her. "What a beautiful home."

"It's thanks to your dealmaking that I have it."

"Are you on the security committee yet?"

"Never," she said. "I don't want to become Oakdale's Amos Tatum."

"You're an owner, he's a renter. That's a big difference. In a few months, you could be running this place."

"That has zero appeal to me."

"We'll see." Linwood held out the bag to her. "I brought you some jam and crème fraîche."

Eve took the bag. "Thank you. It will go great with the buttermilk biscuits and donuts."

She gestured to the food outside. Linwood looked past her and saw all the guests. "I'm surprised to see Vince here."

"So am I," she said. "Is it going to be awkward for you to see an ex-client?"

"We're about to find out."

Vince came over to Linwood, his arms outstretched for a hug. "Linny!"

"Vinny!" Linwood said. They hugged like old, dear friends. Linwood pulled back, looking at Vince at arm's length. "You look terrific. What's your secret?"

"Tantric sex and prunes."

"I hope not both at once," Linwood said, then took the bag back from Eve. "Excuse me, I need to get this into a refrigerator before it goes bad."

Linwood hustled to the kitchen, leaving Eve and Vince alone.

Vince watched after him. "Don't be fooled, hardnose. He's not your friend. He's in this for himself. He'll betray you the second he thinks it will make him an extra buck."

"But until then, he's out there fighting for me," Eve said. "Except for Duncan, I'm not used to that from the men in my life."

"You've got me," Vince said.

Eve laughed.

He said, "I'm fighting for you every day on the set."

Eve raised her hand in a halting gesture. "Please, Vince, just stop. Don't say another word to me about us or the show or I'll shoot you. Think of it as my housewarming gift."

"Okay, but I already got you a toaster."

Eve just walked away, joining her guests outside.

The next few hours went along just fine. Her mom didn't embarrass or antagonize her, and neither did Vince. The food was delicious, the weather was great, and everybody seemed to be having a good time.

Eve sat on a chaise longue, eating chicken and having one of Eddie's beers, feeling completely relaxed.

This was what a home was supposed to be. A peaceful place where you could feel safe, rooted, and appreciated, surrounded by family, friends, coworkers, and lovers.

She'd wanted a real home her whole life and to finally have one now made her so unexpectedly happy that she almost cried.

Linwood took a seat on the edge of the other chaise longue beside hers and she forced back the emotions.

"Good things are happening for you, Eve."

"I was just thinking about that."

"The network is ecstatic about the publicity you're getting on the Winslow case," he said. "It's millions of dollars in free, global advertising for the series."

Those weren't the good things she'd been thinking about, but it did raise a thought.

"Did you contribute to Lansing's last campaign for sheriff and urge everyone you know in the industry to do the same?"

"I did. He's a good man."

"Would you support him financially if he runs for reelection or for another office?"

"Yes, I would," Linwood said.

"Did you suggest to him that it would be a good idea to put me on the Winslow case?"

Linwood smiled at her. "I didn't have to. He's a very smart man."

"When he assigned me to it, was he thinking about what was best for the case or what would benefit his political ambitions?"

"What's good for one is good for the other," he said. "You two aren't the only ones benefiting from the publicity. Have you heard the news about the Winslows?"

"No."

"Their series is being retooled. It's going to become a true-crime reality show, focusing on the murder, the trial, and the aftermath."

"There isn't going to be a trial, at least not of LilGlok9," she said. "He's dead. We can't prosecute a corpse."

"It doesn't matter. The genre is superhot right now and this is a natural transition. *Life with the Winslows* has received a two-season pickup. That's worth millions of dollars."

"Good for them," Eve said.

"What would you think about being a recurring character on their show?"

She stared at him. "You're joking, right?"

"You'd just be doing the job you're doing already but with cameras watching," Linwood said. "You won't even notice them."

And that was when she looked past Linwood and saw the drone hovering over the hillside ravine at the edge of her property, its camera pointed at her house.

"Excuse me." Eve set down her plate, got up, and found Kenny playing Frisbee with Cassie on the lawn. She went up to him. "Can you please take Cassie inside for a minute, maybe get her decorating ideas for her guest room?"

"Why now?"

"There's something I'm going to do that's not safe for children."

"I don't want to miss that," he said.

"Then have Rachel take her in. It will only be for a few minutes."

He took Cassie by the hand and went over to Rachel, who was talking to Jen.

Eve went straight to her bedroom, opened the gun safe, and took out her Glock. She marched back outside, her gun held down beside her leg. Cassie and Rachel were gone.

Vince spotted her coming at him with the gun and backed away. "What did I say?"

Eve ignored him, walked to the edge of her yard, and took aim at the drone. The aircraft abruptly banked away, but not fast enough. She fired one shot, a direct hit.

The drone blew apart, the pieces raining down on the hillside as the gunshot reverberated in the air.

Eve turned to Tom, who rushed up to her side. "Would you mind getting the pieces of that drone for me? I have to go answer the phone."

Tom said, "It isn't ringing."

"It will be."

She lowered her weapon and marched back into the house, but not before she heard Linwood say to her in passing, "That has got to go in the show."

She went back to the gun safe, put the weapon away, and returned to the living room, where Duncan was waiting.

"You really are just like Tatum," he said.

"I didn't have one of his drone zappers or I would have used it," she said. "That was a paparazzo's drone invading my privacy, and that's against the law."

"So is the negligent discharge of a firearm."

"That wasn't negligent," Eve said. "I'm a trained firearms professional. The target was out in the open, away from homes, vehicles, or individuals, and I hit it with one shot, endangering no one. I even sent my niece to a bedroom, far away from the shooting."

But Cassie was out now, running into the backyard ahead of Rachel, who shook her head at Eve like she was a misbehaving child.

Duncan said, "Well, at least now I know what I'm getting you for Christmas."

"I don't need a drone zapper."

"I was thinking of a Stetson."

The house phone rang in the kitchen.

"I'll get that," she said. "Could you call the station and let them know they can ignore calls of a shot fired from Oakdale?"

"Sure."

Duncan took out his cell phone to make the call and Eve went into the kitchen to pick up her phone.

"Hello," she said.

"This is Harvey Mapes at the guard gate. I'm getting calls about gunfire on your street."

"It was one shot and it was me," Eve said.

"What did you shoot?"

"A rattlesnake."

"The HOA frowns on homeowners firing weapons in the community," Harvey said.

"How would they feel about a five-year-old girl dying from a snake-bite?" Eve said. She felt bad about lying . . . but only a little.

"I'll let them know the situation is under control."

"Thanks." Eve hung up and went into the backyard, where her brother greeted her with a big smile on his face.

"This is the best housewarming party ever," Kenny said.

"Just because I shot a drone out of the sky?"

"That and the amazing fried chicken, biscuits, and donuts," he said. "Rachel was convinced you'd just order pizzas."

"I'm an adult," Eve said. "This isn't a frat party."

Tom and Lisa came up to her with the wreckage of the drone in their hands.

"What are you going to do with this?" Tom asked.

The portion of the drone with the battery and card slot was intact. She popped out the microSD card, then removed the battery, revealing a sticker with a serial number inside that began with three letters: *FAA*.

"Confiscate the video, use the FAA registration number to track down the owner, and return the drone to him."

Lisa said, "How far are you going to shove it up his ass?"

"Until he can chew it with his teeth," Eve said.

CHAPTER
TWENTY-FIVE

Although it was a Sunday morning, Eve figured that gossip was a 24/7 industry, so she visited the international headquarters of *Star World News Service*, which was in an unmarked storefront on a Van Nuys side street. The drapes were closed on the barred window and there was a Ring doorbell camera beside the front door, which was behind a mesh-iron gate.

Eve leaned on the doorbell. A voice crackled out of the cheap speaker.

"We're closed."

"I thought you might want this back." Eve held up the clear plastic evidence bag full of drone wreckage to the camera.

A moment later the door opened and she saw Delano Staggs, the paparazzo Tatum had lassoed, on the other side of the gate.

"Well, well," she said.

"Our lawyer is going to contact you tomorrow, Ronin. We have what you did on video. It's low-rez, but good enough to show in court."

"You're not going to court," she said.

"The hell I'm not. I'll have your badge," Staggs said. "You can't go around shooting drones out of the sky."

"I can when they are over my house," Eve said. "It's illegal to take pictures of someone where they have a reasonable expectation of privacy, like in their own backyard."

"Not if it's visible from public spaces."

"It's not," she said. "The hillside behind my home is also private property."

"The sky is a public place," he said.

"Really? That's going to be your argument? *The sky?*"

He folded his arms and shifted his weight between his feet. "And you're a celebrity who solved the murder of another celebrity. You are a legitimate news story."

Eve felt a little silly standing on the street, having this conversation through a gate, but she could understand why Staggs felt threatened, given what Tatum had done to him and what she had done to his drone.

"Maybe if the murder or arrest happened in my backyard, but it didn't. You have no justification for filming there while I am enjoying time with my family. But you're right, I'm newsworthy."

"Damn right," he said, taking the small victory.

"It just occurred to me that I look great shooting down the drone and I've got it in high-def. Why don't I post it? It's certain to go viral."

"You can't," Staggs said. "The video is mine."

"Who do you think the public will be cheering for when they see it? Me or you? Blake Largo's career and his billion-dollar *Deathfist* movie franchise were destroyed overnight by my first video. What do you think will happen to you and your little business?"

"You can't post it. The microSD card and everything on it belongs to me. It's stolen property."

"It fell in my yard and it will make a great promo for my TV series. It might even get me another promotion. I'm so glad we talked. I have a whole new perspective on this."

She smiled and walked away. Staggs opened the gate and hurried onto the sidewalk after her.

"Wait, wait. Stop," he said. "What do you want?"

Eve turned around, nearly at her Bronco, and tried to look baffled. "What do you mean?"

"You came down here to make demands," Staggs said. "So make them and I'll decide what my ass can take."

Eve liked that analogy. She came back over to Staggs. "Whatever I do in my job, or out in public, that's fair game for you. But keep your cameras out of my backyard and respect my family's privacy."

"Or what?" he asked.

"I'll post the video," she said.

"This is backwards," he said, shaking his head. "This is not how this was supposed to work."

"Do we have an understanding or not?"

He nodded. They had a deal. She handed him the evidence bag and turned back to her car.

But Staggs had a parting shot. "Are you taking lessons from Tatum in press relations?"

Eve faced him again. "We both enforce the law and protect the public, if that's what you mean."

"Is that what you call what he did to me?"

"You were trespassing," she said.

"Yeah, I was. But show me in the penal code where the penalty for that is being roped and tied, dragged through shit, paraded down the street, thrown in a cell, and having your equipment destroyed."

She couldn't argue with him about that. "It's not how I would have handled the situation."

"You might have settled for the Blake Largo approach, a good beatdown," Staggs said. "But I get it—there's the law for the rich and famous, and the law for the rest of us."

"Largo was rich and famous. He thought he was above the law. I showed him he wasn't."

"Okay, maybe that wasn't the best example. But we both know how it works," Staggs said. "The sheriff's department offers concierge service for wealthy celebrities. They get priority. Kitty Winslow gets robbed and killed in her home, that case gets solved in three days. A woman in Compton gets robbed and killed, that case will never be solved. Never. If someone wealthy disappears, the entire LASD is mobilized to find him. But if it's someone like me who disappears, a freelance photographer, you do absolutely nothing, because we're the enemy."

Eve leaned her back against her car like Tatum liked to do. "How many freelance photographers have gone missing?"

"Only one that I know of, but he's a good example," Staggs said. "He's been missing for five years, but because he revealed the raw truth about celebrities, because he spoke truth to power, nobody has tried to find him."

Everybody counts or nobody counts. That's what Harry Bosch always said in Michael Connelly's crime novels and she'd taken the fictional character's philosophy to heart, if not his approach.

"What's his name?"

"Like you care," he said.

She did. She needed to prove to herself, if not to him, that his characterization of LASD wasn't true. "I'll look into it. Consider it part of our deal."

"Max Gareth."

"Where did he live?"

"Silver Lake."

It wasn't her jurisdiction, but so what? If Regan could work all over Los Angeles, so could she. Hell, she wasn't in her jurisdiction now, either. "How old was he?"

"In his late thirties. He was single, but he had a sister out in Santa Monica. I never met her, but I'll never forget her name. Maxine. Can you imagine that? What kind of parents give their kids joke names?"

Moon Unit and Dweezil Zappa came to her mind. "Were they twins?"

"Yeah. Good guess."

She was tempted to say, *Don't be an asshole. I'm doing you a favor here.*

Instead, she decided to take the high road. "I'm a detective. We call our good guesses brilliant deductions." That actually got a smile out of him. "What were the circumstances of his disappearance?"

"We're a pretty tight group. We'd run into each other a lot chasing the same celebs, but we stopped seeing him . . . and he was hard to miss on his cop chopper."

"Cop chopper?"

"A BMW R1200RT-P, just like the motorcycle cops use. And white cruiser helmet, too. He wasn't impersonating a cop, but it sure helped him cut through traffic and security. He's going so fast, people don't see it says PRESS, not POLICE, on the side of his ride, and LAPC, not LAPD."

"LAPC?"

"Los Angeles Press Club," Staggs said. "The LAPD tried to cite him for it, but it was entirely legal. You can see why the police weren't motivated to find him. You hate him already and you never met him."

He was right. "Anybody check his place?"

"I did, in case he'd OD'd or something, but the place was empty."

"You broke in?" Eve asked.

"Yeah, I did. You going to arrest me five years later?" Staggs said. "His motorcycle and camera equipment weren't there, either."

"Was he using drugs?"

"We all do," he said. "Mostly just to stay awake. This job requires a lot of stakeouts, and if you fall asleep, you could miss a $100,000 shot of a drunk movie star pissing in the street."

"You certainly wouldn't want to sleep through that," Eve said. "Do you know if a police report was filed?"

"No, I don't."

"Maybe the reason the police didn't investigate is because they never knew anything about it," she said. "How do you know he didn't just decide to leave LA and do something else with his life?"

"Because he loved the job . . . and he was great at it."

"Okay," she said, then started to walk around to the driver's side of her car. "I do have one more question. You have showered since Thursday, right?"

Staggs said, "Of course I have. Like a dozen times because I can't stop smelling the horse shit. I finally decided it's gotta be my imagination. Why? Do you smell it? Even standing outside?"

She opened her door. "Maybe it's my imagination, too. Forget it."

But she knew he wouldn't, which was why she asked the question, even though all she smelled was Dove soap. It was a cruel thing to do, but she was still pissed at him. He was in the business of ruining and embarrassing people whose only crime was being famous.

Eve got in her car and drove off.

As much as she disliked Delano Staggs, and his business, she would do her best to find Max Gareth. Her fear was that she already had.

Eve called Lost Hills and got Biddle on the line. He was working the weekend shift. She asked him if he'd do her a favor and run Maxine Gareth through the system. He griped a bit about not being her personal secretary, but he got her a current address in Santa Monica anyway.

She entered the address into the Google Maps app on her phone and headed off.

◆ ◆ ◆

Maxine Gareth lived in a Craftsman-style bungalow with a detached garage on Yale Street, just north of Colorado Avenue, that was wedged between 1960s-era apartment buildings on three sides and faced a new condo building across the street. The house was maybe 1,200 square feet, but Eve figured it was probably worth well over a million dollars and that Maxine fielded offers from apartment developers every single day.

Eve knocked on the door and it was opened by a freckle-faced woman in her forties wearing a tie-dye T-shirt, stylishly shredded jeans, and flip-flops.

"Yes?"

"Are you Maxine Gareth?"

"Who is asking?"

Eve flashed her badge. "I'm Eve Ronin, a detective with the Los Angeles County Sheriff's Department. I'm here about your brother."

The woman stepped aside to let Eve in. "I'm Bonnie, Maxine's wife. She's in the closet right now."

"No worries. Her sexuality really isn't any of my concern."

Bonnie laughed and blushed with embarrassment, deepening her freckles. "I'm sorry, I said that without thinking. She's an audiobook narrator and we converted a closet into a recording booth. I'll let her know you're here. Can I get you tea? Coffee?"

"Nothing, thank you."

Bonnie walked away and Eve glanced around the tiny living room, which was decorated with secondhand furniture in a wide variety of styles, all appointed with colorful pillows and blankets. Framed vintage concert posters decorated the walls. Bright rugs covered the restored hardwood floors. The galley kitchen was filled with all kinds of jars holding pasta, cookies, rice, flour, and other items. Eve liked it. Very homey. She was tempted to take a picture for reference when warming up her own kitchen.

Bonnie came back a minute later, picked up a teapot, and held it under an instant hot water dispenser in the sink.

"Maxine will be out in a second. She drinks pots and pots of tea while she narrates a book. It helps her voices. She's narrating a crime novel now, an American translation of a Swedish noir, which is really forcing her to test her dialect skills."

"I bet," Eve said.

"I keep telling her not to stress over it. If people could accept Kenneth Branagh as Inspector Wallander, and he didn't even attempt a Swedish accent, nobody is going to mind her American accent doing a different Swedish cop."

Maxine shuffled into the room wearing an oversize sweatshirt, baggy sweatpants, a bathrobe, and slippers. She was in her thirties, with a round, rosy-cheeked face and bright, intent eyes.

"Please excuse how I'm dressed, Detective. One of the great things about my job is nobody sees me. I like to be comfortable when I perform."

"It's okay," Eve said. "I'm intruding on your Sunday . . . and I won't take up much of your time. I'm looking into your brother's disappearance."

Maxine sat down at the kitchen table and gestured to Eve to do the same. "Why now? Has something changed?"

Eve sat down. "His case just sort of fell out of the sky into my backyard. Did you ever file a missing person report?"

Maxine shook her head. "We weren't close, even though we were twins. And it wasn't unusual for him to just jump on his motorcycle and ride into Mexico for a few weeks . . . or take a sudden road trip across the country . . . or hole up someplace, getting crazy drunk or high. But as the months turned into years, I figured he was probably dead."

Bonnie brought a plate of sugar cookies and the teapot to the table. "He was bipolar and a drug addict. The funniest guy and the biggest asshole I ever met."

"He was a character," Maxine said. "He loved the thrill of chasing celebrities . . . like a hunter going after big game. All it took was one big money shot of an athlete doing a line of coke, or a sitcom star picking up a hooker, and his bills would be paid for a year."

Eve remembered those scandals and the photos and the talk show apology tours both celebs embarked on.

"But when he had a dry spell," Maxine added, "he'd fall hard and hit me up for money."

"Or steal from you," Bonnie said as she returned with three mugs, each with a tea bag and spoon inside, and set them down on the table.

"We don't know he did that." Maxine picked up the teapot and poured hot water into her mug.

"I do," Bonnie said, taking a seat. "He'd show up to ask for money, and when he left, whether he got a check or not, something always ended up missing or we'd get a break-in a few days later."

Maxine poured hot water into Bonnie's mug. "When he disappeared, his landlord evicted him and we had to go out to Silver Lake and get all his stuff. We didn't find anything of ours."

"Because he sold it for cash and then snorted it up his nose," Bonnie said.

Maxine offered the pot to Eve, who shook her head. "What happened to his motorcycle?"

"It's probably wherever he is," Maxine said. "That was his one constant companion."

"Did he have any enemies?"

"Tons," she said. "Everybody he ever took an embarrassing photo of."

"Any threats?"

Maxine took a sip of tea and nodded. "Death threats and actual beatings. He seemed to enjoy the beatings—he wore the bruises like medals."

Bonnie took a cookie from the plate. "And they were reasons for doctors to give him legit prescriptions for painkillers, which he'd eat like M&M's."

"Somebody even broke his arm once," Maxine said.

"Max didn't press charges?"

"No, because he probably got caught peeking in some celeb's window."

"Which arm did he break?"

"The right," Maxine said, and drank some more tea.

Eve made a mental note of that. "You said you had his stuff. Can I look at it?"

"Sure, it's in the garage," Maxine said. "The boxes are all marked 'Max Shit.' Take whatever you need."

"Thanks. Do you happen to know who his dentist might have been?"

"Intimately. It was our dad," Maxine said. "He passed away years ago, but our dental care for life was part of the deal to buy the practice . . . or Max's teeth would have fallen out years ago." She studied Eve for a moment. "You want the X-rays in case you find his bones, right? That's also why you asked which arm he broke."

"Yes, it is," Eve said.

"I perform a lot of police procedurals. It's kind of surreal now to be living one." Maxine went on to give her the name and contact information for the dentist's office in Brentwood.

"Can I have your email address?" Eve asked. Maxine gave it to her.

Eve took out her phone, went online, downloaded the Records Authorization Form, and then emailed it to Maxine. "I've just sent you a form to sign and forward to the dentist so I can get the records."

"I'll do it tonight so they have it tomorrow morning."

"Thank you." Eve stood up. "You've been very helpful. I'll let you know if I find out anything."

Maxine stood up with her mug of tea. "I've got to get back to the closet. Bonnie can open up the garage for you."

Bonnie got up and led Eve outside to the detached garage, unlocked the door, and rolled it up. There was a Prius parked inside. The rest of the tidy garage was filled with gardening tools, bags of potting mix and fertilizer, and shelves of file boxes neatly labeled with the contents. The ones marked **MAX SHIT** were easy to spot.

"The sad thing is," Bonnie said, "Max really had talent. He was an artist with a camera. He didn't just capture what you could see but also what was happening below the surface, what the people were feeling."

Bonnie left Eve alone with the boxes. Eve spotted one that said **MAX SHIT PHOTOS**, pulled it off a shelf, and set it on the floor. She lifted off the lid. Inside were several scrapbooks.

She took one out and opened it on the hood of the Prius. It was filled with celebrity pictures, most of them candid, taken at the beach, in their backyards, at grocery stores, at outdoor restaurants, or even through the windows of their homes. They were a lot like surveillance photos, but Bonnie was right—Max somehow managed to capture the emotion of the moment. The attraction, the boredom, the sadness, or the anger of the people he was observing. There were also the usual shots of celebrities arriving at or leaving parties, airports, and industry events.

But there were also plenty of photos of celebs picking up their kids at school, or getting a coffee, doing normal, domestic things. And many embarrassing photos of actors and actresses in bathing suits or at the gym, without the benefit of makeup and lights, where they revealed their age and imperfections and not-so-perfect bodies.

She went through two more scrapbooks before she found one filled with photos of LilGlok9 having sex with Sissy K in their pool, on their chaise longue, even on one of the fake boulders. But Max's skill at capturing emotion also captured the absence of it. These photos all looked posed, not candid, as if they knew they were being watched. There were others of the couple, clearly taken when they didn't know he was there, that had a more raw, natural look to them . . . taken through open windows between blinds, presumably from hiding in the Preserve.

There were also lots of shots of the Winslows—particularly Brandy, Skye, and Kitty—at their home, at the Commons, at industry events, or just eating or buying groceries. There were many shots of Kitty making out with various men, even kissing some women. There were photos of Skye sunbathing topless in their backyard, and making out with various men, and partying with other celebrities her age. And there were also photos of Brandy, in stunning dresses at award shows, in her bikini at the beach, and a series of shots taken through a window of her home, straddling someone on the couch, presumably Caleb, while obviously having sex.

She also found several photos of Max in action, carrying his cameras like guns and ammo, a war photographer in the battlefield of Hollywood. Always with his cop chopper nearby. He looked like a rock-and-roll star, giving off a Mick Jagger vibe.

Eve took pictures with her phone of the shots that interested her of LilGlok9, Sissy K, the Winslows, and Max, put everything away, and left, taking PCH up the coastline to Topanga, then north to Calabasas.

When she got home, she made a list of all the actors, singers, models, and athletes she'd recognized in Gareth's photos, then cross-checked their names against the list of Hidden Hills residents that Tatum had given them.

About half of the celebrities Gareth photographed lived in Hidden Hills, which made sense to her given the high cost of the homes, the cachet of the neighborhood, and the proximity to the movie studios. It was also the place all the newly minted celebrities seemed drawn to. The other celebrities were probably equally divided between Malibu, Bel-Air, and Beverly Hills, with the remaining handful living in Ojai, Santa Barbara, and Newport Beach.

Even so, it seemed to Eve that Max Gareth had spent a lot of time creeping around Hidden Hills, spying on people.

CHAPTER
TWENTY-SIX

Eve got up early Monday morning to beat the rush-hour traffic and was in Brentwood at 8:00 a.m. when Max Gareth's dentist opened to see patients. Luckily for Eve, Maxine Gareth had sent the signed Records Authorization Form on Sunday as promised, so there was no trouble getting her brother's dental chart and X-rays.

She grabbed a croissant and coffee to go at Caffe Luxxe at the Brentwood Country Mart across the street, then headed for downtown Los Angeles, getting mired in the rush-hour traffic on the eastbound Santa Monica Freeway. On the plus side, she could eat and drink without worrying about spilling anything on herself.

She gave Duncan a call and told him she'd be late getting into the station.

"How did it go with the paparazzo?" he asked. "I watched the news last night just to see if they reported on you shooting the drone or the owner, but I got nothing."

"The owner and I came to an understanding. Nobody is going to see the video."

"You sure that's what you want? It'll go viral, and there's a fifty-fifty chance that it won't get you disciplined but promoted instead," Duncan said. "You could become captain."

"I'd rather earn my next promotion the old-fashioned way," she said.

"Merit? Experience? Skill? That's too much work. Social media is a lot faster and requires less effort."

"The guy I met, Delano Staggs, told me about another paparazzo, Max Gareth, who went missing five years ago," she said, "which happens to be how long that skeleton Daniel found has been in the dirt beside those dead Chilean gang members. And both the skeleton and Gareth broke their arms."

"Lots of people break their arms," Duncan said. "It's hardly unique."

"There were indications on the hip bones that the victim spent a lot of time on a horse or motorcycle," Eve said. "Gareth went everywhere on a motorcycle."

"Lots of people ride motorcycles, too."

"I looked at his photos. There were many of the Winslows and LilGlok9. Not only that, but half of his other subjects also lived in Hidden Hills."

"Because that's where the rich want to live now," he said. "Beverly Hills, Malibu, and Hancock Park are passé."

"You're right, but nobody has found the bodies of any paparazzi buried outside the yards of celebrities in those places."

"Not yet. And we don't know that we've found one here. But there's an easy way to find out. Do we have his dental records?"

"We do now and I'm on my way downtown to deliver them to Lopez myself," she said. "That's why I'm going to be late."

Very late. She'd moved only about twenty yards since the conversation with Duncan began.

He sighed. "Okay, let's say you're right, the dead guy is Max Gareth. What's your theory? That LilGlok9 killed him, too?"

"It's not a big leap," Eve said. "We're talking about a man we already suspect killed five people . . . and four in his own neighborhood."

"But those guys were shot. This guy died from blunt force trauma to the head."

"Maybe LilGlok9 caught him in the act and didn't have a gun handy."

"And he just grabbed the nearest crowbar or baseball bat?"

"Something like that," Eve said.

"What happened to his motorcycle?"

"It was probably left at one of the trailheads into the park and was eventually stolen."

"Or it was cited by a deputy or ranger for a parking violation and was eventually towed away," Duncan said. "There might be a record of it."

"Good idea," Eve said.

He ended the call so he could chase down that possible lead and Eve continued her crawl to the morgue.

◆　◆　◆

Eve walked into the morgue as Lopez was making an incision into a young African American man with several obvious bullet holes in his body.

Lopez looked up, surprised to see Eve. "I don't need you coming down to nag me, Eve. I told you I'd have the autopsy results on Charles Newton today and—"

Eve interrupted her. "That's not why I'm here. I'm hand-delivering dental charts."

"For which case?"

"The bones Daniel—I mean, Dr. Brooks—dug up on Thursday." Eve hoped she wasn't blushing over her slipup.

"You can set them on my desk over there." Lopez tipped her head toward a desk in the corner of the room. "I'll get back to you on that later this afternoon."

"I was hoping you might compare the dental records to his teeth while I'm here," Eve said. "I can wait until you're done with what you're doing."

"Those bones have been in the ground for years," Lopez said. "I have live cases, no pun intended, that I need to do first, like this man who was killed last night."

"Understood, sorry." Eve set the charts down on Lopez's desk and headed for the door.

"Don't you want to know about LilGlok9?"

Eve stopped and turned back to Lopez. "You've done the autopsy?"

"First thing this morning," Lopez said. "I was going to call you right after I finished with this man."

"What have you determined?"

"Charles Newton, a.k.a. LilGlok9, was murdered."

"What gave it away?" Eve asked.

Lopez walked around the table and stood in front of Eve. "LilGlok9's cause of death was a cut throat. It was a long, deeply incised laceration along the front of his neck that started below the left ear and gradually deepened as it went, severing the left carotid artery." She used the scalpel in her hand to illustrate on her own throat, though she didn't touch the blade to her flesh.

"That makes sense. He was right-handed."

"Except I will usually see hesitation cuts. I didn't see any. This cut was straight and true."

"Maybe he was very determined," Eve said.

"He was also very drunk," Lopez said. "His blood alcohol level was 10 percent, so his motor skills would have been impaired, so not only should I have seen hesitation cuts but also some wobbliness, and inconsistent depth, in his stroke. I didn't. It was straight. And that brings up something else. Cutting your throat hurts. It would be natural to react to the pain and to the bloodshed, so I would expect the beginning of the wound to be deeper, but a lot shallower as it goes. It was the opposite here . . . shallow to start, deeper at the end."

"Because a killer isn't feeling the pain or the blood, he's feeling his rage," Eve said. "Or he's a pro, feeling nothing and just getting his job done."

"That's right, and there's a more subtle clue," Lopez said. "The victim wasn't gripping the knife."

"The knife was in his hand," Eve said. "I saw it."

"Yes, but it wasn't clutched tight. Slitting your own throat will cause a cadaveric spasm, an intense muscular contraction, in the hand at death." Lopez again demonstrated with the scalpel in her hand, her firm grip on the blade suddenly becoming a fist.

"The death grip," Eve said.

"His was a loose grip," Lopez said, loosening her fist so she still held the scalpel, but not nearly as strongly.

"You think the knife was put in his hand after death."

Lopez nodded. "The grip isn't conclusive by itself, but given all the other factors, it fits with everything else to create a clear picture. This was murder."

"Thank you, Doctor."

"Let the DA and sheriff know, will you? I don't want them calling to nag me."

"Will do," Eve said and hurried out, resisting the urge to remind Lopez to compare Gareth's dental chart to the skeleton's teeth.

◆ ◆ ◆

Traffic was much better heading westbound. On the way, Eve gave Duncan another call and shared the medical examiner's determination that LilGlok9's death was a homicide, explained the reasoning, then said, "Lansing and the DA are not going to be happy about this."

"Why not?" Duncan said. "It doesn't change anything."

"Because we stood up in front of the media and told the world that the case was solved." Not that she'd believed it, but that hadn't stopped her from trying to sell the public on it.

"You were referring to Kitty Winslow and the three corpses in the park," he said. "Those cases *are* solved. I don't think anybody has forgotten how awkwardly and repeatedly you avoided saying how LilGlok9 died."

That was true.

"So my embarrassing performance at the press conference worked out for me," she said.

"It was a cunning move by a master strategist."

"Yes, that's exactly what it was," she said. "I'm always ten steps ahead of everybody else."

"So am I," Duncan said. "I have a pretty good idea who killed LilGlok9."

"Great," she said. "Let's go arrest him."

"It was the same shooters who took out Kitty and 2Fast, silencing the one guy who could finger them."

"Where's the proof?"

"It's on the security cameras," Duncan said.

"There's nothing on them," Eve said. "They were turned off."

"That's the proof," Duncan said. "LilGlok9 was expecting the Crips to visit him and didn't want any evidence of the meet. They probably came in on foot . . . just like they did before."

"How did the Crips know we were coming?"

"They didn't know exactly when we'd show up with handcuffs, but they figured we would eventually, and when we did, that he'd give them up to save himself."

She couldn't see a flaw in his reasoning. "It makes perfect sense."

"I've been doing this awhile," Duncan said. "About as long as you've been alive."

"The only problem is that it's all conjecture—there's no actual evidence," Eve said, knowing that she sounded exactly like Rebecca Burnside.

"That won't stop Lansing and the DA from accepting it as fact and essentially closing the case."

Duncan was right.

◆ ◆ ◆

As soon as Eve got back to the station, she and Duncan went to see Captain Dubois, who brought Sheriff Lansing into the briefing by speakerphone. When Eve and Duncan were finished, Lansing agreed with Duncan's take on the evidence.

But Lansing went one step further. He decided that finding the Crips who were responsible would become the gang unit's problem and took the case away from Eve and Duncan.

Dubois and Duncan were clearly relieved by the decision, but Eve knew the gang unit would probably do nothing about it or, if they did, their efforts would go nowhere.

The investigation was over.

The captain told Eve and Duncan to write up everything and send the files over to the gang unit ASAP, as if there were actually any urgency to the case.

The only rush, Eve knew, was to get the case out of Lost Hills as fast as possible.

As they left the captain's office, Eve said to Duncan, "This is wrong."

"Why?" Duncan asked, a definite bounce in his step. He was a happy man.

"You know the case is going on a shelf."

"We only have so much time and resources," he said. "Besides, nobody has any sympathy for a killer who gets killed by other killers."

"Sympathy isn't our job," she said. "Justice is."

"You ought to get that on a T-shirt. It would make a great tagline for the TV series, too."

They entered the squad room, which they had to themselves.

"I'm serious, Duncan."

He went to his desk and sat down in his chair, which squealed like an injured animal under his weight. "Some would argue justice has been done. LilGlok9 got what he deserved . . . and, someday, so will those Crips."

"You *hope*," she said. "But I believe solving LilGlok9's murder deserves the same effort as Kitty Winslow's."

He swiveled around in the chair, making it shriek in protest. "Really? So you'd say, for example, that finding whoever killed an innocent pedestrian with a stray bullet in a drive-by shooting deserves as much effort as finding whoever killed the drive-by shooter if he gets himself killed."

"Yes." She dropped into her own chair, which made no sound at all.

"I don't think the public would agree with you."

"Murder is murder," she said.

"That's another T-shirt." He pointed at her. "You're good at this."

"Before we hand everything over to be mothballed, we can still do a little more work, at least for another day or two."

"We don't know anything about the Crips," he said. "The only gangs out here are the HOAs."

"We know some other suspects."

"You think one of the Winslows, or Benji, Kitty's would've-been-spurned fiancé, killed LilGlok9?"

"It's possible," she said.

"Based on what? None of them knew LilGlok9 had Kitty's ring until we found it under a rock on Friday and told Caleb."

"Unless whoever killed him planted the ring there for us to find," Eve said. "Or maybe he was killed by his wife."

"Sissy K was in Paris," Duncan said. "There are hundreds of witnesses and the fingering photo to prove it."

"Maybe that's why Sissy K did something so stupid in front of cameras, so the photo would go viral and cement her alibi."

"Okay, let's say she is some kind of brilliant Professor Moriarty supervillain capable of pulling off an incredibly complex plan involving body doubles, or fake photos, or time travel—"

Eve interrupted, "Or let's say she hired someone to do the killing for her."

"Or that," Duncan said. "What's her motive?"

"Maybe she really was having an affair. Maybe she knew LilGlok9 killed Kitty, or that he'd be a prime suspect, and she saw an opportunity to get out of the marriage with everything. Maybe she was the one who suggested to the Crips that her husband would talk if he got cornered."

"I lost count of how many times you said 'maybe,'" he said with a sigh. "But I can see we're going to be annoying a lot of people over the next day or two anyway."

"That's our job," she said.

"I thought it was justice."

"That's how you get it."

They agreed to divide the work, that he would finish the reports and prepare everything to be sent to the gang unit while she explored alternate theories. With only one of them doing the paperwork, it could buy them the extra day or two Eve wanted.

As Eve was getting up to go, Duncan said, "Don't forget your mom's big scene is today."

She went to the door. "I won't."

"I might show up for it, too."

She turned back at the door to look at him. "You mean for the lunch."

"Only because I don't want to do personal business while I'm on the job."

Eve called the Winslows on her way to her car to see if they were home and was told by Brandy's personal assistant, who answered Brandy's cell phone, that they were at the Calabasas house shooting . . . and gave her the address.

CHAPTER TWENTY-SEVEN

Parkway Calabasas ended at the ornate gates to the Oaks, a gated community of expensive estate homes. But within the Oaks, there was a second gated community that was even more exclusive and had even larger homes. And, Eve thought, someday someone would put a third gate in there to create an even more exclusively exclusive community of even larger large homes.

It wasn't hard to spot which house belonged to the Winslows. It was a sprawling Spanish-Mediterranean villa. The cobblestone motor court, the size of a grocery store parking lot, was filled with production trailers, and a private security guard manned the gate in case any A-list movie star neighbors or internationally famous athletes wanted to crash the party for a selfie.

Eve parked, badged the guard, walked past him without waiting for his approval, and went straight into the house, which was essentially being used as a soundstage. A set had been built within the space that was identical to the living room at the actual Winslow house. The landscaping outside the window matched, too, at least until it hit a green wall that had been erected to hide the actual yard. She imagined the green screen would be replaced by a CGI image of Kitty's house, and perhaps even the stable beyond. Makeup and hair team members, grips, production assistants, and other crew members huddled in the entry hall.

Brandy sat between Skye and Maverick on one of the couches. They were all bereft with grief, or at least trying hard to act that way.

Men dressed in black, operating handheld cameras, moved around the room filming the action, if that's what three people sitting around talking could be called.

Skye said, "It's like a bad dream."

"A nightmare," Brandy said, dabbing at her eyes with a crumpled tissue. "How could something like this happen . . . right here in our own house?"

But it didn't happen here, Eve thought. It happened miles away.

Maverick said, "I don't know if I can ever feel safe here again."

"Or anywhere," Skye said.

"I have to pick out her casket today." Brandy sniffled. "Something no mother should ever do."

"I'll go with you," Skye said, taking her mom's hand.

"Me too." Maverick took his mom's other hand, even though it was clutching a wet tissue.

Skye said, "We have to make the casket like Kitty's crib."

"What do you mean?" Brandy asked.

"I mean it's going to be the first Chanel-Vuitton-Hermès coffin ever made," she said, "like something she'd have been proud to wear . . . and fill it with her jewelry."

"Oh my God," Brandy said, breaking into a smile. "That's a great idea."

Maverick didn't seem convinced. "But what about grave robbers? It would be like finding Cleopatra's tomb . . . only without a pyramid on top of it."

"We'll have to bury it in a secret location," Brandy said, as if the thought were just occurring to her, "where nobody would ever think to look."

"That will make it a legend," Skye said.

Maverick nodded in agreement. "When it's dug up in six hundred years, it'll be a sensation, like King Tut's tomb."

"That's so cool, Mav," she said. "Kitty would have loved this."

It sounded to Eve like an idea a writer came up with for the show. It was rife with sponsorship opportunities and a continuing storyline . . . and one that would get people all over the world hunting for the buried treasure. Eve had to admire the cleverness.

Brandy looked up at the heavens. "This funeral is going to be a celebration of your life, sweetheart. To continue spreading your joy . . ."

There was a long silence, then the director said, "Cut." Eve hadn't noticed him before, then realized his voice had come over speakers. Everyone was wiping away tears except for Eve. A woman approached Brandy with a bottle of water.

A harried man, with harried hair and a harried beard, came bounding out of a nearby room with a headset around his neck. From the way others reacted to him, Eve guessed he was the director.

"That scene was so raw, so intimate, so heartbreaking," he said as he came up to the Winslows. "It took courage for you to let people into your home to see that deeply personal moment . . . to see you grieving."

The woman who'd given Brandy water said, "I felt uncomfortable. Like we were seeing you all naked. I had to turn my eyes away."

But not the cameras, Eve thought.

She was also sure they were still on camera now. The director's and the woman's lines were too good.

Brandy sniffled. "Because we were baring something more intimate than our bodies, Wanda. We were baring our souls . . ."

Now Eve was certain this was being filmed, too, as staged behind-the-scenes footage.

Wanda said, "How can you do that? Nobody would blame you for grieving in private."

Brandy took Wanda by the hand and looked into her eyes. "Because America is grieving, too. Kitty touched so many lives. But everyone knows this kind of loss. The truth is, money and fame doesn't protect you from violence and tragedy. When it comes down to it, we are all the same."

And now Brandy paused. She'd spotted Eve, let go of Wanda, and headed over to her, arms outstretched.

"Detective Ronin. Oh my God. We owe you so much. I need to give you a hug."

The cameras were following Brandy to Eve, who stepped back, as if Brandy were advancing on her with a weapon.

"Let's talk where there aren't cameras and after you've removed your body mikes," Eve said. "I want this to be a private discussion."

Brandy came to a stop, her entire demeanor changing. "If that's what you want. But everyone here is like family."

"They aren't your family," Eve said. "Those are the only people I want to talk with. Alone."

Brandy reached into her shirt, unsnapped the wired microphone from her bra, and let the device drop down her blouse and out from her shirttails, where she caught it with her other hand.

Maverick got off the couch, unclipping the mike power pack from his lower back as he did so. "The only rooms in this house without cameras are the crew bathroom and the garage."

"Garage it is," Eve said.

It took a moment for the Winslows to finish unplugging themselves from their mikes and then Eve followed them to a garage large enough to be a second home. It was being used as a crew commissary filled with long tables, folding chairs, and food.

Eve shooed out the half dozen grips eating there. "Could we have the room, please?"

Everyone left, leaving Eve alone with the Winslows.

Now Brandy hugged Eve. "Thank you for getting justice for Kitty . . . and getting her things back so quickly."

Skye joined the hug. "You are an amazing detective."

Eve gave Maverick a warning look, which he took to heart, not attempting to join the hug.

He said, "I'd say you should have your own series . . . but you already do."

"I was just doing my job," Eve said, extricating herself from the two Winslow women, "which is why I have to ask this question. Where were you Thursday night and Friday morning?"

Brandy said, "Thursday night we were working with the writers and director until midnight, then Friday we came here to block out what we'd shoot today. Why do you ask?"

Skye smirked. "Isn't it obvious, Mom? LilGlok9 didn't off himself, somebody killed him. She wants our alibis."

Brandy stared at Eve. "Is that true?"

"Yes, it is," Eve said.

Maverick laughed. "And you think one of us did it?"

"We have to consider every possibility."

"That makes no sense," Brandy said. "LilGlok9 was already dead when we learned that he killed Kitty."

Eve held up her hands in surrender. "Like I said, I'm just doing my job. Where was Caleb Thursday night?"

"In the stable, I suppose," Brandy said. "Since Kitty's death, he's retreated into himself. It's so sad. I'm afraid we might lose him."

"In what way?"

"To the fantasy world he used to live in," Brandy said.

Skye said, "Sometimes he calls me Sara and tells me how much he enjoys listening to my hymnals on Sundays."

"Who is Sara?" Eve asked.

"She was the schoolmarm character on *Saddlesore*."

"Which is super gross," Maverick said, "because Dad's character had a crush on her."

"Out of curiosity," Eve said, "how much of what I just saw being shot was written?"

Brandy smiled. "All of it, but it came from our truth . . . from what we felt and what we said."

"Even the part about the casket?"

Skye said, "Kitty would have loved it, whether the idea came from the writers or from us."

Eve said, "How do you know?"

Brandy said, "It was the writers who suggested she ought to go out with Benji Stanet, and she loved the idea and ended up loving him, too."

Maverick nodded. "The writers really get us."

"The truth is," Brandy said to Eve, "without the writers coming up with things for us to do, our lives wouldn't be that exciting to watch. At least you have murders to solve."

"I'm not doing a reality show," Eve said.

"You could do this one," Brandy said. "You're part of our lives now."

"People keep suggesting that to me," Eve said. "Do you have something to do with it?"

"No, of course not," Brandy said with a smile that suggested to Eve that yes, of course she did. "But you really are part of our lives now, and we're part of yours. That's a fact, whether you like it or not."

"I don't want my part of it on camera," Eve said.

Skye shook her head. "I can't imagine my life without cameras."

"Everybody's lives are on camera," Maverick said. "They just don't have an audience."

"That's so unbelievably sad," Skye said, and Eve thought the kid actually meant it.

Talking about their TV series reminded Eve that her mother's scene in *Ronin* was being shot soon and she didn't want to miss it. Her mom would never forgive her.

"I have to go," Eve said. "Thank you for your time. I'll be in touch when there are new developments in the investigation."

She left. As Eve walked back through the house within a house, she understood why Caleb was confusing fantasy with reality. The line between the two was hopelessly blurred in his life.

But then she remembered the vertigo that she'd felt standing outside the Lost Hills station for the press conference and wondered how long she'd be able to see that line clearly herself.

CHAPTER
TWENTY-EIGHT

Ronin was shot in an unmarked warehouse in an office park near the Van Nuys Airport that had been converted into a studio soundstage. Nobody driving by on Balboa Boulevard knew it was a studio because all of the production vehicles, mobile dressing rooms, catering trucks, and the tent for serving meals were in the parking lot behind the building, hidden from the street.

Eve arrived during the lunch break, and everyone was outside eating in the tent, so she had the soundstage, and the Lost Hills sheriff's station set, all to herself when she came in.

She walked down the station hallway into the squad room and was impressed by how closely it resembled the real place—the linoleum floors scuffed and stained, the walls a bleak, institutional gray. But most of all, she was struck by how lived-in it felt, each cubicle decorated in meticulous detail to create a sense that it belonged to a real person. The papers on the desks, the photos and notes tacked on the partitions, even the way the files were stacked conveyed character. If not for the room's missing fourth wall, which left the set open, as if facing a theater audience, she could easily imagine she was at work. Instead of rows of theater seating, there were lights, cameras, and a video village.

She sat down at her cubicle. It wasn't hers, but it could have been. Someone must have taken a picture of her desk and copied it, because it was a startlingly accurate re-creation. Even a picture of herself as a kid with her brother and sister in Santa Cruz had been copied, with a young Erin Casey and two other actors she didn't know.

Eve picked up one of the files on the desk to see if the attention to detail extended to the papers inside or if it was just blank paper.

"Don't do that!" someone yelled.

Eve, startled, turned to see Zach, the assistant director, standing near the cameras.

"Do what?" she said.

"Touch anything," he said. "We were just shooting here. This is a hot set. Nothing can be moved. Put the file down exactly where you found it."

She did as she was told.

"I didn't realize it would be a big deal." She started to get up, pushing the chair slightly away from the desk.

"Even the placement of this chair is important," he said.

"Sorry," Eve said, making sure the chair was back in the same spot it was in when she sat down.

"If you moved a file, or put it back in the wrong place, it may seem like nothing now, but it will be a huge problem when we come back to shoot."

"I don't understand," Eve said. "Why would anyone watching the show care what files are on the desk?"

"A scene is made up of multiple shots from different angles edited together," Zach said, and as he did, the crew began filing into the soundstage. Lunch was over. "If the file behind your head in one shot is blue, then becomes yellow, then becomes blue again, it's like a blinking light. Not all continuity errors get spotted, but some become legendary. Like Dorothy's pigtails changing size in her first scene with the Scarecrow."

"I've seen *The Wizard of Oz* a hundred times and never noticed that," Eve said, "and I'm a trained detective."

"Because you're caught up in the story, or at least we hope you are, until the magical moving files pulls you out."

"Got it," she said. "I won't make that mistake again."

Eve looked back at her desk, and the files stacked there, and felt a sudden chill. Something about it bothered her . . . but what? Did she move another file without thinking about it? Perhaps it was simply how close she'd come to making an embarrassing mistake.

The actors and the extras, the background people with no lines, came into the soundstage and so did Duncan, carrying a plate nearly overflowing with prime rib, mashed potatoes, grilled fish, and chicken wings.

"What are you doing in here?" he said. "The food is out there."

"Just soaking up the vibe."

"Creepy, isn't it?" He ate a spoonful of mashed potatoes.

"You're only just beginning to notice that?"

"I'm bringing you to 7-Eleven this afternoon," he said.

"Why?"

He sat down in a folding chair, set the plate on his lap, and nibbled on a chicken wing as he talked. "Because the Powerball jackpot is up to nearly a billion dollars and I want you standing next to me when I buy a lottery ticket. You've got amazing luck. Case-solving clues literally fall out of the sky into your hands."

"The bones Daniel dug up are Max Gareth?"

Duncan nodded, swallowed, and said, "I heard from Dr. Lopez just before I left the office. The dental records match. What are the odds of that? And I heard back from the park rangers. Five years ago, they ticketed Gareth's motorcycle, which was parked at the Mureau Road entrance to the Preserve. They came back a few days later and found it pretty much stripped by vandals, so they towed what was left of it away.

What happened after that is a mystery. But I'll tell you what isn't: I ate caviar and potato chips with a big-time killer."

"We can't tie him directly to Max Gareth," Eve said. "At least not yet."

"But we can tie him to Kitty," Duncan said. "Nan confirmed the gun buried in his yard was the murder weapon."

Jen came over to them wearing a sheriff's deputy uniform. "About time you got here, Eve. When I didn't see you here for the first shot before lunch, I thought you'd forgotten about my scene."

"I'm a real cop," Eve said. "I couldn't sneak away from work until now."

"It's probably good you're so late," Jen said. "Now that I've rehearsed it a few times, I've really honed my performance to reveal my character's inner turmoil."

"What turmoil?" Eve said. "Your character doesn't even have a name. It's just 'Desk Officer.' In fact, why are you even in this scene? You're supposed to be at the front desk."

Before Jen could answer, Vince took his seat in the director's chair in front of the bank of monitors and called out, "Positions, everyone!"

Jen hurried into the station hallway, where Erin Casey was already standing, getting ready to enter the squad room set, which was filling up with extras playing detectives and deputies.

Vince turned to Eve. "Hey, hardnose, glad you made it. Sit up here, close to the monitors. I saved you a seat."

He patted an empty chair next to him with a smile. Like a proud father offering his daughter a seat right next to him so she could watch him at work.

The seat for Daddy's special girl.

There was a time she wanted that. Desperately. But that time was long gone. Now the gesture made her nauseous.

"No, thank you," she said.

"You can see all the angles here," Vince said. "We're shooting with three cameras to get the coverage with the master."

"I can see fine from where I am."

"I can't." Duncan got up from his seat with his plate and took the chair beside Vince instead. "Much better."

Eve remained standing. "Where's Simone?"

Vince said, "In her office, writing the next nine episodes. Hanging out on the set is a luxury."

"I'll say," Duncan said. "The prime rib is primo."

Zach, the AD, called out, "Settle, everyone. Quiet."

The second assistant cameraman stepped onto the set and stood in front of the camera with the electronic clapboard. "Scene 47, take two."

Assistants for the other cameramen did the same in front of their cameras. And when they were all off the set, Vince yelled, *"Action!"*

The squad room bustled with activity as Erin Casey, playing Eve, came in.

Eve tracked Erin from different angles on the monitors showing the feeds from all three cameras.

The cameras were cleverly positioned to shoot one wide angle of the whole room, one close-up of Erin, and one midsize angle all at the same time without being seen.

Eve had to admire Vince's skill. His shrewd camera setups would save the production time and money shooting all the other angles individually. This was obviously why he'd had such a long career. He was fast and cost-conscious.

Jen intercepted Erin, turning the midsize angle into a perfectly framed two-shot. Eve watched the scene play out.

Eve turned to the deputy, who usually worked the front desk. "What are all these people doing here?"

The deputy said, "After the news conference last night, the tip lines lit up. The captain had to bring in more bodies to answer phones."

"We could make better use of these people out on the street."

The deputy shrugged. "You're the task force leader. Start tasking."

The deputy walked away, leaving Eve to feel the full weight of her new responsibility in a job she still wasn't sure she deserved.

"Cut! Print," Vince said with a single clap of his hands. "Let's move on to the next scene."

"Wait a minute," Duncan said. "I was the one who told Eve that. Why is the front desk officer doing it?"

"There's been a little rewrite," Vince said. "We were getting too Duncan-heavy."

"But I was there, and the desk officer is supposed to be at the front desk. That's why she's called the desk officer."

Zach came over, his head down, as if dreading a scolding. "I'm sorry, Vince, but we have to do it again."

"Why?" Vince demanded.

Duncan said, "Because I'm obviously supposed to be there. Desk officers don't give detectives orders."

Zach said, "The B camera operator caught a continuity error."

Eve felt a stab of guilt, afraid this was her fault for moving that file. She was going to be embarrassed in front of her father. She'd rather take on the corrupt deputies who wanted her dead than face this humiliation.

"What error?" Vince asked.

"The detective in the background of the two-shot put down his phone during Eve's line in the previous takes, but he put it down on the desk officer's line in this one. It's not going to cut together in coverage."

Vince scowled. "Good catch, but damn it, Zach, keep the monkeys in line."

"I will."

Vince stood up. "Okay, one more time. Positions, everyone."

Eve watched the same scene unfold again, but now she focused on the background decor and activity in every angle and saw just how active everyone was, silently "talking" and moving papers around. The detective who'd made the mistake before put the phone down on the right line of dialogue this time. Everything would match.

And then she felt the snap.

It was a familiar feeling to her now, the moment when all the pixels that meant nothing by themselves aligned to create a crisp, clear picture in her mind.

She'd solved the case. Instead of feeling a sense of accomplishment or a jolt of excitement, she was angry at herself.

I'm an idiot. I should have seen it right away.

She didn't deserve her badge. She didn't even deserve the fake one on Erin Casey's belt.

But this wasn't the first time Eve had thought that she was stupid, and blind, and slow, or had felt a snap like this. Maybe this was just her process. Maybe she should embrace it, accept it, and with it the flaws it exposed and the frustrations it caused. At least it worked.

She'd think about that later. Now that she saw everything clearly, she looked at the case anew and had another realization. She took out her phone and opened her call history from Friday, and then she urgently tugged Duncan's coat sleeve.

"We have to go," Eve said.

"Are you sure? If we leave now, your mother might take your part, too."

"She might be better at it," Eve said. "We got it wrong, Duncan."

He got up and set his plate down on the seat. "Got what wrong?"

Vince turned around and grinned at her. "*All of it.* I know these lines. They're at the end of the script. The big scene where you figure it all out."

Eve said, "Because either I never learn or I'm doomed to keep repeating myself. I'm not sure which it is yet."

She pulled Duncan aside, out of Vince's earshot, and said, "I know who killed Kitty Winslow, LilGlok9, Max Gareth, and the Chileans."

Duncan said, "One person couldn't possibly have done all that killing."

"I didn't say it was," Eve said.

CHAPTER
TWENTY-NINE

Eve held up her badge to the guard as she drove through the residents' gate at Hidden Hills, Duncan in the seat beside her and Rebecca Burnside sitting in the back. She'd called ahead to Brandy and learned that the Winslows had returned to their house from "the set" at the Oaks. Eve told her to stay where they were, that there had been a new development in the case, and that they needed to talk about it immediately. Their conversation was short.

They arrived at the Winslow house and Eve was pleased to see that Tatum wasn't already waiting. But he'd undoubtedly be there soon, once the gate informed him that Eve had come through. It wouldn't take long for Tatum to figure out where she was heading.

Meanwhile, just outside the frame of the security cameras at all the gates, LASD patrol cars were stationed nearby, ready to lock down the entire neighborhood if necessary.

The three of them got out and approached the Winslows' front door. Brandy opened it before they got there.

"What's the urgency?" she asked.

"We have some new evidence to show you that changes our entire perception of the case," Eve said, then gestured to Rebecca Burnside. "That's why she's here."

Burnside stepped forward and offered Brandy her hand. "I'm Rebecca Burnside, an assistant district attorney. Is your whole family here?"

Brandy shook her hand but seemed very confused. "Yes, Skye and Maverick are inside, and Caleb hasn't left the damn stable since Kitty died. I don't understand what's happening or why you're involved."

"Because catching and charging your daughter's killers is a top priority for us," Burnside said. "I'm the one who will have to prosecute the case."

Eve said, "We have to move fast so nobody else gets hurt, but we can't do it without your help."

"Of course, we'll do whatever we can. Come in." Brandy beckoned them in.

They walked in to find Skye and Maverick on the living room couch, in the same spots they were in when Eve first met them.

"Can we go in the editing room?" Eve said. "I have some video to show you."

They all filed into the editing room, Duncan stepping in last and closing the door behind him.

Eve handed Maverick a thumb drive. "Please put this up on the big screen."

"No problem." Maverick sat down at the editing bay and plugged the thumb drive into a port on the keyboard. "What is it?"

"This is the video from your surveillance cameras the night of Kitty's murder," Eve said. "It's the main display with all the camera angles, from the moment the intruders run out of Kitty's house until you three showed up to find her body."

The image came up on the big screen. The footage from all the different cameras appeared in their own windows, playing simultaneously, and it was on a loop.

The cameras showed the hooded figures running into Kitty's house through the unlocked door. There was a gunshot, then a moment later, the intruders dashed out again, running toward the back fence, a rabbit darting out of their path. Caleb rushed out of the stable with his gun and fired off several shots at the intruders as they disappeared from his view behind the guesthouse . . . where another camera picked them up running to the fence, climbing over it, and dropping into the weeds before fleeing into the darkness. Caleb hurried toward Kitty's house as Brandy, Skye, and Maverick came rushing up in their bed clothes.

"It's horrible," Brandy said. "It's as if I'm living it all over again."

Skye hugged herself. "At least there was no camera in Kitty's house . . . That would be unbearable."

Maverick stared at the screen. "I wish Dad had shot them all."

Eve let the loop play again from the beginning as she talked.

"Every scene in a TV show, even yours, is made up of a master, which captures the whole scene, and the coverage, which looks at the same scene from various angles but is often shot at different times, over several takes, due to the need to adjust performance, lighting, move cameras, that kind of thing. The final scene, once it's edited together, is a mix of the master and all the other angles."

Baffled, Skye pointed to the screen. "That isn't our show. That's real life."

Duncan said, "I thought your show was real life."

She stabbed her finger at the screen again for emphasis. "That isn't a script. That isn't a scene. There is no master. There is no editing. You can see it all right there as it happened . . . and it's fucking horrible."

"Skye is right, Duncan," Eve said. "When you shoot a scene in a fictional show, continuity between shots is very important, because if something is out of place, it can create an embarrassing and distracting mismatch. But all of the angles in this security camera video were shot at once and don't need to be edited into a scene, so that's not an issue."

Brandy sighed with irritation. "I don't understand why you are giving us a lesson in basic video editing while making us all relive this horror. We know how it works and this is just cruel. You said you had important new information about the case. Let's hear it."

"If this was all shot at once, why are there continuity errors?" Eve hit the pause button on the keyboard, stopping the footage as the intruders dashed out of Kitty's house and across the lawn. "Here you can see a rabbit darting out of the way as the three intruders pass this camera across the lawn . . ."

Eve pointed to a different camera window. "But that same rabbit is missing when you look at the scene from the opposite direction, the guesthouse camera that they are running towards."

"Who cares?" Brandy said. "It obviously went into a rabbit hole or something."

Duncan said, "Oh, there's definitely a rabbit hole, and we all fell into it."

Eve hit play and pointed to another camera view. "On this angle, the three intruders run behind the guesthouse as Caleb shoots at them. And from these two other angles, from cameras positioned in the eaves of the guesthouse, we can see them climb over the fence and land in the weeds on the other side, in the Preserve."

"We already know what happened," Brandy said. "What's your point?"

Eve hit the pause button, walked up to the big screen, and pointed to the fence. "Do you see those weeds?"

"Yeah, so what?"

"There shouldn't be any," Eve said. "The weed-abatement crew trimmed them all to the ground on Monday. And yet, there they are. It's another continuity error, just like the disappearing rabbit. How are these errors possible if all the angles were shot at the same time?"

Duncan said, "Because they weren't."

Eve faced the Winslows. "You're the three intruders who robbed and killed Kitty."

Duncan looked at Brandy in disgust. "Your own daughter."

Maverick said, "Stepdaughter."

Brandy turned to her son. "Shut up, Mav. Don't say another word."

Eve glanced up at the screen. "The footage of you running out of her house, and escaping over the fence, was shot days *before* the killing and edited into what was supposedly the live feed. You actually ran into the guesthouse, ditched your hoodies, and ran back around to Kitty's house. That's where you really came from, not the main house, when Caleb saw you."

Skye whacked her brother on the back of the head. "Some fucking editor you are."

"Keep your mouths shut," Brandy said, her expression hard. "Both of you."

Eve walked back to the editing bay. "You're wrong, Skye. The action was so compelling, and tightly edited, that we only focused on the characters. We didn't notice what was going on in the background. That's what directors count on to cover their continuity mistakes. The storytelling almost saved you all. Your mistake was framing LilGlok9 for it and participating in his murder."

"We didn't do that," Skye said.

Brandy grabbed Skye and Maverick each by an arm and said firmly, "Don't. Say. Anything. Understand? Shut your mouths. Our lawyer will do the talking."

"It's okay," Eve said. "We know that none of you actually slit LilGlok9's throat. Someone else did the dirty work."

Ever since LilGlok9's death, the big question for Eve had been how he, or whoever had killed him, could have possibly known when and why they were coming to arrest him. Only Eve, Duncan, and Burnside knew about the ring and that they'd deduced that the studio was burned down to cover up the executions of the burglars.

But then, on the *Ronin* set, Eve remembered that wasn't true . . . that she'd made a call from Burnside's office that had sealed LilGlok9's fate.

"It was Amos Tatum who killed LilGlok9 and buried the lockbox with the jewelry and the gun in his yard," Eve told the Winslows. "He was the only one who knew we were coming to arrest LilGlok9 and why. In fact, I was the one who told him."

She'd called Tatum to ask about the date of the studio fire, and that's when he'd realized they knew about the jewelry, that the building was burned down to cover up the evidence of the executions, and that they would be arresting LilGlok9 within hours. And that LilGlok9 would do whatever he had to do to save himself from a life sentence.

At the *Ronin* set, Eve looked at her Friday call history and discovered that the time period when LilGlok9's cameras were turned off and the likely time of his murder were both within an hour of her call to Tatum.

LilGlok9's killer, she knew then, had to be Tatum, acting fast to silence him before he could be arrested and, to cut a deal on a reduced sentence, reveal the deputy's role in the killings.

Duncan faced the Winslows. "You thought Tatum was framing LilGlok9 to help you, but he was really doing it to save himself. What Tatum didn't tell you when he asked you for Kitty's jewelry was that he was using you to cover up three other murders he'd committed with LilGlok9."

It seemed to Eve that the Winslows were more shocked by this revelation than her outing them as killers.

Burnside had been standing quietly in the back of the room, listening and observing, but now she stepped forward and spoke.

"That's why I am here, to make you a limited-time offer. Only one of you shot Kitty in the face—the others are accomplices." Burnside looked at Brandy. "I don't care which one of you three actually did it. But if you confess to killing Kitty and testify against Tatum, then I'll give your horrible kids a chance to get out of prison before they are collecting Social Security. Otherwise, you all go away for life without the possibility of parole."

Brandy stared defiantly at her. "I want to talk to my lawyer."

"You can call him, but then the deal is off the table," Burnside said. "We need to know your answer now, before we arrest Tatum . . . and certainly before we take you into custody and he knows for sure that we're coming for him next. The man is armed. No word can leave this house yet."

Duncan said, "He's probably waiting for us outside, and we'd like to avoid a shoot-out in the street."

Burnside glanced at her watch. "You have two minutes to decide."

"I'll testify against Tatum," Maverick blurted. "He came here Thursday night, said he knew everything we'd done, but that it was okay, that he could help us."

Brandy grabbed her son by the arm again. "Shut up, Mav. How many times do I have to tell you?"

Maverick yanked his arm free from her. "It's him or us, Mom. I choose us."

"Me too," Skye said, turning to Burnside. "The marshal said all he'd need was the jewelry and the gun and we'd never have to worry about getting caught."

Burnside nodded, then looked straight at Brandy. "I need to hear it from you, too."

Brandy's shoulders sagged. "We'll take the deal. Okay? Shit. This is so unfair. It's blackmail."

She sat down in one of the editing chairs, defeated.

Eve read them all their rights. When she was done, and the Winslows all acknowledged that they understood their rights, Eve asked, "Did Tatum tell you what he was going to do and why?"

Brandy looked at Eve with contempt. "He said we'd find out soon enough and it was better if our reactions were genuine."

"He thinks we can't act," Skye said. "He's obviously never watched our show. We deserve fucking Emmys."

Duncan asked, "How did he know it was the three of you who robbed and killed Kitty?"

Brandy shrugged. "All he said was that he knew it was us as soon as he saw the security video."

Eve guessed he'd immediately noticed the continuity issue with the weeds. But there was something she didn't understand at all.

"Tatum calls himself the law," she said. "Why didn't he arrest you all on the spot?"

Brandy started to cry and turned away from her children. "Because he loves me."

"You and Tatum were having an affair," Eve said, stating it as a fact, not a question.

She nodded. "Caleb lost interest in the sexual aspect of our marriage years ago."

It must have been Tatum, Eve thought, that Brandy was having sex with in the photo Max took of her through their window. Perhaps there were other photos somewhere that actually showed Tatum's face. Or they were still in Max's camera when he was beaten to death. She assumed it was Tatum who did it, but there was an easy way to find out.

"There was a paparazzo who caught you and Tatum together," Eve said. "His name was Max Gareth. What happened to him?"

Once again, Brandy appeared to be stunned by what Eve knew. "I didn't know his name. All I knew was that some photographer wanted a lot of money for the photos or he'd sell them to the highest bidder. I couldn't match what the *Inquirer* or one of the other scandal rags could pay. Amos said not to worry, that he'd make it go away. He did. That's why I gave him the jewelry and the gun. I knew he'd take care of me again now."

"You mean that instead of arresting you for murder," Burnside said, "he'd help you get away with it."

Brandy wiped the tears from her eyes and glowered at Burnside. "Yes."

"Which brings us to the obvious question," Eve said. "Why did the three of you kill Kitty?"

"Not the three of us. *Me*. I shot her," Brandy said. "I found out the selfish bitch was leaving the show and cutting us out of her new one, betraying the family and everything I'd spent decades building. I created her. But without her, the show was finished . . . and so were we. I was protecting my kids. Simple as that."

Duncan said, "You've done a hell of a job of it, too. You've protected them right into prison."

Brandy ignored him and looked at Burnside. "But not forever, right?"

"That's our deal," Burnside said. "If you plead guilty to all charges and testify fully and truthfully against Tatum."

Eve remembered what Linwood had told her the morning after the murder, that *Life with the Winslows* would surely have been canceled after Kitty left unless something big happened to change their fate. Kitty's murder certainly qualified. It got the Winslows global publicity, guaranteeing their revitalized show would have a massive audience and earning them a two-year renewal. Brandy's plot might have worked if not for the bodies of the three Chileans, killed two years ago, being unearthed in the Preserve.

There was a knock at the door. Duncan opened it. Deputies Tom Ross and Eddie Clayton came in.

Duncan asked, "Did anybody see you climb the fence from the Preserve?"

"Just the old man," Tom said.

"Cuff these revolting kids." Duncan gestured to Skye and Maverick, then took out his handcuffs and looked down at Brandy. "I'll take the witch. Get up and put your hands behind your back."

Brandy did as she was told, turning her back to Duncan and facing Eve. "When you got here, you said you needed our help so nobody else got hurt. Who the hell were you talking about?"

"Your neighbors," Eve said. "We're going to arrest Tatum and he's armed. They could get hurt in the cross fire if he resists arrest. Did you tell him we were coming over?"

Brandy shook her head. "Tatum said we shouldn't contact each other for a while."

"Keep them here," Duncan said to the deputies. "Until we tell you we have Tatum and it's safe."

"Understood," Ross said.

CHAPTER THIRTY

Eve and Duncan left the editing room and went to the storage room that held the security monitoring system. They looked at the camera views on the screen. There was no sign of Tatum, just Caleb riding his horse out of the stable toward the house.

"I'm surprised Tatum isn't outside," Eve said. "It's the first time he hasn't shadowed us into the community."

"Maybe something came up that required him to do his job."

"Or he figured out it was over for him as soon as we drove in and he tracked us on the city's surveillance security cameras heading to the Winslows' house."

"Let's go to his office and see," Duncan said.

They walked outside and were heading for their car when Caleb met them on his horse.

"I saw your deputies climb the fence and go into the house," he said. "I got to wondering why and decided it was an arrest." He glanced at the house, then back at Eve and Duncan. "It was my wife and kids, wasn't it? They killed Kitty."

Duncan nodded. "I'm so sorry, Mr. Winslow."

Caleb grimaced. "I've lost my entire family."

He turned his horse around and headed back to the stable. It broke Eve's heart to watch him go. The man had nothing left. How do you live with that kind of loss and betrayal?

She said, "I hope he doesn't put his gun in his mouth before we get back. Even loaded with blanks, it'll do the job."

Duncan said, "I'll call Tom on our way down to Tatum's office, ask him to keep his eye on Caleb."

He took out his phone and made the call as Eve drove them to Tatum's Old West marshal's station in Bill Crocker's front yard.

Tatum's patrol car was still parked there. That was a good sign.

Eve and Duncan got out, pulled out their Glocks, and approached the door, flanking it on each side. She knocked on the door.

"Tatum? Are you there? It's Eve Ronin. I need you to step outside."

There was no answer. She glanced at Duncan. He nodded and covered her. She reached out, turned the unlocked knob, and opened the door. They both spilled into the room, Eve to one side, Duncan to the other, ready to shoot.

But the room was empty.

Duncan's cell phone rang. He holstered his gun, took his phone from his pocket, and answered it. He listened for a moment, then ended the call with, "Shit. Thanks for letting me know."

"What is it?" She holstered her gun.

He pocketed the phone. "That was Tom. Caleb is gone. His horse is, too."

They heard someone coming toward them outside. They both drew their guns again, but it wasn't Tatum who came through the door.

It was Bill Crocker, who immediately raised his hands. "Whoa! It's just me. What's the big emergency?"

Eve and Duncan holstered their guns, and Duncan asked, "What do you mean?"

"You were ready to shoot me and the marshal tore out of here on horseback a few minutes ago."

Tatum knew we were coming for him, Eve thought. "Where is the key to the ATV that's in the stable?"

"In the ignition," Bill said.

Eve turned to Duncan. "Tatum is heading for the Preserve, making a run for it. I'm going after him."

Duncan nodded. "I'll lock down the gates anyway, get a helicopter up to search for him, and alert the rangers. Be careful."

She ran to the stable, fired up the three-wheeled ATV, and sped out, heading up the street, then down the horse trail that she and Tatum rode on Thursday.

Tatum had a few minutes' head start, but Eve figured she had the advantage. The ATV was faster than a horse, and she hoped the animal would run out of energy before she ran out of gas.

Eve burst into the Preserve. A hundred yards to her left was the excavation area that Daniel and several CSU techs were still working. She kept going forward and, as she rounded a stand of oak trees, saw Tatum two hundred yards ahead, riding toward two hills and the hidden gulch that separated them.

She chased after him just as he disappeared into the fold, leaving a cloud of dust in his wake that was as good as an arrow for her to follow. He wasn't going to get away from her.

Eve charged into the gully moments after he did.

There were two loud cracks, her front wheel exploded, and the ATV flipped end over end.

She flew into the air, arms out in front of her, and slammed hard into the ground, the impact knocking the air out of her lungs. But she instantly rolled over and saw the ATV about to crash on her. In that split second, Eve half rolled again, the ATV landing inches from her head, shaking the ground beneath her.

As she lay there, struggling to draw air back into her empty lungs, she reached for her gun, but a sharp pain in her wrist stopped her. Her wrist was broken. Before she could try again, someone yanked the gun from her holster and tossed it away.

Eve looked up to see Tatum standing over her, aiming his gun at her head.

"Stay down, Eve," he said. "Or I will put you down permanently."

It took her a second, but she was able to gather the air to gasp out, "You'd kill a cop?"

"If I killed you, I'd be the most popular deputy in the department," he said. "They'd pin a medal on me."

Eve managed to draw in another breath, feeling a stab of pain in her sides, and then breathed again, though not as deeply. "You won't kill me. When it comes down to it, you're a lawman. Isn't that why you executed those three Chilean gang members?"

"LilGlok9 shot one of them, then called me. I shot the others and buried them."

"Why?"

"It was in the best interests of the town if nobody knew about the home invasion and shooting . . . and the disappearance of the burglars sent a strong message back to the Chilean gang leaders: 'Hit us and die.' No gangs ever struck Hidden Hills again. It kept the peace."

"And what was your excuse for beating Max Gareth to death? Trespassing? Or is that the penalty in Hidden Hills for taking pictures of you and Brandy mating?" she said. "Not to be crass."

Tatum's face tightened. He wasn't amused.

"I won't kill you, Eve." Tatum moved the muzzle of his gun away from her head and aimed it at her hip instead. "I'll just maim you for life. You'll be finished as a real cop, but there's always TV."

She steeled herself for the agony she was about to feel.

But then she heard Caleb say, "I hoped you'd fight."

Tatum sighed and looked to his left. Caleb stood a few yards away, his horse even farther back. "Go home, old man."

"No home to go back to. Nobody's left," Caleb said. "I can't shoot my wife for what she's done to me, Kitty, and my kids, but I can shoot you."

"This isn't *Saddlesore* and your gun is full of blanks."

Caleb shot him twice, knocking Tatum off his feet, the gun flying from the deputy's hand.

Eve scrambled for Tatum's gun, grabbed it with her left hand, and crawled over to him. He was on his back, gasping for air like Eve was only moments ago, two bullet holes torn into the chest of his uniform.

But there was no blood. He was wearing a Kevlar vest underneath his shirt.

Caleb looked down at Tatum and said, "It's not my gun."

Eve looked over her shoulder. Caleb was holding her Glock.

Caleb said, "Is he still alive?"

"Yes," Eve said.

He aimed at Tatum's head. "I'll finish him."

"I can't let you do that." She moved protectively in front of Tatum and raised the gun in her left hand at Caleb. It was heavy and awkward in her hand.

"You're right-handed," Caleb said, his aim not wavering. "You aren't going to be much of a shot with your left."

"I don't have to be with you this close."

"Maybe you'd be doing me a favor," Caleb said. "What have I got left to live for?"

"Everyone who ever watched *Saddlesore*. That is your legacy."

An LASD helicopter streaked overhead, then circled over them, drawing their attention for a moment, though neither one of them lowered their guns. They'd been spotted.

Eve went on. "Is this how you want them to remember you and your character? As a man who died trying to shoot a cop? Then what will your life have been worth?"

Caleb looked up at the helicopter again, then down at Tatum, thought a moment, then dropped the gun and walked slowly back to his horse.

Eve glanced at Tatum, whose breathing was coming back, and shoved the gun barrel hard into his groin in case he was thinking of making a move against her.

"I'm the law," she said.

CHAPTER
THIRTY-ONE

Eve sat at a table in an interrogation room at the Lost Hills sheriff's station facing a handcuffed Amos Tatum, her right wrist in a temporary splint that the paramedics made for her at the scene. The paramedics also suspected she had broken ribs, but she refused to go to the hospital until her job was done. Each breath she took hurt. Rebecca Burnside sat beside her, a yellow legal pad in front of her, staring at Tatum.

"In return for the statement you're about to give," she said, "and pleading guilty to all charges, I'll guarantee that you will be held in isolation from the general prison population for your safety wherever you are incarcerated for the entirety of your term, which will be life with no possibility of parole."

"You'll also guarantee that I have full library privileges," Tatum said. "I want to catch up on all the reading I never got a chance to do."

"Agreed. Now let's start with what actually happened the night of LilGlok9's home invasion two years ago."

"The three Chileans broke into the main house. They didn't know he was on the property. He was in the studio and saw them on his cameras. So he grabbed a gun, walked into the house, and caught them in the act."

"Why didn't he call you or 911 right then?"

"Because that's not what Crips do," he said. "They handle things themselves. And he was mad. He thought it was personal."

"It was more than that," Eve said. "They'd seen the jewelry he'd already reported stolen, and he didn't want the police knowing about that."

Tatum nodded. "That's something I didn't learn until last week. But yes, it explains a lot."

"Go on," Burnside said. "What happened next?"

"He led them at gunpoint into his studio and demanded to know which rival gang sent them," Tatum said. "When they didn't answer, he executed one of them . . . and when they still didn't answer, he decided it wasn't personal, that he was probably targeted at random. So he called me."

"Why would he call you then," Burnside asked, "after he'd committed a murder in front of two witnesses?"

"Because he saw reason and knew I'd do what was best for maintaining law and order in my town."

Eve laughed ruefully at that. "What made you think that executing the two Chileans, burying them, and burning down the studio where the killing took place was better for 'your town' than following the law . . . and arresting the two of them and reporting the shooting of the third?"

"Think about it," he said. "You have an ex-Crip living in Hidden Hills . . . who executes a gang member who broke into his house. I didn't see how he could argue self-defense, given that it was obviously an execution, and if he went to trial, how he could prevail with his own gang background."

"So he goes to prison for murder," Eve said. "What do you care?"

"That ugly incident and his conviction would permanently tarnish the reputation of the town," Tatum said. "It would send the message that we're a haven for rich, violent gang members."

Burnside said, "What if we'd bought the self-defense argument or if he won the trial? Did you think about that?"

"It would be just as bad," Tatum said. "It would glorify him and might even encourage others like him to move into Hidden Hills. It was also likely in either case that those two Chileans would skip out on their bail and return home . . . and talk about what happened. That would have led to reprisals against our community in the form of more home invasions . . . or worse. But even if none of that happened, the simple fact that there was even one violent home invasion would frighten homeowners and send the wrong message about the safety of Hidden Hills."

Eve said, "So you decided protecting a murderer was the best option."

"They brought it on themselves," Tatum said. "He was protecting his home."

"And so were you?"

"That's right."

"Whose idea was it to burn down the studio?" she asked.

"Mine," Tatum said. "It was the only way to be sure there would never be any evidence tying the gang members to that house."

"But then you learned on our horseback ride that we'd unearthed the bodies of the Chileans and Max Gareth," Eve said. "You knew where that might lead, and if that happened, you had to find a way to end the investigation and wrap everything up with a nice ribbon on top. That's why you went to see Brandy that night. How did you know they killed Kitty?"

"When I saw the security video and weeds on the other side of their fence. It couldn't have been shot that night. I knew the weed-abatement crew had trimmed it the previous day."

The same thing Eve had noticed . . . only days later. He was a more observant cop than she was. But she had to give herself a break. He was also more familiar with Hidden Hills and had information she didn't have at the time.

"You kept your mouth shut because you loved Brandy," Burnside said.

Tatum shook his head. "I did it for the town. The Winslows are globally famous. Their arrest for the killing would make Hidden Hills known all over the world for all the wrong reasons."

And yet now it was happening anyway, only much worse.

"When I called you on Friday and asked about the studio fire," Eve said, "you knew we'd tied LilGlok9 to the killings and would be coming to arrest him."

Burnside added, "You were certain he'd give you up to me in exchange for testimony against you and a lesser sentence."

Tatum nodded. "I called him and said we needed to talk . . . but nobody could know. He turned off the cameras and told me he'd be relaxing in the hot tub."

Eve said, "You came in from the park, got a knife from his kitchen, walked up to him from behind, and slit his throat."

"I'm not proud of it," Tatum said. "At least he never saw it coming."

"You showed up at the scene immediately after we did," Eve said, "so if any forensic evidence tying you to the scene was found, we would have assumed it was left then, not before. But there wasn't any. You left nothing behind."

"Then what was my mistake?"

"Bad timing and bad luck," Eve said. "Once I realized that Brandy, Skye, and Maverick killed Kitty, the one thing that didn't fit is why they'd frame and kill LilGlok9. And why on Friday? They had no idea we were onto him for another crime or that we were close to arresting him. Then it hit me. You were the only one who knew it all. And my call to you asking about the studio fire was like a time stamp—it coincided with LilGlok9 turning off his cameras."

"I knew it was a big risk," Tatum said, "but you didn't give me any choice. I had to act fast."

"It was all for nothing. In fact, you made it worse," Eve said. "Not only is everything you covered up coming out . . . but also the revelation that Hidden Hills was protected for decades by a serial killer."

"I'm not a serial killer," he said. "I killed to enforce the law and protect my town."

"How does that argument justify slitting LilGlok9's throat and beating Max Gareth to death? Brandy told us everything, and we've got the pictures, so there's no point lying to us now." The pictures didn't show Tatum's face, but Eve didn't see any reason to tell him that.

"They were two terrible individuals, a murderer and a blackmailer, and I can't protect the town if I'm arrested for doing the right thing."

"And what about the others?" Eve said.

"There aren't any others," Tatum said.

"Dr. Brooks found another body out there today," Eve said. "How many more is he going to find?"

Tatum stared, hard and cold, at Eve.

Burnside said, "This deal applies to all of the people you've killed. Leave any out, and it's voided. You'll get the death penalty, if you aren't beaten to death by inmates first."

Tatum didn't break his stare.

"Seven," he said. "All worthless gang scum."

Eve got up and walked out of the room.

She entered the hallway just as Lansing stepped out of the captain's office, where he, Duncan, and Dubois had been watching the interrogation on CCTV.

"I didn't hear about any other bodies," Lansing said.

"Because we haven't found any," Eve said. "But now we will."

Daniel's instincts were right. It was a mass grave, just like the others he'd excavated all over the world.

Lansing smiled. "Nice bluff. You just love taking down deputies."

"You would have preferred that Tatum got away with a dozen murders?"

"I would have preferred not to have one more scandal and one more bad cop on my watch," Lansing said. "I have to step outside now, stand in front of a hundred reporters from all over the world, and tell them what's happened today. Even though I inherited Tatum and didn't put him in Hidden Hills, he's my responsibility. This will probably finish me in politics."

"I'm not going to shed any tears for you."

"Then shed some tears for yourself," Lansing said. "I put that badge on you, so I had a vested interest in you succeeding. But the next sheriff? He'll inherit you, just like I did with Tatum."

"I'm not Tatum," she said.

"You could be a liability to the department in an entirely different way," he said. "Are you going out there with me for the press conference?"

"Hell no," she said.

"Smart lady. I'll walk the plank alone." He walked away.

Dubois and Duncan came out of the captain's office after letting Lansing say his piece.

"You did good work," Dubois said. "Now would you please let Duncan take you to the ER?"

"Yes, sir." Eve wasn't looking forward to being on the receiving end, once again, of her sister's concern. But she really needed some Vicodin. Everything below her chin was hurting.

Dubois went back into his office. Eve and Duncan headed down the hall to the parking lot.

Eve said, "Just once I'd like to close a big case without ending up in the ER with broken bones. You said this wouldn't happen again if I changed my approach to policing. I tried. I really did . . . but here I am, on my way back."

"Your mistake now is that you don't watch enough westerns," Duncan said. "I told you that a few days ago."

"How would that have helped me?"

"There's a lot of good stuff in westerns about what it means to be a lawman."

"That didn't help Tatum much," she said.

They walked outside into the parking lot and toward their plain-wrap Explorer.

"You'd have known not to chase a desperado on horseback into a ravine. Everybody who has ever watched a western would've known he'd ambush you," Duncan said, opening the driver's side door. "What you're supposed to do is sneak around the other side, like Caleb did."

They got into the car. Eve put on her seat belt with her left hand and said, "Then I guess it was fitting that a TV character showed up to save me."

"You are a TV character." Duncan started the car. "We both are."

"No, we're not. We're real."

They drove out of the official vehicles lot and past the mob of reporters attending Lansing's press conference on the station's front steps and learning the news that Kitty Winslow was murdered by her own family.

"The Winslows are real, too," Duncan said. "But I can't tell the difference."

"That's because they stopped being real a long time ago."

Duncan turned right onto Agoura Road and headed east toward Las Virgenes Canyon Road. "When is that going to happen to us?"

"Never," Eve said.

They were silent for a long moment, and when they reached the intersection, she could see Duncan feeling the gravitational pull of the McDonald's on his right instead of any urgency to turn onto the freeway on his left.

He who holdeth the steering wheel decideth whether to driveth-through or not to driveth-through.

She figured it was probably the promise of hospital food, which he loved, rather than concern for her health that gave him the willpower to turn onto the 101 instead.

Duncan said, "How long do you think it will be before we see *Lockup with the Winslows* as a weekly series?"

"I'll bet they are already in negotiations," Eve said.

ACKNOWLEDGMENTS

This is entirely a work of fiction, so any similarity to real people is unintended and coincidental. That said, the City of Hidden Hills *does* exist, and they do have a dedicated Los Angeles County sheriff's deputy, among others, who patrols their streets.

But that deputy doesn't live there, he doesn't wear a cowboy hat, he doesn't ride a horse, and he doesn't have a western-style marshal's office to call his own (though there are a couple of homes designed to look like they're western sets—one even has the entrance to a fake silver mine in the front yard). And he's not a serial killer . . . At least I hope he's not.

A lot of very nice Hidden Hills residents, enthusiastic fans of the Eve Ronin series, invited me into their community, gave me guided tours, and answered all of my questions about the history and the lifestyle. They asked me not to name them, for obvious reasons. I appreciate their support, and I hope they don't feel betrayed by my depiction of their community, which they dearly love.

I can see why. Hidden Hills is a beautiful, peaceful, inviting, and remarkably safe place to live. And yet, it's also a strange, surreal, and oddly unsettling place. If aliens from another planet wanted to create a zoo for human beings and put it under a dome, it would be Hidden Hills.

I could probably have depicted the city in a much more positive light, but I've written a crime novel, and that wouldn't have worked. I hope my friends in Hidden Hills will forgive me.

The Commons, the Oaks, the Lost Hills sheriff station, and several other Calabasas locations in the book are also real, though obviously the events I have taking place there are imaginary.

Chilean burglary tourists are, unfortunately, very real. In a bit of irony, while I was writing this book, the neighbors on either side of my house were both burglarized by intruders that sheriff's investigators strongly believe were Chilean, so it really hit home to me. We've significantly upgraded our security system and stopped complaining about our dog barking at every leaf that drops around our house. Now we're thankful for our four-legged, overly protective security guard.

I am indebted to Dr. Alexis Gray, forensic anthropologist; David Van Norman, deputy coroner investigator, San Bernardino County Sheriff's Department; Danielle R. Galien, criminal justice professor, Des Moines Area Community College; Pamela Sokolik-Putnam, retired supervising deputy coroner investigator, San Bernardino County Sheriff's Department; Chris Lizarraga at LA Sound Panels; and jewelry designer Cynthia Wolfe for sharing their experience and technical expertise. Any errors or creative contortions of fact are entirely my fault. I know I've taken some liberties that will probably make them cringe.

I found many articles useful in my research, but especially "Inside Hidden Hills, Shangri-La to the Kanye Set" by Chris Lee and "Thieves in the Night: A Vast Burglary Ring from Chile Has Been Targeting Wealthy U.S. Households" by Mark Wortman, both for *Vanity Fair*; "Forbidden City" by Paul Ciotti, "Hidden Hills Likes Its Politics Out of View" by John M. Glionna, and "Outsiders Will Be Insiders Thanks to Annexation in Hidden Hills" by Bob Pool, all for the *Los Angeles Times*; "Foreign Theft Gangs Rife in Region" by Becca Whitnall for *The Acorn*; "How South American Theft Groups Target Ventura Homes" by Jeremy Childs for the *Ventura County Star*; and "Chilean Burglary

Gangs Causing Havoc in Southern California" by Scott Schwebke for the *Orange County Register*.

Several reference books also came in handy, including *Practical Homicide Investigation, Fifth Edition* by Vernon J. Geberth, *Introduction to Crime Scene Investigation, Third Edition* by Aric W. Dutelle, and *Advances in Forensic Taphonomy*, edited by William D. Haglund and Marcella H. Sorg.

Finally, I am certain you wouldn't be holding a fifth Eve Ronin adventure in your hands now if not for the continuing support of my agent Amy Tannenbaum, the creative contributions of my devoted editors Gracie Doyle, Megha Parekh, and Charlotte Herscher, and the marketing and promotional work of Megan Beattie, Dennelle Catlett, Allyson Cullinan, Sarah Shaw, and everyone at Amazon Publishing / Thomas & Mercer. I am grateful for everything they've done for me and Eve.

About the Author

Photo © 2013 Roland Scarpa

Lee Goldberg is a two-time Edgar Award and two-time Shamus Award nominee and the #1 *New York Times* bestselling author of more than forty novels, including the Eve Ronin series and the Ian Ludlow series. He has also written and/or produced many TV shows, including *Diagnosis Murder*, *SeaQuest*, and *Monk*, and is cocreator of the *Mystery 101* series of Hallmark movies. As an international television consultant, he has advised networks and studios in Canada, France, Germany, Spain, China, Sweden, and the Netherlands on the creation, writing, and production of episodic television series. You can find more information about Lee and his work at www.leegoldberg.com.